PROFESSOR RENOIR'S
COLLECTION OF
ODDITIES,
CURIOSITIES,
and
DELIGHTS

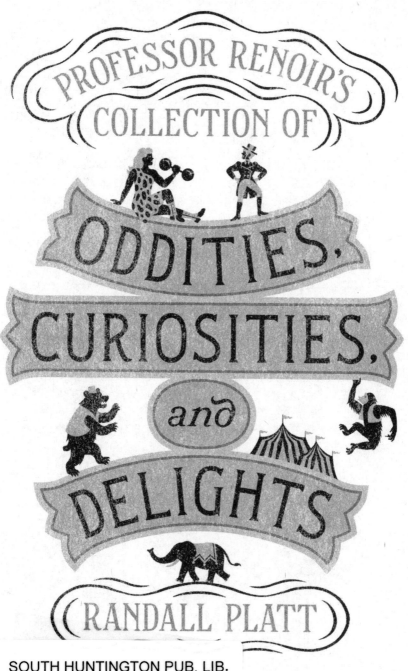

PROFESSOR RENOIR'S COLLECTION OF ODDITIES, CURIOSITIES, and DELIGHTS

RANDALL PLATT

ublishers

Professor Renoir's Collection of Oddities, Curiosities, and Delights

Copyright © 2019 by Randall Platt

Library of Congress Cataloging-in-Publication Data

Names: Platt, Randall Beth, author.
Title: Professor Renoir's Collection of Oddities, Curiosities, and Delights /
    Randall Platt.
Description: First edition. | New York, NY : Harper, An Imprint of
    HarperCollinsPublishers, [2018] | Summary: In 1896, fourteen-year-old
    "giant" Fern "Babe" Killingsworth joins a traveling carnival where she
    befriends a dwarf and some animals, with whom she escapes the clutches of
    a corrupt businessman.
Identifiers: LCCN 2017057333 | ISBN 9780062643346 (hardcover)
Subjects: | CYAC: Size—Fiction. | Dwarfs (Persons)—Fiction. | Freak
    shows—Fiction. | United States—History—1865–1898—Fiction.
Classification: LCC PZ7.P7129 Pr 2018 | DDC [Fic]—dc23
LC record available at https://lccn.loc.gov/2017057333

Typography by Joel Tippie
19 20 21 22 23 PC/LSCH 10 9 8 7 6 5 4 3 2 1

First Edition

For Kristi

"Babe, put that dang runt pup down and get over to the store! Someone come to see you! Come all the way up the mountain from Boise, so don't keep him waiting!"

"Ain't giving up," Babe called out to her father, gently nudging the puppy's tummy. She hoped her big, clumsy thumbs didn't break anything inside. "He's got life some-wheres inside and I'm finding it!" Babe had found the pup's mama, a starving stray mutt, hiding in a deserted mining shack earlier that week. Her two other pups were beyond saving, but this one still had some struggle inside.

Babe blew her warm breath into the pup's face and stroked his wet black fur. "Come on, come on. Breathe." She ignored her father's boot steps coming closer. The small mama dog looked up with pleading eyes as her tail tapped lightly on the bed of straw.

"Now!" her father growled.

Then came the sweetest sound—snorts of puppy breath as the newborn squiggled in Babe's hands. The mama inched closer, sniffing. The pup sniffed back, head bobbing as he nosed around for his mama.

"Look at you," Babe whispered down to the pup, so tiny in her large, cupped hands. "You ain't no bigger'n a runt rabbit."

Her father stepped closer, stealing the lamplight.

"Babe!" He tugged on her long thick braid. She ignored him and yanked her braid back.

"Here's your baby," she said softly, placing the pup next to the mama's face. "He's all you got, so take good care of him." The mama licked and nudged more life into him.

"Girl, I told you to ditch that ugly dog or I'll do it! Just like I did all them other strays you dragged home! Can't be dragging home every worthless stray you find! You're thirteen and . . ."

"Fourteen, Pa. Turned last month."

"Time you growed up!"

"Criminy, Pa, you been saying 'time you growed up' since I was three. How much more 'growed up' do you think I can be?"

"Don't want none of your lip!"

Babe stood full up, her knees creaking like an old woman's. Her father took a step back. Her shadow cast looming and dark over him, forcing him to crane his head up to look at her—his little girl, his giant.

His face stayed hard. "Put something clean on, and then get over to the store."

"Ain't got nothing clean."

"Didn't I have a new dress made just a year ago?" he demanded.

"Outgrew it just six month ago."

"Well, at least wash up. You smell like a barnyard."

"Seems fittin', since I live in a barn," she mumbled.

"No lip!"

"I don't want my picture tooken, Pa."

"Who said anything about pictures?"

"Ain't it always when you want me cleaned up?"

"It's different this time." He stepped back out of her shadow. "Now, shake a leg! We got important comp'ny."

As soon as he turned to leave, Babe pursed her ample lips, lifted a leg, and gave it a shake. "How's that?" she said to the barn door. Her breath showed in the chilly morning air. "You warm enough?" she asked the mama dog. She pulled off her shawl and snuggled it around the dog and her pup, then closed the stall door. With a push and a pull, she moved a wagon against the door to hold the dogs in safe and sound and away from her father. She looked down at them, smiling at the dog murmurs between mother and babe.

"Don't you worry none. Ain't letting Pa get rid of you.

Your Babe'll figure something out."

She shared her room in the barn—the only room large enough to give her standing, walking, and breathing room—among harnesses, saddles, barn cats, rats, and bats. She poured water into a bowl, soaked a rag, and ran it around her face and hands, then ran a jackknife under her fingernails. The bottle of lemon verbena stared up at her. It had been given to her, along with other "lady things," by a committee of churchwomen. Their "lady things" seemed to be their cure-all for the "unlady things" in Babe's life . . . her huge and awkward size, her rage at the constant teasing and taunts, her fights, her punishments, her dismal future.

A mirror hung nearby on a nail, but she kept it reflection-side in. She wondered why she even bothered. Washed up and smelling like a garden didn't mean anything was going to be different this time. "Ain't gonna make me pretty or small or smart, or make folks take to me," she mumbled. She turned her gaze to the row of newspaper clippings, mostly yellowed and curled up, tacked on the wall in order of date, her escalating ages, and her escalating sizes. She learned early on: when you're a spectacle, curiosity comes calling. Two dollars for a photograph, but if it was for a newspaper, her father charged a buck extra.

Pointing her finger along the headline of one of the clippings, she read it out loud, slowly and sounding out the big words:

LITTLE IDAHO GIRL ISN'T SO LITTLE
AMAZING GROWTH SPURT
P. T. BARNUM? HAVE YOU MET THIS GIRL?

Also tacked to the wall was her birth certificate. It reminded her that she, Fern Marie Killingsworth, was born on January 2, 1882, weighing seven pounds, six ounces, and was once perfect and perfectly normal. Right as rain, she whispered each time she looked at it, putting her thumb alongside her two tiny ink footprints. Her thumb was three times as long now, not counting the lump of a wart on the end. Yes, right as rain—for the first three months.

Then it all changed.

A bell clanged in the distance. Nine o'clock. Time for the kids who weren't giants to go to school.

"Baaaaaabe!" her father screamed out across the street as though answering the bell. "Get your fat rear over here!"

Babe clenched her jaw and swallowed the temptation to scream back. Instead, she muttered, "Great. Now the whole dang town knows I got a fat rear." She grabbed her coat off a nail and trundled out of the barn. Some boys, on their way to school, spotted her, and she ducked back into the barn. Didn't need their taunting and laughter. Neal, Idaho, was a mining town—tough, poor, and played out— and it seemed to attract bullies of all ages, shapes, and sizes. Babe was a constant, ripe target. At least the mud pies and horse apples the boys slung could be slung back. But the girls were sometimes worse than the boys, slinging their snippy teases and taunts. . . . How could she forget that rope-jumping song they made up?

Fat Babe Sprat
Et just fat
If you tell her that
She'll squarsh you flat
How many kids did Babe squarsh . . . ?
One . . . two . . . three . . . four . . .

Babe had stepped in, grabbed the rope and gave it a tug, yanking the two twirlers clean off their feet and tripping the jumping girl. Grunting and growling, face growing red, she pulled and pulled the rope until it frayed, then snapped in two. Then she tossed the pieces high into the trees. The girls screamed, cried, tattled. Of course.

Those pieces of rope, dangling—*nah-nah-nah*—in the treetops, was the last straw. She was dismissed from third grade for not being a "good fit." Or not fitting good. Which was fine with Babe. Being full adult-man size by the time she was eight, Babe and school didn't "fit" very long anyway. Her desk and chair had been set back as far as they could make it, but she still didn't fit. The time she stood up fast and brought up the whole hooked-together row, spilling out two little girls, she figured it out. Babe didn't "fit" anywhere.

That was the birth of the beast, that day when she'd been asked to leave school for good. The beast inside the beast, she called it. Something that roiled deep down—a gnawing pain that doubled, then tripled in size, just as she had, and then exploded. That day, the enraged beast overturned another row of desks, pulled down the schoolhouse curtains, and slammed the door so hard, a hinge broke loose.

Once the schoolboys were gone, Babe pulled her skirts up through her legs, hitched the hems into her belt, and slogged across the street. Her men's boots laced up to the knees made a sucking sound in the thick, spring mud. A warm Chinook wind had blown in, melting the February snow and turning the streets into streams of mud and slush.

A fancy black-and-red wagon with yellow lettering scrolled along the side was hitched up in front of her father's mercantile store. Her face hardened. "'Nother dang circus," she growled as she walked around the wagon, carefully approaching the two horses with soothing words and gentle pats. She'd been spooking horses since she was six.

"Well, hello, Babe," a woman said from the sidewalk. "What's all this?"

"'Morning, Miz Frazier," Babe replied. "Reckon it's a circus wagon."

The woman read aloud, "'Professor Renoir's Collection of Oddities, Curiosities, and Delights.' My, how fancy. You finally leaving us?" The woman adjusted the scowling toddler on her hip. The child gripped a partially gnawed cob of corn.

Babe looked at the corner entrance to her father's store, then back at the wagon. "Might could be."

"Well, everyone knows that's the best thing for a girl the likes of you," Mrs. Frazier said. "Harold, quit kicking!" The child went to her other hip. "I'm sorry. You scare little Harold."

Babe smiled weakly. "Sorry."

"Well, good luck, dear!" Mrs. Frazier said, continuing along with her morning errands.

Babe watched her walk away and dodged the corncob that her little brat Harold tossed at her.

Just then, the store window opened and her father appeared. "If maybe you could honor us with your presence, missy!" Slam! The window crashed back down.

Babe released a long, heavy sigh, gave each horse a nose pat, and climbed the steps up to the elevated boardwalk. Looking at the town around her, her eyes roamed from the high bell spire of the school; her father's run-down barn; the tired, lopsided bustle of Mrs. Frazier as she trundled along the sidewalk; and then finally the store.

Maybe it would be different this time.

"A hundred down, fifty in three months, and that's my last offer," the man said, looking Babe up, looking Babe down. He scratched his goatee and mustache so much Babe wondered if he also offered a flea circus in his show. "And that's a far sight more than I've paid for any other act, Mr. Killingsworth."

"Well, Professor Renoir, I got to reckon she's cheap at twice that price." Babe glanced at her father. That wasn't pride in his voice; it was greed. While the men dickered, she took in this visitor: his shiny black suit was patched in places, his high-top boots had worn-down heels, and his dirty starched collar was pinned, not buttoned, down. The fruity smell of his hair pomade wafted up toward the rafters.

"How old is she?"

Mr. Killingsworth looked at his daughter, eyes squinting. "Fourteen, I think."

"In your letter you said seventeen. What state is this? Idaho? What's the legal age of consent here? Don't need the authorities after me."

"She passed consent four year ago," her father said.

"Consent to marry at *ten*?" Renoir barked. "Good Lord!"

"What difference does it make? She ain't marrying, and I can sign for her. I'm her pa, and I'm legal, even if she ain't. She's a bony-fied giant, and they don't grow on trees. And she can read and cipher some. She ain't no lost cause. She's a giant." He grinned like he'd just sold a salted silver mine to a wide-eyed flatlander.

Read and cipher some? Babe read that eagerness in his voice and she ciphered this was the fifth time her pa had tried to sell her off. Two chautauquas, one minstrel show, and another traveling circus. She examined this Renoir from the corner. Sort of handsome. Talked good. And all that money! Best offer by far.

"Come over here, Babe, so's Professor Renoir here can see your size full up. Quit stooping in that corner," her father said, tugging at her sleeve. Babe jerked her arm away. "Don't you look at me that way, girl!" Then, to Renoir, "She's always a bit cantankerous in the morning. Once she gets her belly full, she's more come-at-able."

Babe stood now in the center of the room, where the

beams were higher and she was able to stand up to her full height. Renoir walked around her, fiddling with the tip of his black goatee. "She *is* big, I'll give her that. Does she talk?"

Babe opened her mouth to speak, but her father beat her to it.

"Does she talk? Of course she talks! And she sings some, too! Babe, sing that one about Winsome Winnie from Winnemucca."

Once again, she opened her mouth but was stopped.

"Don't need a bawdy singer," the carnival man said, cutting her father off. "I need a strongman, uh, strong-*woman* act. I run a carnival, not a burlesque show. In fact, is there a Mrs. Killingsworth? Women have different opinions about what becomes of their daughters. Even ones like this."

"Her ma died after Babe was born."

"And who can blame her, huh?" Renoir said. The men chuckled together.

"Ain't my size what killed her!" Her voice boomed in the confines of the room. They stopped laughing and looked up at her. "I was birthed right as rain. She died of fever of some sort. Tell him that's so, Pa."

Father and daughter locked eyes. So seldom did they ever discuss her mother, the right-as-rain birth, the lingering death, who knew what was behind her father's chilly expression?

Renoir broke the uncomfortable silence. "Shall we get back to the issue at hand?" He took a circle of glass hanging from a ribbon around his neck, placed it into his eye socket and looked down at the papers.

"Of course, Professor Renoir, of course," her father said. "Let's talk about her care." Now came the groveling, the backing down, the upping of the ante. This was the best part. "Naturally, Babe here deserves nothing but the best. And, say, here's something—she's still growing! No telling how big she's going to get! What do you weigh now, Babe?"

Babe felt her jaw tighten. Her fingernails cut crescents into her palms. "Three-forty-two," she answered, looking down.

"There! You see? Why, she's up four pound in just two week! We have to weigh her on the livestock scale down at the butcher's," he went on, shaking his head and grinning. "How tall're you this week, Babe?"

She walked to the grow plank propped in the corner. Floorboards creaked under her no matter how lightly she tried to step. The sign on the grow plank read:

HOW BIG WILL BABE GET?
PLACE YOUR BETS

"Six foot, nine inch," she said, feeling the latest notch carved there . . . but she ciphered from her rising hemlines she was about a half inch taller. If this kept up, soon she'd be able to go back east and look the Statue of Liberty eye to eye.

"And strong? Babe, show Professor Renoir how strong you are."

If only she had a dime for every time she'd been asked to put her strength on display. There was a bin of wood next to the potbelly stove. Grabbing a handful of kindling, she stared at her father, snapped the bundle like it was a teacher's hickory stick ruler.

"See there? I seed her carry a crippled colt over her shoulders like it was a newborned lamb. I tell you, if you don't sign her, someone else will. I've writ to P. T. Barnum, you know."

Renoir itched his chin again and studied the notches, inch by inch, on the grow plank. "Well, bona fide giants *are* rare," he said. "Tell you what, I'll add another fifty to the pot. That's two hundred. One fifty today, but the last fifty comes only when I know how she'll work out. I usually know within three months. Not every freak takes well to being put on display. Had a bearded woman go stark raving mad and nearly killed a boy who displayed his backside to her without the benefit of trousers."

The two men had their laugh like they knew something she shouldn't. She knew all about bare backsides and teasing and taunting and wanting to kill someone on account of it. She got teased and taunted anyhow, why not get cash money for it?

"Whereabouts you go with your carnival show?" Babe asked.

"Well, we have several circuits. All around the country during different seasons," Renoir answered. "We don't normally run this far north in the winter, but the weather's been fair and folks just love coming out for a carnie—uh, carnival—no matter what the weather."

"You got anyone famous in your carnie?" she asked.

"Babe, stay out of this and . . . ," her father said.

"No, let her ask. As a matter of fact, we have several very famous people in our troupe. In fact, I've just signed a world-famous elephant act."

Money, travel, maybe even fame? Babe's wheels started to churn to life.

"You have anything else you have to ask, Babe?" her father snapped. He went back to the papers. "So, let's see . . ." He held the contract up to the light and squinted. "How long this contract good for?"

"Just a year, and then it automatically renews," Renoir replied. "With her consent, of course. When she's sixteen, she can sign for herself. Naturally, her board and her wages are all spelled out. Very boilerplate. It's all right there. Just need your John Hancock and the date, February third, 1896. I think you'll find this fair commerce, Mr. Killingsworth."

"Shouldn't I look at that? After all, I'm the one it's writ about."

"Get out of my light, Babe," her father grumbled. "You might be legal to marry but not to sign nothing. You just leave these legal things to us men."

"Who gets that cash money?" she asked Renoir. "The two hundred dollar?"

Her father glanced at Renoir, then stepped in to answer. "Now, Babe, you know I'll keep that money for you. For when you're older and know how to handle it. Sure. I'll set up a special account at the bank and—"

"No you won't," she said, breaking him off.

"You got no idea how much your upkeep is, Babe, and how . . ." His words fell away as he looked at his daughter, then at Renoir, and finally, down at the papers on the counter.

"Sign that paper, take his money, Pa. Reckon you have it coming for what my doctoring cost last fall."

Her father gave her a long, hard look. "You want to go, Babe?" The pen in his hand was ticking back and forth. A signal? Maybe he was just holding out for more money or maybe . . .

"Go ahead. Sign it, Pa."

"And remember, Mr. Killingsworth, she'll be among her own kind." Renoir stepped in. "Think of this as a mercy. I mean, what else can the poor thing do? And, Babe—may I call you Babe?—you'll come to love carnie folks and carnie life. We're all just one big, happy family."

"Of freaks," she said, looking down at her father.

Would he up the ante, fold, or was he bluffing? Did they really want to be shed of each other? Was it time? What did she have to offer her father here? Food bills and doctor bills and help unloading the delivery wagons. What did her father have to offer her? A cold barn, drowned dogs, and ridicule.

"And food! I have the best cooks on the circuit!" Renoir went on. "And a seamstress—a genius with needle and thread—to sew you beautiful clothes!"

Babe considered the cards she'd just been handed: travel, money, fame, food, and clothes. Quite a poker hand to draw to. For some time she'd been thinking there was no place big enough for her. What was she, after all? Just an ugly giant with more mouth than sense and all in the company of the beast inside the beast.

"What sort of critters you got in your outfit?" she asked. "Me and critters get along, once they get used to my size. Critters is folks to me."

"Critters galore!"

"She loves her critters," her father said. "Sometimes I think she's more animal than—" He stopped when he caught her eye. "Well, anyway, critters take to her real natural-like. You got critters, she'll be happy. Won't you, Babe? Won't you be happy?"

"Reckon so," she said. The cash and the contract for her future sat on the counter. She walked over, ducking the lamps hanging from the rafters, took a twenty-dollar gold piece, and slipped it into her pocket. "Need me ten minutes to pack my grip," she said to Renoir. "You can have your barn back, Pa. So that makes us both happy."

Her father didn't even flinch. The scratching sound as he signed the contract answered her question—it *was* different this time. They *were* both happy to be shed of each other.

Back in the barn it didn't take long to pack her things. BVDs, socks, underthings, all men's sizes, dirty and worn and patched together. She had a few childhood things in a trunk. The lid was swollen, and she had to jerk it open. The smell of mold and things forgotten and neglected drifted up. There, on top, the delicate doll—what had she named it? Alice? Annie?—smiled up at her, her eyes closed in repose. She picked up the doll and noticed how much smaller it seemed now in her giant hands. The eyes opened with a click as she held it upright. Such a perfect porcelain face, such China-blue eyes, such elegant lashes, such a sweet red bow of a smile. Alice or Annie was perfect, and Babe remembered why she'd tossed her into the trunk when she was seven. She wasn't even sure how or when she'd gotten it. Perhaps taken in trade at her father's store. More likely, she'd swiped it from some teasing little girl.

She reached in and pulled out the wooden cigar box of lead soldiers. Setting Alice or Annie aside, she dumped her tiny army out on the floor. Grinning down at them, she was reminded how she bent them, twisted them, and maimed them, lead being as pliable as clay in her hands. Soldiers no more—just a boxful of tiny little freaks of nature.

Those were left where they had scattered. She rummaged through the trunk and found nothing she would want or need.

From there, the wall opposite her bed. She ripped down the photos and clippings and made sure her birth certificate was well hidden at the bottom of the old leather valise the "lady things" had arrived in.

Last, her one pretty, the one thing she loved so much that she never used it—a silver mirror and brush set. It was all she had from her mother, except her life itself. Carefully, she pulled the set out of a bin under the window. Strands of her mother's long black hair were still intertwined deep in the bristles of the brush. Babe closed her eyes and breathed in the faint aroma. Slowly, she raised the mirror and found her eyes reflecting back.

"You're doing it, Babe," she whispered. "You know it's time and you're doing it." She dared a small smile, then quickly packed the mirror and brush safe and sound among her clothes.

One last look around and she closed the door on her room. She stopped, standing in the center of the barn. Eloise, the cow, was still in her stall, dozing.

"Gonna miss you, Eloise," Babe said, tossing another handful of grain into her manger. "Thanks for all the milk. Sorry I run you dry so much. Things'll be better now."

Then Bo Bo, the old delivery horse, murmured from his stall. "Got some oats for you too, ol' man," Babe said. "Thanks for helping me deliver all of them groceries up to the mine. I pushed and you pulled up all them big hills. I saved us skidding downhill a few time, too, huh?" She gave his nose a rub, smiling at the feel of the ageless velvet.

Next, she walked to the back of the barn and opened the small hatch to the outside chicken coop. She poked her head out and tossed some grain. "Thanks for all the eggs, girls. Reckon you can all relax some now that your Babe's leaving."

There was no reply. She closed the hatch.

She looked around the barn. "What else?"

The tiny rustle from the stall answered her question. The mama dog and her one pup. She pushed the wagon aside and opened the stall door. Kneeling down, she whispered, "Hey, mama dog. How's he coming?" She found the pup nestled down—happy and warm and fed. The mama nudged her hand and licked it.

"You're welcome, girl." Babe's giant hand gently encased the dog's head as she pet it. "You're welcome."

Renoir's wagon rolled up outside the barn.

"Babe? You ready?" her father called in. "Professor

Renoir says it's a good twenty mile to the railhead. Better git gone."

"Like hell he's going to ditch you," she said to the dogs. "You're coming with me."

Her valise was packed up full, so she looked around for something to hide the dogs in. She grabbed a box, popped the lid, dumped the contents, made a bed with her shawl, and gently nestled the dogs inside.

"Just going us on a little trip." She put the lid back on and carried it close to her chest.

The two men were talking over the wagon bed but stopped when she approached.

"What you got in there, girl?" Her father pointed to the box. "You ain't stealing any of my chickens, are you?"

"Just the dog and her pup, Pa. Gonna ditch 'em off the bridge on the way out of town. Just like you said."

"Well then," her father grunted. "See that you do. This town don't need no more stray dogs and——"

"I said I'll do it!"

"You watch your tone, girl. You might be leaving, but I'm still your pa and . . ."

"And what?"

He didn't answer. After a few moments of silence, Babe said, "You said yourself things is different this time." She turned to Renoir as he climbed aboard the wagon. "You need to move them boxes about some." She pointed to the cargo in the bed of the wagon.

"What for?"

"Well, unless you want them horses heading skyward once I set in the back of the wagon . . ."

"Oh! Oh, yes! Yes!" Renoir said. He climbed over the seat and rearranged the load.

Babe tossed in her valise, eased herself into the back of the wagon, and put the box on her lap. Her father took a few steps back. "Bye, Pa."

Babe hadn't cried in four, maybe five years. Why should she? Crying never did her a speck of good. Crying was for little girls and sissies, not giants. No tears even now, looking at her father, standing there, saying nothing, not even a little wave goodbye, the played-out town and all she'd come to know behind him. She set her chin, turned, and looked ahead.

Renoir clucked his team. The horses groaned as they pulled forward. Her father walked away and disappeared into his store. "Well, that's that." She lifted the lid to the box to give the dogs some air. She smiled at the mama dog as she poked her head out. "Shed is shed, ain't that so, mama dog?"

Renoir stopped the team just outside of town.

"Why you stopping?" Babe asked.

"So you can let those dogs go." He pointed his whip to the box in Babe's arms. "Like you told your father."

"My ol' man knew I was lying. These critters is coming with me."

"Now, you just wait a minute, Babe, I didn't say any-thing about . . ."

"Or I climb out right here and you're out your money and your strongwoman show," she said, surprised at her tone and her threats.

Renoir stared at her across the wagonload. "We'll settle that when we get there, girl." He turned and clucked the team on.

Babe pulled the mama dog out of the box, pet her, and ran her fur along her cheek. "Don't you worry none. Your Babe's got you."

"Get out," Renoir said, pulling the tarp off Babe's head. "Get your grip and get aboard that train. The hog engine will be here any minute and we still have to finish take-down."

Babe looked around her and blinked. Hog engine? Take what down? "Where are we?"

"Just outside Boise," he said over his shoulder.

Babe got out and looked around. What was this world? She'd seen trains and even some traveling carnivals, but not in this state—half in and half out of the train. She raised her nose to the air and took a deep breath in. Popcorn, something sweet, and—deep breath—roasting peanuts? Her stomach sent out a rumble.

Renoir had disappeared into a tent, and people were yelling, calling orders—Do this! Do that! You do it! My hands are full!—as the carnie was being folded up and put away into railroad cars.

What might have been a cow pasture yesterday was a muddy field of turned-up ground and big puddles of rainwater. Babe left the mama dog and her pup in their box and put up the tailgate of the wagon to keep them safe inside.

Walking between two steaming cook fires, she followed her nose toward food. No one paid her any attention, as though a giant girl walking among them was nothing unusual. Tables and chairs were being folded and stacked, boxes and crates were being filled with little dolls, popguns, shiny dishes, and trinkets. Off in the distance, a train engine hooted three times and people started moving faster, cursing and shouting even louder.

Someone untied a handful of red balloons and they bounced on the muddy ground, catching a breeze. Babe shaded her eyes, watching them drift away and wondering where they might end up—maybe a child will find one, or what if one spooks a horse down the road?

A man tossed some rubbish from a large can onto a fire. The smell of smoldering food drew Babe closer. A whole Sunday picnic! Corncobs, sandwiches, apple cores, popcorn balls—all half-eaten but good enough for Babe. She devoured a half sandwich in one bite, then poked around the trash can for more. She salvaged what fit into her pockets to have for later and for the mama dog.

Thirsty now. There were three metal mugs on a nearby

table. Sure enough, soda pop! One was nearly full, and she downed it in one gulp, burped, then finished off the others.

"I said put your back into it!" a man hollered from up toward the train. Three men struggled under the weight of the pole they were carrying uphill. The rope on one end trailed behind them. The last man in the line was as short and skinny as a matchstick. He tripped on the tail end of the rope and slipped in the mud, bringing down the other two men. The pole rolled downhill as people yelled and dashed out of the way. It rolled pell-mell toward Babe, who picked up the trash can with one hand and, holding a mug in the other, stepped out of the way.

She set the can down, finished off the soda pop, tossed the mug, then walked to the pole. Lifting her skirts and stooping down, she picked the pole up at its dead center and hoisted it to her shoulder. Everyone stopped cold and stared.

"Where you want this thing?" she asked.

A man pointed up the siding, toward the railcar. Babe toted it while the other men gathered the trailing ropes and wires. With barely a grunt, she pushed the pole to the top of a railcar, where it was tied down and ready for travel.

Babe looked down at the carnies watching her. She reckoned folks knew she was here now.

Something was tugging at her skirt.

"You're strong," a creature stated. Babe looked down,

took a step back to see . . . this who, this what? A masculine face but wearing a dress, only about a third of her height. The head, much too small for the body, seemed to point skyward and was topped with a knot of hair, tied with a pink ribbon. A filthy doll was tucked into her belt of rope.

"You're strong," she said again, still tugging Babe's skirt. She grinned up, displaying huge, gap-toothed buckteeth. "You're strong." She stuck her thumb in her mouth and sucked earnestly.

"Twenty minutes! Twenty minutes!" a man hollered, walking toward them. The man bent down to Babe's first "oddity" and said, slowly, as if he was talking to a three-year-old, "Now, JoJo. We're busy here, so let's take you to your car, okay?"

JoJo ignored him and pulled on Babe's skirt. "You're big. You're strong."

"Thank you," she said. "You're nice."

"I like you!" JoJo now grinned ear to ear as she stroked her doll's nearly bald head.

"You got to watch it with this little pinhead. You give her an inch, and she'll take a mile," the man said. "You come with me now, JoJo." He offered her a finger, which she grasped, childlike. She waddled off with him, waving a shy bye-bye to Babe.

Someone from up the hill yelled at her, breaking her stare. "Hey! You! Yeah, you giant! Come on! Shake a leg!"

Babe flashed back to her father's warning from just that morning. She shook her leg at him, then trotted back to Renoir's wagon. The horses had been unharnessed and taken away. The boxes and crates inside were gone.

"Where's my grip? Where's my dogs?" she asked a woman carrying a satchel.

"Ladies go into Car C."

"Where's that wood box?" Babe asked, feeling a heat inside rising up. "Had me a mama dog and her pup inside."

"You mean that?" the woman said, pointing her nose to the trash pile. "Renoir said to toss it."

Babe rushed over and snatched the box. She sat down, opened the lid, and pulled out the mama dog. "You still got your baby?" She reached in and pulled the whimpering pup out. "You okay, baby dog?"

"Well, would you look at that," the woman said, kneeling down. She wore an exotic, shiny robe of reds and embroidered golds. Babe tried not to stare at the woman's powdered face, blue-lined eyes, bloodred lips—as red, white, and blue as the Fourth of July!

"Renoir knew these was my pups in this box," Babe said, putting the puppy to her cheek and giving it a gentle kiss.

"Well, Renoir isn't very fond of animals," the colorful woman said. "Strange, for a carnie man, huh?"

"Then I ain't fond of Renoir," Babe grumbled.

"Look, do yourself a favor," she said, giving the mama

dog a pat. "Give the dogs to Donny. He's our dog act—Donny Davis and His Doggone Dogs. He'll see to it they're both taken care of. Maybe even get that pup into the act. Just don't let Renoir know. He doesn't like his orders being disobeyed."

"Where's this doggone man?"

"Usually in Car B, the men's smoking car." The fancy woman smiled at Babe. "Lord, you're built from the ground up! Every bit the giant Renoir said you were. Saw your first performance with the tent pole. Brava!"

"What's a brava?"

The woman chuckled. "It means 'nice job.'"

"Oh," Babe muttered, pulling her eyes away from the woman. "Sorry for staring, ma'am. Ain't never seed a face like yours . . . I mean . . . all painted up . . . I mean . . ."

The woman smiled so wide a gold tooth in back shone bright. "Well, that goes for me, too. Don't reckon I've ever seen a girl as big as you." She offered Babe a slender, white-as-snow hand. "I'm Cora Epstein." Her long, sharp fingernails were painted as red as her lips. "My stage name is Madame de la Rosa. I'm the mitt reader in this mud opera."

"Ma'am?"

She gave a deep laugh, mixed with a cough, and said, "I read palms. You know, a fortune-teller?"

"For true?"

"Sure! Here, give me your hand."

Babe's hands were always rough, cracked, dirty, ugly and that wasn't even considering the warts. "No."

"Oh, come on." The fortune-teller grabbed Babe's hand and turned it over, inspecting the palm. "What's this?"

"Peanut shell, looks like."

Madame de la Rosa flicked it away. Babe looked at the woman's head while she traced the lines of her palm. Her mahogany-black hair was snowy white at the roots.

"There. Uh-huh, uh-huh, uh-huh," the woman muttered.

"Uh-huh what?"

"Just as I suspected. Long life, lots of love, and many, many, many adventures are ahead for you."

Babe pulled her hand away. "Don't say no such thing. Giants don't live long. My ol' man told me."

The woman smiled and winked. "Well, in folklore, they do." She pulled out a leather tong necklace and shook out the charms dangling on it. "For ten cents extra, I sell a juju to make sure good fortunes come true."

"What's a juju?"

"It's anything you can hustle—sell—to make a person feel good." She took one off the tong. "Here."

"I don't got ten cent."

"On the house," she said, handing it to her. "You're going to need all the good luck you can get with this broken-down outfit. And believe me, I've seen them all!"

The train tooted again. Madame de la Rosa hurried off, calling, "See you in the car! We have to hurry. That train'll leave us here to walk to the next stop if we're not on it. By the way, what's your name?"

"Fern Marie Killingsworth!" Babe hollered after her.

"Glad to meet you!" she called back, her long robe flowing behind her.

"Folks call me Babe!" She smiled down at the juju—a small wooden disk with a frog painted on it—then pocketed it. She tossed some food in the box for the mama dog, closed it, and climbed the hillside toward the train, the box safe and secure under her arm.

She continued along the side of the tracks, counting twelve cars and a pink caboose. The first car after the firewood car was painted faded red, black, and gold. "Professor Renoir's Collection of Oddities, Curiosities, and Delights" was painted on the side in fancy white letters, chipped and dirty with soot. A painting on another car caught Babe's eyes. The huge creature had red eyes spitting fire, sharp long tusks, barreling through a crowd of terrified people.

"Car-lot-ta." Babe sounded out the writing. She stepped back and squinted while she sounded out "El-e-phant."

She glimpsed someone peeping at her through the window at the front of the elephant railcar. A curtain came down with a snap. The back of the car had no windows but narrow slots too high up for Babe to peek into. Sniffs and snorts came from inside.

People shouting, engine panting, steam hissing—all

such foreign, strange sounds. Babe felt her heart pound and her breath come faster. Excitement or fear? Was she really about to climb aboard this train and go . . . where? Her few belongings were already on board, but she had her twenty-dollar gold piece in her boot and her two dogs under her arm. Maybe she could just turn around, walk away. Contracts, Renoir, her father, her future be damned! If she was going to turn tail and run, now was the time, she warned herself.

A long, shrill whistle startled her as it echoed off the grounds and the train gave a jerk forward. "Hey! Giant! You coming?" a man called as though he could read her thoughts from three cars ahead.

Was she? The train began to inch away. She looked down on the empty field, back at the pink caboose, up at the engine. Yes, she was coming!

Babe broke into a bone-jarring trot, then a clumsy lope. Gravel shot up behind her. People on board laughed and pointed through the open windows.

She finally caught up, and with the help of the man who had signaled her, she pulled herself aboard.

"Where's . . . that man . . . with the dogs?" she gasped, peeking inside the box to make sure the dogs were all right.

"Donny? He's up there in the men's smoking car. Bald as a baby's butt. Can't miss him." The man pointed to the car ahead.

Babe struggled with the railcar's double door. It didn't push; it didn't pull.

"It slides," the man advised.

She looked at the casing, then understood. Like a barn door. She tried it, but it stuck.

"Got to unlatch it first." He pointed to the handle.

She grabbed the handle and slid the door with such a force it came off its tracks, sticking and now only half open. She jiggled it. Still stuck. She tried to edge her way through the door ignoring the sound of men's laughter.

Now *she* was stuck! "No!" Babe growled. Roars of laughter erupted as two men on both sides of the door pulled and grunted to get her and the door unstuck. Finally free, she burst into the car, where a wave of heavy cigar smoke hit her. She looked around through the fog.

Not one bald man did she see. "Need me that baldy man with the dogs!"

"Hey, baldy man!" someone called to the back.

A man walked toward her. "I have the dog act," he said, smiling kindly at her. "Ignore all those laughing hyenas."

"You ain't bald," Babe said, noting the man's full head of hair.

More laughter came from the crowd that had gathered around them.

"Oh!" He reached to his head and pulled off his toupee. "Now I am." Roars of laughter!

Babe gasped. She knew women wore wigs sometimes,

but men? "What're they laughing at?" Babe asked the short, stout, bald man.

"Oh, I was taking a bow after my act yesterday and my rug fell off."

"Rug?"

He shook his toupee under her nose, and the car exploded in more laughter, boos, hisses, cuss words. With more voice than Babe figured a man of his size could muster, he shouted, "Shut the sam hill up! Can't you see there's a young lady present?"

More laughter at "young lady."

"Who *can't* see her?" another man shouted.

"Don't listen to them. Come on." Donny tried to make his way toward the platform between the cars, but Babe was blocking the way. She backed up into an empty seating area. "Yep. You're the giant all right. Renoir said he was chasing a strong act. So, what can I do you for?"

"That mitt reader, Madame Something. She said you'd make sure these critters get tooken care of."

He opened the box. "Lookee there. Just a wee one and not very old."

"Borned just this morning. She had three, but the first two was already goners coming through."

"Mama's a tired old girl. Terrier, I'd say. Smart dogs, terriers."

"Maybe you can help her come around," Babe said, scrunching the dog's ears.

"I'll do my best," he said, smiling up at her. "Say, you better get to the ladies' car. Renoir doesn't like fraternizing while on the road."

"Ha!" another eavesdropper muttered, chuckling over his newspaper across the aisle.

"Reckon mama needs some water. Gave her a few bites of sandwich. Her poor youngin's had a hard day."

He smiled at her. "I know just what to do. You go on." He nodded toward the car door. "Say, what's your name?"

"Babe. Can I come visit them?"

"Sure. Any time."

"You won't let that boss man, that Renoir, get rid of 'em?"

"Of course not."

"Okay, then."

Babe paused, then lumbered back through the car, this time carefully sliding the door open and closed behind her. She stopped on the vestibule.

"Sure is a wonder," she whispered, looking back on her first day ever away from home—from helping the mama dog birth her pup, and her father and Renoir bartering for her, to the strange people she'd met. And now watching the greens, browns, and blues blurring as the train now zoomed toward whatever—whomever—was on the tracks ahead. "A wonder for sure."

"You sleep in there," Madame de la Rosa said, moving aside the thick black curtains to a short and narrow berth in the ladies' sleeping car.

Babe poked her head inside. "What half of me?"

"Oh," Madame de la Rosa said, putting a delicate hand to her mouth. "I see what you mean." Babe gripped a handle to keep her balance as the train waddled back and forth. Madame de la Rosa swayed like a seasoned sailor, her sea legs well under her. "Well, here. Come with me and we'll set you up in the ladies' lavatory."

"Ma'am?"

"Latrine? Privy? Uh, outhouse?"

"A necessary room? Here on a train?" She massaged her shoulder, already cramping from bending over in the train's passageway.

"Come, dear," she said, leading the way toward the back of the car. "I'll show you."

The "necessary room" was bright with shiny white tiles reflecting light from the gas lamps. "Don't tell me you've never seen a lavatory before," Madame de la Rosa said.

"Not like this," Babe whispered, folding herself in half to get through the door. She peeked into the stall. "Got a chain pull and everything." Babe recalled the only other necessary room she'd seen—the infirmary in Neal, and that was not a pleasant memory, considering the broken porcelain commode. "Can I give it a pull? See the water gush and all?"

"Be my guest." Madame de la Rosa smiled as she watched Babe pull the chain, lean over, and watch as the water flowed out and then back in. Another pull and a third. "Sure comes and goes hellity-split. Where's it all go?"

"Down on the tracks, of course. But here, here's a couch. At least you might fit better. Maybe you can hang your legs over the edge. Better than those sleeping berths." She swiped away some magazines scattered on a long, low fainting couch. "Here. I'll go round up some bedding."

Babe picked up a magazine and sounded out the cover story. "Peo-ple. Who. Are . . . Dif-fer-ent." She eagerly flipped through the pages. Madame de la Rosa returned with an armload of linens, and Babe put the magazine behind her back.

"What'd you have there?"

Babe's face went scarlet as she handed over the magazine.

"*Sideshow Monthly*!" she snapped, tucking the magazine into her belt. "No, young lady, you're a bit too young for this."

"Sorry. I don't read so good, so I was just looking at the pictures. Them's my beddings?" she said, quickly changing the subject. "Uh, that couch is nice, ma'am, but reckon I'll just set me up on the floor."

"Okay. But hang on to those pillows and blankets. People around here have a tendency to swipe them." She winked at Babe.

"Folks have a hard time swiping anything from me." Hundreds of times she'd easily hung on to something while three or four others tried to take it away. Babe always won at tug-of-war. She was a team of one.

"Oh, and the food cart comes along around six. You sure you don't have any money on you?"

"For what?" she asked, remembering her twenty-dollar gold piece resting safe and warm in her boot. She wasn't about to let it cool off.

"Well, you see, we pay for food on the cart or else Renoir takes it off your pay. No, never mind. I'll just sign and we can settle up later. You're so green."

Babe put her hand to her face. "I feel okay."

"No, no. Green—greenhorn. Fresh fish. Ha! You'll learn the lingo."

Babe's eyebrows grew together as her face scrunched.

"The way we carnies speak."

"You're a carnie?"

"Yes, and you're one now, too. You'll catch on. We have a language all our own."

Babe rolled out a huge sigh and said, "Got me a lot to learn."

"Baby steps," Madame said, smiling up at Babe.

"Never once took me one of them," Babe said, smiling down at the woman.

Madame de la Rosa threw her head back and laughed. Babe was charmed by her new friend—from the colorful splash of her silk scarves right down to her bespangled wrists. "Don't worry. You'll learn."

Babe carefully tested the strength of the couch before sitting down full load on it. Her knees rose up to meet her chest. "Don't do well learning. Quit school after third grade, second try."

"Well, what I meant is, there's plenty of stuff to know about carnie life. Us." She pulled a cigarette from a silver case. "Cigarette?"

"No, thank you. It'll stunt my growth."

Madame smirked around the cigarette dangling from her painted lips. She swiped a match along the wall with a dramatic flare and inhaled her cigarette to life. Babe fanned away the smoke as it wafted up.

"You know, I've been with this outfit a few years now,

and I think you might be the one and only real performing freak we've had."

Babe had been called a freak a hundred times, a thousand times! But never a "real performing freak." "Ma'am? I mean, Madame?"

"Well, there's JoJo the Astonishing Pinhead."

"JoJo? I met her. Him?"

"Her. But JoJo doesn't have an act. She's what we call a nondescript. She's not this; she's not that. She just goes on display and sometimes, if she feels like it, holds up the signs for the next act. Mostly we're all just fakes here on this circuit. Renoir seems to attract fakes like dogs attract fleas, because he's just a cheap fake himself. You'll see."

"You got yourself a elephant. That can't be fake." Babe recalled the painting on the railroad car of the charging elephant with fire-blazing eyes.

"No, you're right. The elephant is real, but that Carlotta! Ugh, what an *enfant terrible*!"

"What's that?"

"A first-class brat. Anyway, she's the elephant's handler, and talk about a no-talent little blister. I heard Renoir say he hopes the elephant will just squash Carlotta flat and then we could get a real handler! One who might stir up some excitement. Anyway, Babe, you're young and you're the genuine article. The rest of us, we're pretty much old, tired, and fake."

"You ain't fake. You're about as real as anything. The only . . . *carnies* . . . I ever seed up the mountain was dog and pony shows, magic men, jugglers and such. Punch and Judy puppets beating each other to hell . . . I mean to doll rags. Nothing fake about them. They was puny but not fake."

"Honey, there's something called wool, and this show is all about pulling it over the eyes of people paying hard-earned money just so they can be fooled. Well, plenty of time for that. Nothing wrong about it. It's the biz. Just saying, you're . . . you're . . ."

"A giant. Don't that show?"

"I know, but you're a *real* giant."

"Excuse me, but how can there be a fake giant? I mean, either you're a giant or you ain't. . . ."

"The fat-woman act," she said, breaking her off. "You don't want to end up being that."

"You get a act for just being fat?" Babe balanced herself as the train lurched.

"If you're really, *really* fat you do. The fat woman sits in a huge chair, wears a tent for clothes, and tells folks about being fat. How much she eats, how much she weighs. She has to make like she's jolly and laughing all the time. Then folks usually throw food at her and poke fun. I've seen it in other outfits. The fat-woman act is about the lowest act there is. And the fat, jolly woman is usually the saddest one in the whole show. So don't you ever let Renoir make you a fat-woman act. Now, come with me and I'll introduce you around."

Babe looked down at her own belly, sucked it in, and thought back on what Renoir had told her father. *She'll be among her own kind.* If Madame de la Rosa was "her own kind," maybe things were going to be okay. Even so, she knew she better watch what she ate.

The air in the dining car was steamy and stuffy. Cigar and cigarette smoke rose to the top and mixed with the aroma of food cooking somewhere, forcing Babe's stomach to churn. The smells, the movement of the car . . . Babe's burp was a warning.

Madame introduced Babe to the performers and crew as they went through the car. But Babe barely had time to say how do, let alone remember names. Every one of them made a comment about her size. Babe ignored it all and was glad to fold herself into a row of two empty seats.

"Make way, make way," a man said, wearing a white coat and carrying a tray high above his head. "Dinner for Little Miss Full of Herself! Coming through!"

His passage was greeted with boos and hisses. Someone hollered, "Aw, let the little snot come eat with us peasants!" Laughter and nasty comments. Several voices clashed together with a singsongy *"Car-laaaa-taaaaaa!"*

Babe looked around. "Who's that?"

"That's who I told you about."

"The one Renoir wants squarshed?"

Madame de la Rosa laughed. "Well, she *is* spoiled rotten. Renoir bought her act a few weeks ago. The kid and her elephant got stranded in Spokane."

"Probably paid big money for them!" a man called out.

"Money he don't have!" a woman added.

Another man jumped in. "We get slop and she gets her food made to order and served on a silver tray. La-de-dah!"

"Car-la-de-dah!" a few others called out, laughing.

"And talk about a no-talent, sad act! The elephant can dance a jig better'n she can," another person said.

Still another person leaned into their conversation, gesturing wildly with what looked like huge lobster-claw hands. "Claims she's got royal blood. My clawed foot! I'd like to spill some of that blood!" She opened and closed her hands to gesture snapping. Babe's eyes widened. "Quit staring," the woman said, flashing her hands under Babe's nose. "These are just hands. They can do everything yours can do."

"Yes, ma'am." Babe quickly looked away, feeling a rush of dizziness.

"That's Lucretia the Lobster Woman. This is Babe, our new strong act. Show her your feet, Lu."

"That's okay," Babe said, her stomach giving another churn. She looked outside the window and tried to keep her eyes on the horizon. She stifled another deep, angry burp.

"Uh-oh. You're green," Madame de la Rosa said from the seat across.

"I know. You already told me I'm a new fish," Babe muttered. The smell of tobacco smoke mixed with the scent of sticky-sweet perfume.

"No, I mean you really *are* green. You feel okay?"

"My stummy ain't fond of moving so fast." She rubbed her middle and hoped the leftover food she'd found and bolted down earlier didn't bolt back up in full and with bonuses.

"Here. Switch seats. You should be looking forward, not backward."

"This window open? Could use me some fresh air."

A man pushing the food cart stopped beside them. There were two large kettles simmering on a gas burner. Overripe fruit dangled from hooks on the side, and slices of bread were stacked on a shelf below. Beer sloshed from a large growler attached to the cart. "Got yesterday's hog hash and tomorrow's red cabbage," he announced flatly, lifting the lids, allowing the clashing aromas to drift up.

"Need air!" Babe said, sensing impending doom. She stood up fast and hit her head on the iron luggage rack overhead, bringing all eyes up to her just in time to see—and hear—her giant-size puke into the only vessel she could find—the huge growler of beer. Immediately, people yelled, moaned, tossed things at her, and ordered her to get out and get out now!

"Follow me," Madame de la Rosa said. "Move that cart out of the way, Simon!"

"Damn you! That was the last of the beer in the keg!" Simon yelled back, tossing a towel over the growler.

Madame de la Rosa pulled Babe along to the aisle and out onto the open-air vestibule. Babe got her balance and inhaled deep gulps of fresh air. She leaned out, puked again, then leaned against the car. Tears rolled down her reddened face.

"You okay?"

"Never been more hurt-faced in all my whole life," she said. "All them people. Won't never live that down." She nodded toward the dining car.

"Yes, you will. Here, blow your nose."

Babe looked at the delicate lace-trimmed hanky and handed it back. "You ain't never seed a giant blow her nose. Almost as ugly as cascading into a beer bucket. I got this." She pulled out a large, crusty red bandanna. She wiped her tears, blew her nose, and stuffed the bandanna back into a pocket.

"Thank you, Madame de la Rosa."

"Call me Rosa."

"Thank you, Rosa." They rode in silence. "I'm okay now, if you want to go get your vittles."

"I'm enjoying the fresh air, too." Rosa lit another cigarette.

Babe leaned out and looked toward the cars behind

them. "Where do the critters travel? I'm thinking I'll be better off bunking with them."

"Cars F and G, down the back. Right after Carlotta's car. Renoir has them crammed in like sardines, poor things. But you're not a 'critter,' and you don't ride with them."

"Yes, ma'am."

"You feeling better now? You look better."

"Think maybe I can go lie down? Been a long day."

"Sure. I'll go with you. Make sure you're okay."

She led the way back to the ladies' sleeping car.

"Oh, that sweet little JoJo," Rosa said, looking down on Babe's made-up bed on the floor of the ladies' restroom. There was a wilted wildflower on the pillow. "She must be quite smitten by you. She leaves flowers for people she likes. Dead rats for those she doesn't. Renoir's gotten his fair share! And that Carlotta! You should have seen what JoJo left for her!"

Babe smiled down at the flower. "JoJo's nice."

"I'll warn you now, Babe, she'll become a pest if you let her." She tapped her head and added, "She's forty-two but has the smarts of a three-year-old. And whatever you do, never touch that doll of hers. Thinks it's a real baby."

"Who watches out for JoJo?"

"We all do. She used to winter with family, but they up and left, so now we're her family." She pointed to Babe's valise and asked, "Your pajamas in there?"

Babe felt her face go red again. "Alls I got is BVDs."

Just then, a woman stuck her head in the door and shouted, "Hey, Rosa, you coming? Game's starting up in Renoir's car and he's backing all bets."

"You going to be okay here?" Rosa asked Babe.

"I'll make do. I'm good at it."

Alone in the room, Babe looked around. She shucked down, a layer of clothing at a time, to her BVDs, praying no one walked in on her. Using the couch to help ease her down, she spread herself out and pulled the blankets to her chin, exposing her legs to the knee.

Her eyes popped open wide. A new, strange screech. She held her breath and listened. Scream? Growl? Howl? What? It was pitched high and held long. Babe sat up. She could feel the hair on her arms rise up as the screech came again, this time muffled. Babe had heard wolf, cougar, wolverine, and maybe even once the howl of a tommy-knocker mine ghost. But never a sound like this.

She settled back down and closed her eyes, trying to envision what sort of creatures Renoir kept. And an elephant! She'd seen a drawing of one in a picture book, but to think, here and now, in a railcar not far behind her, there was an elephant with fiery eyes and razor-sharp tusks!

She let that thought, the *humhumhum* of the wheels, and the gentle sway of the car lull her to sleep.

5

Babe opened her eyes, blinked as she looked around. Where was she? Oh! On the floor of the necessary room of a train. But they were no longer moving. She peered across the floor, into the toilet stall. There was what looked like a stepping stool set in front of the commode.

Then the person inside the stall scooted the stepping stool toward the back of the commode.

"Uhh! Uhh! Dag rat it! They did it again!"

Who did what again? Who was in there? She heard another small *Ooof!* followed by the toilet chain clanging against the wall. Babe quickly sat up as the door to the stall opened.

"Nothing but a bunch of no-talent jerks in this cheesy outfit!" the person snapped as she came out of the stall.

Even sitting, Babe looked down on this little person. It wasn't the diminutive JoJo.

Babe blinked in disbelief. This person was the most beautiful thing she'd ever seen, even more beautiful than the porcelain doll she'd left behind and not much bigger—maybe thirty inches tall. Jet-black hair that curled around a delicate white face, large emerald-green eyes, and a perfectly formed tiny body, encased with an elegant silk robe of cream and gold, tied with a sash around a tiny waist.

The girl stopped, locking eyes with Babe. She ticked her head toward the toilet and said, "Pull that flusher, will you? Some joker raised the chain too high. Again! Make yourself useful, giant!" Her words might have been harsh and demanding, but her voice was delicate, high-pitched, childlike.

The girl carried her stepping stool over to the sink, climbed on it, and proceeded to wash up. She looked at Babe in the mirror. "Well, hop to it! That toilet isn't going to flush itself!"

Babe couldn't "hop" to anything. There's only one way a giant can stand up. All fours, rear end up, walk hands back, then a final unfold to a stand. She edged into the stall and pulled the toilet chain.

"Reckon you're that Carlotta folks've been talking about," Babe said, keeping her distance. "They said you was teeny tiny, but I didn't know you was a midget."

At this, the girl turned around, her face full of toothpaste, which she spat out on the floor. "I am a dwarf! Not a midget!"

"Yes, ma'am," Babe offered.

"And I'm not a ma'am, I'm a miss! But I'm not a child, either. Wish people would get that straight!" She turned back to the sink and swished her mouth with water from the community glass.

"What age do them words change?" Babe asked.

Carlotta cast Babe a confused, cold look reflected in the mirror. "What?"

"When does a miss get called a ma'am? I'm only fourteen, but I get called ma'am sometimes. Reckon it's my size."

"Well, I'm only fourteen, too, and anyone calls me ma'am is going to get one of these!" She offered up a fist so tiny, Babe couldn't help but laugh.

"You mean one of these?" Her own fist was huge.

Carlotta turned, leaned into the counter, looking up at the giant girl with the huge fist. "Yeah. That would work better."

She put her toothbrush in her robe pocket, picked up her stool, and started for the door.

"My name's . . ." But Carlotta had already left. "Babe."

Babe shook her head. A dwarf—as small and dainty as Babe was big and awkward! As beautiful as Babe was ugly! She walked to the window, wondering if maybe she could see where Carlotta had gone. She looked right and left, then took in the beautiful valley below the railroad siding. What a dang miracle! Rain and gray and mud yesterday and now sun and shine and green!

Babe washed up quickly, dressed, and grabbed her valise to discover her first day in the employment of Professor Renoir's Collection of Oddities, Curiosities, and Delights, wondering which she was going to be.

She stepped down onto the railroad platform. Things in the clearing below were bustling and busy, just like yesterday, only going the other direction. People were bringing back out what just a few hours ago they had put away; rushing here and there, toting, shouting orders and ignoring the giant girl, standing with valise in hand. A hitching post had been erected, and already a few carriages and horses were tied up with curious onlookers standing about watching the hustle and bustle of a carnival breathing to life.

The whinny of a horse brought her head around. She followed the sound toward the end of the train, staying well in the shadows. Some men were leading horses down a ramp and another team was already hitched. Ropes and poles were lying on the ground, not far away, set out in an order of escalating sizes. Huge rolls of canvas were placed between the poles, ready to be pulled back to life as tents.

"Need two more men for the hammer gang! Two tickets for one hour's work!" a man from the crew called out. Babe watched as a few boys, hands raised, shouting, "Me!

Me! Me!," shoved their way to the man.

Babe held her valise to her chest and watched it all, grinning with the same sense of wonder and excitement she felt in the air. Already the come-hither smell of roasted peanuts and popcorn floated up from a tent below. Then coffee and bacon and maple syrup! Oh, food!

A ruckus from the other side of the train started up. She trotted past the caboose. Trunks, crates, boxes, hay bales, cages, and more people milled everywhere, watching or offering to help.

Another sound. A high-pitched whine this time, more familiar to Babe. A little girl, bawling to beat the band, pointed and cried, "My dolly! My dolly! That monkey took my dolly!" She hit a note so high and hurtful, Babe's ears rang. "My dolly! My dolly!" Another huge, looooong scream.

Babe stepped around and stopped cold. There was a wagon with a large cage and sitting on top of that cage was . . . was *what*? Looked like a gorilla but wasn't gorilla-big like Babe had seen in picture books and heard in scary stories. There was a chain around its neck and it was hooked to a ring inside the cage. The creature was playing with a rag doll.

"You there! Back away! Don't get too close to him!" a man warned Babe. "He'll take your face off!" Then he called out, "Someone get a wrangler so that brat'll shut her pan!" He then tipped his hat toward the mother and added, "All due respect, ma'am."

The little girl doubled her scream when she saw how Babe towered over her mother. Babe gave the girl an extra-mean look that shut her up and sent her hiding behind her mother's skirts.

"What is this?" Babe asked the man, nodding toward the creature. "I'm Babe. Going to be a new strong act."

He tipped his cap. "I'm Vern Barrett, head roustabout."

Babe indicated the buildings beyond. "Where are we?"

"This jerkwater? Glenns Ferry, Idaho."

"What sort of critter is this?"

He looked around like he didn't want anyone, maybe even the critter, to overhear. "This is Euclid. He's really a chimpanzee, but someone cropped his ears to make him look like a pygmy gorilla. Look close up and you'll see that's shoe polish on his face and gray hairs."

"He looks puny for a gorilla, even a pretend one," Babe said, trying to catch the creature's eye.

"They say he was something in his day, but he's just a shrunk old man now. Bet he don't weigh more'n a hundred pounds."

Euclid started chatting with the girl's rag doll like it was long-lost kin. The little girl's mother said, "Are you going to get that doll, or do I have to call the authorities? That beast's a menace and should be put down, the way he went after my daughter's doll! He might have killed her for it!"

"How'd he get out of his cage?" Babe asked the man.

"Are you kidding? That devil can slip a latch in his sleep. Someone didn't lock it. Well, it wasn't me. I hope Renoir doesn't hear about this. Euclid gets out all the time, but when that kid shook her doll in his face, teasing him and all . . . Between you and me, I don't blame Euclid. Poor ol' guy's been teased at his whole life. You have no idea. . . ."

His words faded away as he looked up at Babe. "I reckon I got a idea," she said, stepping closer to the cage. "Hey, feller," she whispered. The creature stopped chattering at the doll and looked over at Babe, his eyes wide and staring. He looked her up and down.

She smiled at him and spoke softly. "What are you gawking at? Ain't you never seed a giant before? They call me Babe. Look here, want to see a pretty?" She reached into her valise and pulled out her silver hand mirror and held it up. Euclid looked at his reflection and raised his lips in a hiss. He grabbed for it, but Babe held it back and reached for the doll. But he held the doll even closer to his chest now, and hissed again.

"How 'bout we trade?" She offered him the mirror and reached again for the doll. Nothing doing. A third time and a fourth. A crowd had gathered and silenced as the bartering commenced. Finally, trust taking its own sweet time, they swapped on the sixth offer.

Babe tossed the doll to the little girl's mother, who huffed and scurried away with her daughter. People applauded. Babe ignored them and kept her attentions on Euclid.

"Got me a apple." She pulled out a half-eaten apple from her pocket and offered it to Euclid. "Want it?" Euclid gave an indifferent sniff but watched the apple out of the corner of his eye. Babe took a small bite, then offered it to him. She felt Euclid's uneasy, sly glances. "You ain't never seed a critter like me, have you?"

Slowly, cautiously, he took the apple and, like Babe did, snipped a small bite out of it. There were gaps in his yellow teeth and his old-man breath made her wince. They each looked thoughtfully at each other. Babe did everything Euclid did. He chewed, Babe chewed. He turned his head, Babe turned her head. He scrunched his lips, Babe scrunched her lips.

Someone in the crowd laughed and said, "Look at that! Monkey see, monkey do!"

"You mean, monkey see, ape do!" another man said. "Look at the size of that girl!"

Euclid and Babe ignored the laughter. Euclid hissed at his reflection, and then followed it with some chimp chatting.

"Good luck getting that mirror back," Vern Barrett said, stepping closer and lighting a cigarette.

"Well, least I got that little brat girl to shut up and go away," she said, putting her hand out again. "How's about we trade again, Euclid?" she asked, looking around for something else to trade.

"No closer, Babe. This old boy might look like buzzard bait, but he's strong as a horse."

"Just like me. Strong as a horse but dull as a ox. Least-wise, that's what my ol' man always told me." Euclid chirped at himself as he made more faces in the mirror.

"Look, whatever you do," Vern Barrett said, again low and looking around, "just don't get Renoir involved. Him and this ape are sworn enemies. Oil and water they are. No, gasoline and fire! But if you can get Euclid back in that cage, I'd be grateful."

"I'll see what I can do."

Vern tipped his hat in thanks and disappeared down off the platform.

Babe looked at the sad and soggy remnants on the bottom of Euclid's cage, which could use a good wash out.

Another gaggle of children crept around a railcar. They each grasped a bag and left a trail of peanut shells behind them.

Babe lumbered to the boys, standing in front of them, glaring down with hands on her hips.

"Look! A giant!" one cried out. They all took a huge step back.

"Me . . . want . . . pea . . . nuts!" she growled, giving them an ugly, mean face.

She came back to Euclid in no time with three bags, still warm from the roaster.

"Not going to hurt you, boy. How about I comfy you up a bit?" She unhooked the chain from the ring inside the cage. "There. That better?" But he was more interested in the peanut bags peeking out from her coat pocket.

She opened a bag, shook a few peanuts out and tossed them, shell and all, into her mouth. She worked them around, then spit out the shells and tossed them into his cage. "Hmm. Sure is good."

He looked at the smashed shells, then back at her, giving her what seemed like a look of disgust. So she did it again. "Peanuts for my mirror." She held a bag just out of his reach. Sure enough, he traded her straight across like two old friends passing the time of day together, one peanut at a time.

"You ready to go back in your cage?" she finally asked, holding the cage door open wide.

He looked at her long and hard, like he was thinking things over. Babe wondered what those old, cloudy eyes might have seen in their lifetime.

She held out her arms. "Come on, ol' man. Let your Babe help you back in." Slowly, Euclid climbed into her arms. Holding him, babe-like, she couldn't help but rock him a bit, to and fro, before putting him back in his cage. She took the collar off his neck. The hair was worn thin where it had rubbed, and his skin was red and festering. She gave him the rest of the peanuts, shut the cage door, and set the lock.

Euclid sat down and muttered something that made Babe smile. "Nice meeting you, too, Mr. Euclid."

"If I have told you once, I've told you a hundred times, Mr. Renoir! Egypt is the famous dwarf elephant of Borneo, and she only works our act! She's small and dainty and not for common labor! And neither am I!"

Babe recognized the tiny voice with the big opinions. She paused before she rounded the corner of the railroad car, then carefully peeked around it. The ramp to Carlotta's car was down.

Carlotta was dressed all in tan—jodhpurs, linen shirt, and boots to the knee. She pointed a long pole toward the ramp and said up to Renoir, "I will bring her out so people can watch her eat and drink, but that is all until our show or perhaps one of your silly parades, if any of these jerkwater towns you book us in even have a main stem! Egypt does not lift tent poles or push wagons! You have flunkies and roustabouts for that. You even have that giant to do all that!"

"And if I have told *you* once, I've told you a hundred times, you better refer to your contract!" Renoir shouted back. "That would be the paper that also says you get your own private car and your own private meals, ma'am!"

Babe cringed at the word *ma'am* and peeked to see if Carlotta's tiny fist went up to challenge Renoir.

"I didn't want anything to do with this shabby outfit in the first place!"

"Well, you're stuck with us now for a year, unless you can buy out your contract, and with your salary, I doubt that will happen," Renoir said down to her, his arms folded. "And another thing, missy! I just signed a new girl four times as big as you and I can just as easily build her into the top act."

"That giant? Ha! What can she do? She's dumb as JoJo!"

"She may not be smart, but she's strong! Oh, I know! The Girl Giant and the Elephant! A Battle of Brawn!" He held his hands up as if holding up a marquee.

Babe felt a heat deep inside rise to her cheeks.

"Now get that beast out of that car and put her to work! I'm tired of telling you!" He pointed to the clearing.

Babe looked at them both, wondering who was going to win this. Carlotta's tiny boot tap-tap-tapped on the platform. Renoir stood with his hands on his hips.

"Put that elephant to work!" Renoir repeated.

Carlotta handed a long black pole up to Renoir. "Here's my handler's rod. *You* put her to work! And remember, she hates men!"

He glared down at her, his face shaking. "Fine!" he yelled. He started away, turned, and added, "But let me tell you this, young lady, I run this outfit and you do as I say!"

"Go ahead," she said again, holding the pole up higher. "See if *she* will do as you say."

He huffed off. Carlotta watched him go, then sighed heavily and leaned against the car, covering her face with her tiny hands. Babe wasn't sure, but from the heave of her chest, she might have been crying. Then, out from the opened car door came a curious, sniffing elephant's trunk. The girl touched the tip of the searching trunk, brought it to her check, and kissed it. "I know," she muttered. "I know."

Babe turned to tiptoe away, but her boot crunched up some gravel.

"Who's there?" Carlotta demanded, coming to the end of the car.

With nowhere to turn but around, Babe stepped into the sunlight. "It's me. The giant who pulled the privy chain."

"How long have you been standing there?"

"Long enough to know I'm dumb and to hear him call you ma'am and you not giving him one of these." She held her fist up in the air.

"That was between him and me!" she snapped. "And it's not nice to eavesdrop!" For one so small she surely could scream.

"Sorry," Babe said. "It's my first day. Guess I don't know the rules."

"There's just one rule you need to learn. I'm the star of this outfit." She pointed to the writing on her private car. "See?"

"I'm just the strong act. I don't even know what a strong act is."

"Renoir's been bragging for weeks about getting you signed on. But let me tell you this. I don't give a grease spot how big you are. You'll never be bigger than me!"

Babe's mouth turned down as she considered that. "They say I'm still growing. No one knows how big I'll get."

"No, that's not what I . . ." Carlotta shook her head. "I was being facetious."

"Huh?"

"Sarcastic."

"Sorry?" Babe asked.

"Sorry for what?"

"I mean what language you speaking?" Babe asked.

Carlotta cast her eyes skyward. "Obviously not yours! Just stay out of my way! I have to tend to my Egypt."

"What's your e-gip?"

Again, Carlotta pointed to the side of her car. "Egypt! My elephant! Can't you even read?"

"Not a word I never seed before."

"Well, you're going to *seed* it plenty from now on!"

"How come you're so frothy?" Babe asked.

"Frothy?"

"Miffed," Babe explained, smiling that she had one on her now.

"Miffed?" Carlotta shouted. "I passed 'miffed' about six years ago!"

"Looks to me like you gots lots to be nice about." Babe nodded to the fancy railroad car. "Don't see why you're so all-fired mad."

Carlotta shaded her eyes as she looked up at Babe. She broke out in shrill, high-pitched laughter. "Why I'm so all-fired mad?" she echoed. "How come you're *not* so all-fired mad?"

"I get so mad I could chew fire but that don't make me smaller."

"Well, I'm mad as hell about being small!"

"You reckon that makes you bigger?" Babe asked.

"No, I *reckon* my act makes me bigger! I'm the star of this outfit, and you best remember that! You don't want to mess with me, you big ape!"

"Well, you don't want to mess with me, you little fryin'-size runt! I been fighting my own battles since I was four, when my ol' man set me to chopping my own wood so's I could tend my own fire so's I could cook my own vittles, so whatever you think you done bad, I done good!"

Silence, as the dwarf and the giant stared each other down. The elephant let out a small *trumpet* as though to add her two cents to the argument.

"Kindly step aside, I have to bring Egypt out. Stand over there in the shade while I bring her out. You'll probably spook her!"

"Would you look at that," Babe whispered in awe as she beheld the elephant being charmed by the "fryin'-size runt." Carlotta used only the gentle touch of her handler's rod and her small, calming voice to maneuver the animal. The elephant's leg cuff clanked against the wood as she walked out of the car and down the ramp, which moaned under the weight.

"Why, she ain't so big," Babe said, coming out of the shadows. "Thought elephants was giants."

Carlotta pointed her rod to the railroad car once again. "It says in great big letters right there! Dwarf Elephant! You know, *dwarf*? Like me?"

The elephant stopped fast when Babe appeared. Slowly, her tentative trunk sniffed toward her.

"Do not move!" Carlotta warned. "No telling what she'll do."

Babe let the elephant sniff her outstretched hand, then her face. "Tickles," she whispered. "She like apples?" Babe could look Egypt in the eye, the giant girl and the dwarf elephant being equal height.

"No!" Carlotta snapped. Too late, the apple was out

and already being mauled by Egypt. "Do not ever feed my elephant again!"

"It's only a half-et apple. Afraid it'll spoil her appetite?" Babe smiled at the sound Egypt made as she crunched the apple. "Why, you're cute as a needle," Babe whispered.

"She's not cute! She's fearsome!" Carlotta barked. "Now move away, I have to find her water."

"Don't look fearsome to me. Them eyelashes is like scrub brushes," Babe marveled as she reached out to touch Egypt's face. "And how come she's got such tiny eyes? Don't she need better sight, what with lions and such?"

"Once again, if you would just read my billing! Egypt's from Borneo. That's an island off of India, and there are no lions. Tigers, no lions."

"Can she see 'em lurking?"

Carlotta sighed and gave Babe an impatient glance. "Why don't you just read a biology book? She's got ears to hear and a nose to smell. That's all she needs." She tapped Egypt's shoulder with her rod. "Hut, hut, Egypt. Follow!"

Babe stepped aside and watched in wonder. The dwarf girl leading the dwarf elephant who followed her like a puppy, her tiny tail twitching.

By eleven that morning, the carnie was set up and running. Without an act worked up yet, Renoir told Babe to walk around the grounds, holding the sign:

**TONIGHT! ONE PERFORMANCE ONLY!
CARLOTTA, THE DANCING DWARF, AND EGYPT,
THE FAMOUS DWARF ELEPHANT OF BORNEO
EIGHT O'CLOCK!
ADMISSION 10 CENTS**

Her instructions were clear: Don't talk, just grunt, growl, scowl, scare the kiddies. She got the usual stares and taunts but kept the sign as her breastplate and wandered among the acts, concessions, games, and displays.

Never had she seen anything like it! The ten-in-one sideshow had most of the short acts and displays. Lucretia the Lobster Woman displayed her odd hands and feet and explained she was born that way, along with her seven sisters and brothers. Her act consisted of her doing simple things one would think difficult with her hands—tying a shoelace, opening a can, buttoning a coat. Her finale was her lying on the stage and, using both hands and feet, juggling balls tossed to her by an assistant.

"Don't miss the darling, daring, dancing girls, Ina, Mina, and Tina, the Triplets of Tripoli!" their barker called out. "Step right up, gentlemen! Hurry, hurry! Hot-cha-cha!"

JoJo got her own display. It was just her walking shyly around a small stage while the barker shouted. "JoJo the Astonishing Pinhead was found in the jungles of the Amazon, living with a family of baboons and speaking not a word! Rescued by a kindly family of God, she comes to us today as a testament to what love and caring can bring about." JoJo, dressed now in a robe of floral print, came forward. The barker continued. "JoJo, recite for these fine people the Ten Commandments."

The crowd hushed as JoJo pulled her thumb out of her mouth. "Thou . . . shalt . . . not"—her eyes landed on Babe—"have any other . . . giant! Hi, giant! She's strong! She's nice!" The crowd turned toward JoJo's pointed finger, where Babe stood frozen. She put up the sign to cover her face and quickly left.

She continued through the sideshows, one barker's spiel bleeding into the next.

"Sensational Señor Renaldo! Swallows swords, eats fire!"

"The Fabulous Fabians! World-renowned acrobats! Daring feats! Amazing balance!"

"Donny and His Doggone Dogs! Best dog act in the West!"

"Wire-walking Wallaces! No net!"

Babe snuck a quick look at each act as she passed, mouth open in amazement, just like the rest of the small-town audience. Oohs, aahs, taunts, and applause at every turn.

Each pass through the carnival included a trip through the dog cages to check on the mama dog and her pup, the mess tent for a sandwich and something to drink, ending at a small area, always empty, which featured just two "exotics" in their small, filthy display cages. On each pass, she gave them whatever scraps she rounded up and made sure their water pans were filled. She straightened the signs above their cages.

JUPITER! MAN-EATING BEAR!
DO NOT STAND CLOSE!
DO NOT PUT YOUR HAND INSIDE CAGE!

EUCLID!
WORLD'S SMARTEST PYGMY GORILLA!
ABLE TO CALCULATE SUMS!
DO NOT TEASE OR FEED!

The day dragged on, with three more shows, all leading up to the evening, when the sun stretched west, when the torches were lit, when people came from after work, when kids came from after school, when the main event—the elephant act—was set to go on. The pull of food aromas seemed stronger in the dusk as the concessionaires barked their goods. Popcorn balls! Sausage on a stick! Caramel apples! Corn on the cob! Cold beer! Soda drinks! Pie by the slice! Babe was in heaven!

Madame de la Rosa found Babe coming away from the mess tent, her fifth pass through. "You know, you might save a little for the rest of us," she said, indicating the circle of candy-apple red around Babe's lips.

Babe quickly swallowed. "Sorry, ma'am."

"I was just joking, dear. So, what do you think of our

little collection of oddities and curiosities and delights?"

"Never seed such ever in my life!"

"Yes, we're quite an assortment."

"Them triplet dancing girls sure gots flimsy clothes. Reckon they catch their deaths lots."

"Ha!" Rosa laughed. "First of all, they're not even sisters, let alone triplets! Second, well, yes, now that you mention it, they do sneeze a lot!"

From the center-stage area came a booming voice. Renoir was speaking through his megaphone, calling people to buy their ten-cent tickets to see Carlotta's world-famous act.

"Oh, come on, Babe. You've got to see this," Rosa said, pulling Babe along. Babe finished off the corn on the cob she was holding, then flung it high and over the mess tent.

The six-piece orchestra filed in wearily, plopped down into their seats, and struck up an off-key tune. Renoir stood in the middle of the performance ring, barking his ballyhoo pitch to the gathering crowds as they took their seats ringside. He wore shiny black boots, a red suit coat, black top hat, frilly white shirt, and flashed dashing smiles and winks at the ladies.

"Ladies and gentlemen, meet Carlotta, the world's smallest girl, and Egypt, the famous dwarf elephant of Borneo!"

Carlotta entered the fenced-off area, standing on Egypt's sturdy straight back, acknowledging the crowd with a royal wave of her leather-gloved hands. How they made gloves so small, Babe had no idea. She seemed to glimmer under the lights. She wore a riding outfit of black, a red satin shirt, and a cunning little hat cocked to the side of her head and held in place with a silky white scarf.

She started her act to great applause . . . acrobatics atop the elephant, then dancing a jig on Egypt's flat head. After a few minutes and two stumbles, she finished her act to sparse applause.

"Is that all?" Babe whispered down to Rosa.

"Just about," Rosa said.

"You mean I walked around all day toting this sign and that's all there is? Just a few of them summysaults on Egypt's back? Don't the elephant do nothing?"

"Yeah, eats."

"Been waiting all day to see this." She was unable to keep the disappointment out of her deep voice. "Glad I didn't pay no ten cent."

"The elephant was the draw. Once upon a time, that elephant was the talk of the south, so they say. Used to do a lot of tricks. The girl was part of the deal." Rosa looked up at Babe and added, "Well, remember I told you we're all pretty much just old or washed-up in this outfit."

"Bet I could teach that elephant some tricks," Babe whispered down to Rosa. "I'm good with critters."

"Even Donny's dogs dance better than Carlotta," Rosa said, frowning. "Maybe Donny could teach her some new steps. But she's been with us since Spokane, and those are the same cheap ditties she always does. If you ask me, Renoir got played for a sucker getting saddled with this act." She ticked her head toward Renoir, who was watching from the sidelines, arms folded, not smiling.

"Wait. There goes something," Babe said, pointing. Carlotta was now jumping rope across Egypt's flat back while the orchestra struggled to play an Irish jig.

Carlotta tossed the jump rope down and then gave Egypt a gibberish command. The elephant gracefully dropped to her front knees and stretched her trunk out until it made a long slide. Carlotta took a breath and balanced herself on top of Egypt's head and, one foot in front of the other, slid down Egypt's extended trunk. She did a handspring, a somersault, and then a big finish with several cartwheels, landing off-balance, then falling over, upsetting three people in the front row. Meager applause. She signaled Egypt to come closer, sit back on her haunches, raise her trunk, and issue a long, echoing *RRRRRRR!* That made the crowd applaud heartily.

Rosa said out of the side of her mouth, "She has a wrangler slab axle grease on the elephant's trunk so she can slide down." Rosa started to chuckle. "One performance the other day someone forgot the grease. No grease, no slide! Carlotta fell off—*kerplunk!*—right on her teeny-weeny part that goes over the fence last! Come to think of it, that was the biggest applause she's gotten since being with us."

Babe snickered with Rosa. "Wisht I'd seed that!"

"Oh!" Rosa said. "Got to get to my tent! Someone might need one last fortune before heading home!"

Babe watched her dash off. "Ain't never seed nothing like it," she said with an exhausted sigh. She tossed the sign she'd been carrying around all day onto the ground and slowly made her way back up to the train.

"Babe, you cannot sleep in here! Not in this ... this, why it's a cattle car," Madame de la Rosa said. "It's for those filthy animals. This place smells like a ... a ... cattle car. I won't allow it!"

Three nights sleeping on a hard, cold tile floor in the ladies' necessary room was enough for Babe's joints. So when they stopped to set up in Pocatello, Idaho, Babe got to thinking.

"That Carlotta gets her own car."

"Well, she's different. That car came kit and caboodle with her act."

"She keeps her elephant in there, don't she?"

"Well, not really. It's a duplex car. Half is her personal quarters, the other half is for the elephant," Rosa explained. "I haven't been invited inside, but I hear it's quite posh."

"But she can visit and talk to her Egypt, can't she?" Babe asked.

"Yes, there's a door to her section, but, Babe . . ."

"I want me that, too."

"Babe, no, I just won't allow it," Rosa said, folding her arms.

"Well, that rock-hard privy floor ain't no fancy feather-piller bed. Let me show you around. See?" she said, turning a full circle around the cattle car. "It's warm, it's cozy-some, and it's big. Alls I had to do was move all them crates and trunks around." She went to one corner. "This here's my bedroom." Another corner. "This here's my libarry." She held up the women's magazines she'd swiped from the ladies' necessary.

"Babe, no."

"Criminy, Rosa, I been sleeping in a barn my whole life. I'm used to smells and creaks and drafts. I reckon this cattle car is something of a betterment. Besides, I can take care of Euclid the chimp and that ol' Jupiter bear who gets put up in here, too. I've been feeding 'em, and we're old friends already."

"Not that old, flea-bitten bear! Renoir says Jupiter isn't even worth the price of a vet and is going to have him put down."

"Put down what for?"

"Infected foot or something."

"I'm good doctoring critters. Maybe I could . . ."

"Look, Babe, you're not here to be a wrangler or a razorback."

"A hog?"

"No, a stooge. Common worker. You've been hired as a strong act. You've been with us a week." She tapped Babe's arm. "So, what's your act going to be?"

"Renoir says he's still working on my act. I told him no fat-woman act and he said I'll be a fat woman if he says so."

"What does your contract say?"

Babe's face went blank. "I don't know. My ol' man and him worked it all up."

"Have you even read it?"

"My ol' man kept it," Babe said, low and looking down. Reading a child's poem was trouble enough for her, let alone a contract.

"My dear, you have to . . ."

"Babe, you in there?" Vern Barrett called out from the train platform. "Here's Jupiter and Euclid. Ready for bed. Just need to hear their prayers and tuck 'em in. Hello, Rosa."

Vern and a roustabout pushed the two cages inside the car.

"What's that horrible smell?" Rosa asked as the bear cage went by.

Vern pointed at Jupiter's right foot, and Babe took a closer look, then said, "It's all swolt and oozy. It was puffed out yesterday, but now look."

"Been getting worse by the day. Don't get too attached to him. Renoir says to put him down as soon as we land in a town with a good skinner so's he can pick up his new parlor bearskin rug on the return swing."

"I warned you, Babe," Rosa said, taking a brief glance, then turning away from the smell. "Poor thing."

"Any doc in this outfit?" Babe asked.

"Archie, he's one of the wranglers, he thinks he's a horse doctor, but he's afraid of that bear," Vern said.

Jupiter groaned as he shifted his weight and rolled over. "Got to be something you can do," Babe said, reaching inside the cage and gently stroking the bear's thick ear.

Rosa touched Babe's arm. "He's in pain, dear. He should be put down."

"We did get him doped up two days ago, but dang, this ol' boy's stronger than he looks, and we just couldn't hold him down long enough to drain that toe," Vern said.

Babe turned to Vern. "You reckon he's stronger'n me?"

Vern and Rosa looked at each other, the doubt in their faces slowly melting into shrugs of *Why not try?*

"Well, there's just one way to find out," Vern said, dashing out the door.

"I think he's about as drowsy as he'll get," Archie said, putting away a huge syringe. "Got to work fast, though." Babe gently pulled the grumbling bear out of his cage. She sat down and kept his head on her lap. She wrapped her arms about his neck and held the bear tight, whispering in his ears, "Your Babe's got you. Your Babe's got you."

"Careful now. Everyone ready?" Archie said, taking a deep breath. "Hold him tight, girl. Here goes."

Pus and blood spurted out as Archie dug into the side of the toe. Rosa looked away, and Vern dabbed the incision with cotton. Euclid, in his cage across the car, started screaming. Babe held tight as Jupiter groaned and tried to move. "His paw, hold his paw!" Vern cried.

Babe grabbed Jupiter's large paw in her own two large paws and fought against the bear's struggle. "Got it!" Archie said. "Hand me the nippers. Get your hand away, girl!" He snipped away at the long claw, using the horse-shoeing tool. The bear's long, curled claw had a slit down the middle.

"He's opening his eyes," Vern warned. "Hurry, Archie."

"I got him," Babe said.

"I think I got it all," Archie said. His forehead was beaded with sweat. "Vern, iodine!" He commanded.

"You or the bear?" Vern asked.

"The bear, you clown!"

Babe kept her arms tight around Jupiter, who let out a muffled roar as the iodine soaked in. "He ain't so asleep no more!"

"Can you trim those other claws? They'll just split, too," Vern said.

"I knew you'd say that," Archie grumbled. Babe held

each foot up while Archie worked fast to trim the claws. She had to lean into Jupiter, putting all her weight against him.

Finally, Babe, Vern, and Archie hauled Jupiter back into his cage. "No wonder it got infected," Archie said, pointing to the conditions of the cage. "Shut up, Euclid!"

Babe walked to the chimp's cage and said softly, "Your friend's okay, Euclid. It's okay now."

Just then, the cattle car door crashed open. "What the devil is going on in here?" Renoir demanded. No one said anything. Even the animals grew silent as Renoir stalked around the car. He looked at Jupiter's lanced foot, at the mess, at each person, and then stood in front of Babe.

Babe wiped a wisp of hair from her face. "We got him all fixed up. Easy as pie." She smiled and indicated Jupiter's cage. "He's going to get right as rain now. Won't be a rug after all."

He ignored her. "And under whose authority did you do this?" he demanded, pointing to first Rosa, then Vern, then Archie.

"Well, gosh, Mr. Renoir . . . ," Vern started. "Putting down that bear would have—"

"Shut up!"

"Really, Phillipe," Rosa intervened, "we just wanted to—"

"You, too!"

Archie wrapped his tools in a rag, rose, and started to leave. "Collect your pay at the next stop!" Renoir shouted as he left.

Babe's smile disappeared as Archie left, followed by Vern.

Rosa paused in front of Babe. "Don't let him bully you. We did the right thing here." She squeezed Babe's arm and left, leaving Babe alone and face-to-face with Renoir.

She took a step back. He glared up at her. "And did you have anything to do with this?"

"Held Jupiter down," she said low. "I don't—"

"No, you don't!" he shouted. "Listen, my dear, huge young woman, in *my* outfit *my* orders are to be obeyed! Do you understand that?"

"Reckon so, but—"

"There are no buts!"

Euclid had been watching the exchange and, as Renoir paced closer to his cage, reached out with a scream and grabbed for his shoulder. Renoir raised his hand as though to strike back. Another earsplitting screech, followed by Jupiter's groggy growl.

"Critters don't favor yelling," Babe defended.

Renoir turned on her. "Sit down, you!"

"I like standing," Babe said, hiding the light from the door and casting her shadow down on Renoir. The truth of the matter was, sitting down was awkward and ugly. It wasn't as though she could just gracefully sift herself down.

"I said sit!" Their eyes met. She stifled her groan as she folded herself down onto her straw mattress. Dust shot up as she plopped down.

"My orders were explicit! I had something else planned for that animal, and curing him isn't it!"

Babe wasn't sure she heard him correctly. "But now he can go back on display and . . ."

"And now he's going to start eating again. That's just fine! He was a lot cheaper to keep when he went off his feed."

"But why?"

"He's old; he's decrepit; he does nothing to warrant what I feed him." He pointed toward Carlotta's car. "Everyone in this outfit has to pull his own weight! Especially now because that hay-burner elephant is eating me off the circuit! Cuts have to be made, and I'm making them!"

"I can pull his weight!" Babe shouted. "I'm strong!"

"He's my inventory, and I'll do with him as I please!"

It was no time to ask what inventory was. She took some deep breaths to crush down her rising beast. "How about . . . um, how about I get him his vittles now? Make sure he don't eat too much. And Euclid. He don't eat much, neither, and we can get along on scraps."

"Ha! I've seen you chow down five times a day since you got here."

"I can scrimp back."

"Anyway, that's not what I've come to discuss. It's time *you* start pulling your own weight here."

"I can pull my own weight three times over. I'm strong."

"No, you idiot girl, I mean earn your pay. Everyone in this outfit better earn their pay or they're gone! I'm not made of money. I won't put up with spongers who soak up my generosity."

"You don't make me into no fat woman," Babe muttered.

"No, this is a new act. You and Euclid. That ape's not earning his keep, either. Hasn't done a thing but take swipes and spit and fart at people for over a year now. Ever since his trainer died."

"Critters can wear the willow just like folk, I reckon. Had a cat lost her sister. She wasn't never the same."

The way Renoir looked at her, she felt as though she had corn growing out of her ears. "What on earth are you talking about?"

"Euclid pining after his trainer."

He cast his eyes to the heavens and sighed heavily. "No, animals don't have those kind of feelings. Anyway, Carlotta's convinced me to give him one last chance."

"Carlotta?"

He headed for the door. "Yes, she said you and that Euclid were two of a kind and would make a great knockabout act. And I have the routine notes from Euclid's last trainer. Never was much of an act, but Carlotta had some good ideas about how to freshen it up. You and Ernie Evans begin rehearsing tomorrow. Found a siding outside town, and we'll have a five-day layover, and there's lots in this outfit that needs fixing, not the least of which is reminding people who the boss is!"

Ernie Evans introduced himself as a "this 'n' that" man. Sometimes he did this and sometimes he did that—played the horn, cymbals, and drum; helped in the mess tent; barked acts in the ten-in-one sideshow. Babe liked him for his gap-toothed smile and Southern accent. Didn't make her seem quite so ugly, didn't make her sound quite so hick-like.

"Reckon I'm an animal trainer today," he said, refer-ring to the papers Renoir had given him. "Here's how the chimp's last act worked." He held up his right hand. "And these are scribbles from that midget elephant gal." He looked back and forth at both, screwed up his face. "Okay, says here, your right hand goes to your right cheek when you ask him what's two plus two and he'll count—I mean bark—four times."

He stood in front of Euclid, who was perched on a high stool, uninterested. "How much is two plus two?" Ernie made a very slow and obvious motion . . . his right hand to his right cheek. Euclid spit out peanut shells, sighed heav-ily, looked away, and yawned.

Ernie tried it again, this time raising his voice. Nothing. "Look, you son-of-a-gun monkey! You do what I'm telling you! What's two plus two?" Same hand motions; same disinterest. "It's four, you dummy! It's four!" He chirped out four *arf*s, holding up a finger for each *arf*. "See? Four!"

Babe tried not to snicker at the expression Euclid gave Ernie's performance. "Let me try. Critters listen to me. Once taught me a squirrel to play dead."

"Well, Euclid here won't have to *play* dead if we don't get him to obey."

Babe repeated the question and the hand motions. Still nothing.

Ernie looked at the instructions. "Well, it says here Euclid was born in . . ." His lips moved as he calculated the years. "Heck fire, he's already thirty-nine. Probably gone senile. Here's his ballyhoo. Lemme read the pitch . . . get him sort of warmed up." Holding his hand high, Ernie read dramatically: "'Here we have Euclid, the world's smartest pygmy gorilla. So named after the arithmetician Euclid of Alexandria, for his uncanny ability to calculate sums.'"

"What's that mean?"

"Heck if I know," Ernie said, scratching his head.

"Renoir said this here's a new angle on the knockabout act that Carlotta girl come up with for me and Euclid."

"Look, I have two other acts to frame before we hit

Granger, Wyoming, next week, so y'all'll have to work with him since it's your act. It's all writ up here what you're supposed to say and what Euclid's supposed to do." He stuffed the instructions into her hands. "Wishing y'all good luck!"

Euclid watched as Ernie walked away. He sighed, turned to Babe, lifted his lips to expose his yellow teeth. Babe brushed away a bothersome fly from her cheek.

"Arp! Arp! Arp! Arp!"

"What did you say?" She fanned her cheek again.

"Arp! Arp! Arp! Arp!"

"That's what I thought you said!" She looked at the other notes of hand signals.

Within four days, they were working as a team. They ran a dress rehearsal for the crew, beginning with little JoJo holding up the sign and giggling across the stage, taking long, deep bows.

MONKEYSHINES AT SCHOOL

Babe wore a long black dress, bulging seams, hair in a tight bun—all to make her look the very picture of an elderly, nasty schoolmarm—the sort that girls feared and boys shot spit wads at. Serena, the makeup woman, lined her face with harsh lines and shadows, put white powder on the temples of her hairline, and fashioned a lump of putty for a chin wart complete with a long wire "hair" springing from it. It was the first time Babe was ever someone else, and she loved it.

Euclid wore a little boy's sailor uniform complete with a cap, tied on with baby-blue ribbons. The stage was a schoolroom with a teacher's desk, a student's desk, and a blackboard. The first laugh came from what was on the blackboard: "Miss Higglebottom is a fat cow" with a crude drawing. Euclid sat in the student's desk while Babe called out questions and used her hand signals. The first few questions were easy, and Euclid performed right on cue, receiving his rewards of fruit slices. Babe's lines made fun of her size and stupidity . . .

"No, no, two plus three isn't five, it's eight."

"You can't make a monkey out of me!"

"I'll sit on you and squarsh you flat!"

The action soon turned to the knockabout brawl Carlotta had suggested with Babe chasing Euclid around the desks with a ruler and Euclid throwing the chalk and erasers and fruit at Babe.

"I'll get you and you'll be sorry!" Babe called out. Here, Euclid was trained to stop and start chasing Babe. "Yipes!" Babe screamed, running off stage left and coming back on stage right, chasing Euclid once again.

Finally, a garbage pail of potato peels was passed through the crowd, encouraging people to get into the act by tossing them on the stage. JoJo came back on with a large conical cap with the word *DUNCE* painted on it. She handed it to Babe, who sat, forlorn, in the corner wearing the dunce cap while Euclid hopped on the teacher's desk and ate a banana. The flimsy curtain came down.

Everyone laughed. Everyone except Madame de la Rosa. After the crew cleared, she came up to Babe, the dunce cap still cocked on her head.

"I can't believe you let Renoir do that to you!"

"Do what?"

"Make fun of you like that!" She pointed to the cap.

"It ain't real."

"No, but *you* are!" Babe picked a long potato skin off her dress and munched it thoughtfully. "Babe! I'm talking to you!"

"Don't matter about me. Renoir said Euclid had to start pulling his weight."

"By making a monkey out of you?" She stood, arms crossed, demanding an answer.

Babe looked at the sign for the act leaning on the stage apron. "Ain't that what *monkeyshines* is?"

"For Euclid, not you!" She pointed to Babe's head. "And take that dunce cap off!"

Babe took it off and looked down at it. "Don't even know what a dunce is."

Rosa seized the cap and threw it down. "Not you!"

"Sorry you don't like my act," Babe said, voice low. She pulled off her fake wart by its wire.

"Well, it's bound to flop! You'll fall flat on your face with this gluey act!"

"But Renoir said Carlotta seed a act like this in a other outfit and it knocked 'em bowlegged. I think that's good."

"Carlotta? You mean this was all her idea?"

"It don't make me feel bad, Rosa. Honest. I like Euclid, and him and me get along just fine. I like dressing up, and I don't want to be no fat-woman act, and Euclid has to pull his own weight. Reckon I'm keeping him alive."

"What about your strongwoman act? Isn't that what you were hired for? What about the terms of your contract!"

Babe fiddled with another potato skin in her hand. "Oh, I don't know about them contracts and such. My ol' man said they was for menfolk. Hell, Rosa, I'm having a good time. For once."

Rosa shook her head. "You have so much to learn."

Just then, Renoir came to the foot of the stage. "We leave for Granger tomorrow. Make sure that chimp is cleaned up. He reeks to high heaven. Oh, and Babe, I just talked with Carlotta and I think she's right."

"About what?"

"You need to make more noise when you fall on your butt that second time. You know, give your fanny a bigger rub when you say *OOOOWWW!* Give it plenty of ham!"

"Ham?"

"He means act like a bloody fool!" Rosa snapped.

"Yes! That's it!" Renoir echoed, grinning. "The audience'll love it!"

Rosa and Babe looked at each other. Rosa shook her head, then turned to Renoir. "Phillipe . . ."

He turned and gave her a chilly stare. "What?"

"Babe's act isn't ready for a real audience."

"We leave for Granger, Wyoming, today after lunch. Her act debuts tomorrow. Eleven o'clock show."

He turned and walked away, followed by Rosa.

Babe heard someone snickering from within the folds of the tent. She pulled aside the curtain. Carlotta turned with a grin, then walked briskly away, her long black hair swaying pertly from side to side.

Madame de la Rosa was wrong as wrong could be. Babe and Euclid's knockabout act was a big hit. Over the next two months, as new stage business and snappy dialogue was added, as Babe grew more sure of herself, as Euclid fattened on his rewards, as the audience laughed louder, clapped longer, and tossed pennies and nickels now instead of potato peels and apple cores, Monkeyshines at School inched higher and higher on the bill of acts in Renoir's carnival.

"So, Carlaaaaaaatta," Renoir said, drawing out her name. "You didn't do your second number tonight. Are you sick?"

"I think Egypt was off her feed."

"Oh? Looking at the latest feed bill, I don't think that was the problem."

"She needs at least two hundred and fifty pounds of food a day! She's been getting half that! No wonder she's feeling weak!"

Babe pretended to be busy with her makeup but kept her eyes on Carlotta in the mirror. Carlotta had barely spoken three words to her since her act with Euclid had taken off so well.

Renoir showed Carlotta a poster. "Here. This is what people are expecting to see." Babe had seen the posters at every stop. He held it at arm's length and read, dramatically, "'Carlotta, the world's smallest girl! Egypt, the famed elephant of Borneo. Thrills! Chills!'" He tapped the poster and said down to her, "Note it does *not* say spills!" He went back to reading while Carlotta stood, hands on hips, face reddening. "'You will be amazed! Never before seen! Not to be missed!'" He ripped the poster in half and tossed it down and added, "I could be arrested for conning the public!"

"Well, in this dinky, cheap disease of an outfit, I am not surprised!" She fingered the lapel of her riding habit. "Cheap clothes, cheap makeup, and that swill you feed us can't even be called cheap eats!" She pointed outside. "That jig band you call an orchestra is so lousy, people leave just to get away from the cacophony! And what's the big idea putting *her* on at the same time? I'm the main attraction! Since when do you have a tacky sideshow act at the same time as the headliner?"

Babe quickly looked away as Carlotta pointed her tiny finger toward her, and she hid her face behind the large powder puff of lamb's wool.

"If you don't come up with a better act with that elephant," Renoir went on, "then you'll both be playing a tacky sideshow while Babe gets star billing! I have big plans for that big girl!"

Babe felt two tiny, sharp beads of eyeballs boring a hole in her back. Renoir stomped out, leaving just the giant and the dwarf alone in the costume tent. Babe turned around on the barrel she sat upon, opened her mouth to speak, but Carlotta glared at her, turned with a snap, wobbled a bit, and stomped out of the tent.

Babe's monkeyshines act was now promoted on the fliers
Renoir's advance man plastered on trees, fences, posts,
and storefronts ahead of the carnival's arrival into a
town. If there was a raise in her pay, Babe wasn't aware
of it. She signed her weekly statement, along with everyone else—food on the train billed against her pay, along
with any damages or expenses that might have occurred.
Babe and ciphering did not see eye to eye, so she simply
signed her chit, cared for her critters, and did what she
was told.

They were outside of Laramie, Wyoming, the middle of
April. Spring was coming in chilly, but not as chilly as the
air between Babe and Carlotta. It was easy for them to steer
clear of each other, each living in her own cattle car, each

with her own animal, each doing her acts opposite the other. Everyone in the carnie had noticed the giant and the dwarf, total opposites, and now sworn enemies. Babe felt right at home being at such odds, even though she had no idea what she had done to make Carlotta so nasty. Some people were just born that way, she figured. Just about everyone she'd ever known, come to think of it.

Babe and Euclid were getting ready for their act. Euclid, in his sailor-boy costume, delicately picked away at globs of caramel and kernels from a popcorn ball. Babe gave him one before each performance to keep him distracted. She loaded her pockets with the treats he received for his correct answers and bits of business on the stage.

"You ready, Euclid? Good crowd tonight. Rosa said this here's a cowpoke town and things can get rowdy."

Euclid gave her a nonchalant look.

"Rowdy means rough and tough—like maybe you was in your youth. Come on. Can't be tardy for school."

They walked, hand in hand, in and out of the sideshows, tents, and seating areas toward the two main stages, now set up back to back. No doubt Carlotta was leading Egypt from their train car about now. Both acts started at eight, ten cents a seat.

"Wait up, Babe!" Rosa called out. She attached a sign to her gaudy, multicolored tent.

MADAME DE LA ROSA IS IN
DEEP MEDITATION
AND WILL RECEIVE GUESTS AT NINE.

Babe grinned at the sound of coins jingling as Rosa trotted toward her. "Making good ookus?"

"*Goooood* ookus!" Rosa smiled as she brought out a handful of coins from her pocket. "There's no dupe like a just-paid-cowboy dupe. Here's some advice. If you can, play to the crowd tonight. Cowboys and their money are soon parted. Remember, Renoir can't keep track of your tips!"

"Okay. Euclid's all set," Babe said, lifting the ape and holding him to her hip.

"Have a good show," Rosa said. "I'll be watching!"

"Ain't going to see what Carlotta's been working on? I hear she's got her a new routine."

"I might pop over and take a peek after I go 'meditate.'" She winked at Babe as she headed off.

Rosa had been right—this crowd of rowdies laughed louder, clapped longer, and hissed and cheered more than most. Babe loved the part when someone would shout something and she'd go to the end of the stage, look mean, whack her ruler in her hand—the meanest of all teachers—and growl all the warnings her teachers had growled at her.

Zap! Something had zinged across her stage and hit the blackboard behind her. Euclid was on the stool next to the desk. He whirled around and looked, too. There was laughter from the back of the crowd but the torchlight was too bright along the edge of the stage for Babe to see anyone beyond the first few rows of seats.

Pang! Something else flew by. The crowd howled as Babe, serious now, shaded her eyes and looked for the rabble-rouser. Two more! *Bam! Zing! Whap!* Euclid screeched and grabbed his arm. He jumped off the stool and screamed his rage, showing his long, yellow fangs. Babe quickly scooped him up, but enraged, he pounded on her. People in the front row got up and moved back. There were cheers from the back rows.

"Euclid! Quiet!" Babe said, holding his jaw shut to keep him from biting her. Several more rocks pelted them, hitting both Babe and Euclid in the face and head. Babe's hand went to her forehead and she lost her grip on the struggling, screaming Euclid. He jumped down and ran off the stage and into the darkness.

Total silence. Babe jumped down off the stage, fire in her eyes. "Who done that?" she demanded of the crowd. People parted for her as she stalked toward the back, overturning benches and folding chairs and tossing them aside as if they were nursery playthings.

"Who done that?" she hollered again. One by one, people swept aside as Babe stalked through the area. There at the back stood a young man, a slingshot dangling from his hand. Babe felt it rise, her beast within the beast.

She towered over him. She snatched the slingshot from his hand. The man was turning to go, but she yanked him around by the arm. "How come you done that?" she growled.

"Aw, come on, he was just sportin' you," another young man said. His smell, his stance, his dare reminded her of her father.

She felt blood trickle down her cheek and ignored him. "How come you done that?" she demanded again. "We wasn't hurting you none."

He laughed, and Babe put her hand on his shoulder and squeezed. He yelled and crumpled to his knees. She kept her grip on him. "Why?"

"Someone paid me! Said it was just a joke!" he eked out. "Come on, let up! That hurts!"

She yanked him back to his feet and pulled him up to her nose. "Who paid you?"

"Put me down and I'll tell you," he said, coughing.

She dropped him down. He adjusted his collar and rubbed his shoulder. "It was that teeny-tiny person," his buddy said for him.

Babe's jaw tightened. "What teeny-tiny person?"

"That midget. The one with the elephant!" the man said. "Honest. She said it was part of the act. I didn't know it would—"

"Well, it did! Gimme a rock," she said, holding out her hand. "Someone gimme a rock!" she hollered.

His buddy handed her a rock. Babe loaded the slingshot and drew it back two feet.

"Hey, you'll kill him!" someone said.

"What are you going to do . . . ?"

She shot the slingshot just past the man's ear, then tossed the slingshot far off into the night.

Babe looked at his friend and said, "How much did she pay him?"

"A dollar," he said, backing away.

Again, Babe held out her hand. "Gimme!"

The man quickly complied. "There. There's a dollar. Come on, Willy. Let's get the hell out of this freak show!" They gave her a dirty look and left.

Babe went to her cattle car to check on Euclid. Sure enough, there he was in his cage, shaking and whimpering to himself.

"Your Babe's got you," Babe said softly, petting his neck and back. "That man got tooken care of." There was blood trickling down his face and he kept running his hand over his shoulder, crying softly.

She tended his wounds, wrapped a bandage around her own bleeding forehead, fed Euclid, then went back out.

She stood in front of Egypt's ramp, waiting, watching the people in the carnie below douse lights and slowly make their way back to the train. The last of the audience and revelers mounted their horses or clucked their teams and drove off toward town.

The huge shadow of Egypt approached, and Babe stepped into the light. Carlotta startled but quickly straightened and kept walking.

"Heard you put on quite a show tonight," Carlotta said, not looking at Babe as she walked Egypt to her ramp.

"Reckon you'll want this back." Babe tossed down the dollar bill. It landed at Carlotta's feet. She stopped. Egypt rambled inside her car.

Slowly, Carlotta looked up. Her smug smile faded when she noticed blood oozing from Babe's forehead bandage. "Look, those two rubes were . . ."

"Don't you never talk to me!" Babe growled.

Babe knew if she stayed there any longer, the beast would continue to rise. She turned and disappeared into the darkness, revenge on her mind.

"You didn't!" Rosa said, her hand hiding her smirk. "Tell me you didn't!" Babe and Rosa were having coffee in the mess tent before they were pulling up stakes a few days later.

"Don't you tell, Rosa. Promise?"

"Well, damn," she said, laughing. "The little snot's had it coming."

"Don't think I'll ever get poor Euclid back on that stage, so you're doggone right she's had it coming!"

"But really. How did you . . . ?"

"Ssshh. Here she comes," Babe said, pulling an apple pie closer for another slice.

Carlotta walked into the tent, wearing a baggy cotton dress—a far cry from her usual fashionable wardrobe. She paused at a tent post, backed into it, and scratched her back, up down, down up. Her face and her bare arms were nearly covered in a thick white paste.

Rosa and Babe had to look away to keep from breaking into laughter.

Carlotta walked over to them. Rosa composed herself and said, "My, my Carlotta. What have you gotten yourself into?"

"Just came over to tell you thank you again, Babe, for your peace offering. The bouquet of flowers was just lovely."

Babe laughed out loud. "Glad you liked 'em."

"Especially the brush clippings. Made a lovely arrangement."

"Flowers always make me smile," Babe said, grinning ear to ear.

"I saved a little sprig for you." Carlotta tossed down a paper sack. "With my compliments."

She turned and left, awkwardly trying to scratch the middle of her back.

"Don't touch that," Rosa said. "If it is what I think it is."

Babe opened the sack and pulled out a bright orange,

three-leafed cutting. She ran it along her arms and face.

"Babe!" Rosa shouted.

Babe smiled at her and said, "Ain't never once had poison oak give me a lick of itch."

Babe got her revenge, but she lost her act. Euclid was not just physically hurt during the slingshot incident but frightened beyond forgetting. He refused to even let Babe dress him in his sailor-boy outfit, let alone go on the stage for their act. For the next several stops, Babe was without an act, which made her angrier at Carlotta. Never once did she apologize. But it was a chilly comfort that Carlotta was also without an act until her poison oak rash calmed down. And never once did Babe apologize. So the get-even pranks would continue until someone cried uncle.

Eventually, Carlotta returned to her act, nose held high, once again the headliner, and Babe was told to turn in her schoolmarm costume and report to Serena, the wardrobe woman.

"Don't boo-hoo to me about it. Renoir said make do and piece something together out of wardrobe, and that's just what I did," Serena said. Babe was unsure how old the woman was—whatever years behind her were covered up with heavy stage makeup and red hair dye. "Suck it in." Serena was short to begin with, and standing on a stool next to Babe didn't help much. She slapped Babe's back. "I said, suck it in!"

Babe gulped down air and held it while Serena pinned some seams together. "You grow much more and I don't know what we'll do. Don't want you to become a hoochie-coochie act," she mumbled around a mouthful of pins.

"A what?"

She took three pins out and splayed them between her fingers. "Ina, Mina, and Tina?"

"Oh. Them dancing girls."

"*Those* dancing girls."

"What girls we talking about?"

"Oh, Babe, hold still."

"Air's hot up here," Babe said, picking out the smells of moldy canvas and Serena's perfume mixed with something else. "Mighty whiffy up here, too. What's that smell?"

"Rabbit. Very, very dead rabbit. Well, the skins of the rabbits," Serena said. "There. Turn around." She stepped across the tent to take in her handiwork. "Quit scratching,

and I warn you, one good sneeze and the whole shebang
will come undone."

"Can I look yet?"

"Go ahead. You'll find out sooner or later."

Babe walked to the full-length mirror. Working from
her feet up: her old men's boots now covered with sheep-
skin gaiters, legs and arms covered in the stretchy body suit.
About her middle and over one shoulder were Serena's very,
very dead rabbit skins dyed with spots to look like leopard.

"Reckon there's lots of lucky rabbit feets running
around out there," Babe mumbled.

"Here. Chew this up," Serena said.

"What is it?"

"Black Jack gum. It's part of your costume. And while
you're mawing that . . . no, *all* the pieces! Undo those
braids and let's see your hair."

Babe chewed and unwound her braids and fluffed out
her hair. Serena got back on her stool and took a brush to
Babe's curly auburn locks.

"Ow. That hurts. What're you doing?"

"It's called ratting."

Babe scratched her scalp. "I can see why."

"Sit down," Serena ordered. They looked at the skimpy
folding chair, so Serena pointed to a sturdy costume trunk.
Serena brought over a tray of makeup and started to blot
Babe's face.

"Never noticed before, but you have very pretty eyes. Such a pretty blue," Serena said.

"Some folk say I got evil eyes, devil eyes."

"Well, that's why we're here, isn't it?" she muttered, working on Babe's eyebrows. "High cheekbones are an asset to some women. Think maybe Mother Nature overdid yours. And that jaw."

"Mother Nature overdid everything on me. 'Cept these," Babe said. "My chests."

"How old are you?"

"Fourteen."

"Got the curse yet?"

"Been cursed my whole life."

"You know what I mean. Your monthlies. Got 'em yet?"

"Little here. Little there."

"Well, the chests come full on when the monthlies come full on. One day soon you'll wake up and BOOM! Chests galore!"

"For real? Overnight?" Babe asked, her face full of wonder.

"Well, it can seem like that. Your ma never told you all this?"

"She died after I was borned."

"Well, can't blame her for that," Serena said, under her breath.

How many times had Babe heard jabs like that? "No, it wasn't my size. She got infected. I was regulation size coming out. Right as rain. My gigantism didn't come on me until I was a few months old."

"Do you know what else comes with the chests and the monthlies?" Serena asked, still daubing makeup onto Babe's face.

"More pay?"

Serena laughed.

"Here's some advice. I've been in a theater, a circus, or a cheap carnie all my life. And I'll tell you this. Beware of men who like different girls, and girl, you are different."

"'Course, I know all that. Got that church-lady curtain lecture years ago."

She smiled and said, "Good." Then she stepped back to look at Babe's makeup. "Hmmm, maybe we'll give you a nice, long scar. You have such a huge face and square chin. What a landscape! Yes, let's see . . . maybe something with stitches."

Babe pulled the wad of gum out and held it delicately between her fingers. "What do I do with this?"

"Black out some teeth. Make 'em look like fangs, you know, jagged! Oh, here! Open your mouth." Serena took the wad and pressed pieces onto Babe's large teeth. "Hold it. Not done. Relax your lips."

She painted magenta-red paint onto Babe's large, fleshy lips, then stood back, smiled, and announced, "There! Not bad if I say so myself!"

Babe looked at herself in the mirror, laughing at her

scarred face and gum-snaggled teeth. "Renoir said I got to be a fright, and I reckon I am."

"What's Renoir calling this new act of yours?"

"Magnifica, Queen of the Somethings. I forget."

"There you go, Magnifica. Now, Renoir's waiting for costume and makeup approval. Give me a howl and a growl way down deep in your throat."

Babe gave out a low, menacing growl.

"Put some gurgle into it. You know, like you're gargling," Serena said.

"Grrrrrwwlllllgugglegrrreeee . . ."

"Perfect! You'll have 'em fainting with fright!"

Babe left the costume tent, grateful for the sets of canvas curtains strung between the front and the back lots. She wasn't ready for anybody's opinion on how frightful she looked or smelled.

"Hey! Babe!" someone called out. "Your props!" Babe turned just in time to catch two barbells, freshly painted black with white numbers *250* on each end. She tucked them under her arm and went off to see Renoir.

Renoir walked around Babe, taking in her Magnifica costume, scratching his goatee in thought. "Well, I didn't think it was possible," he said. "Didn't think Serena could make you any uglier than you naturally are. But I think she did it. You look perfectly horrible."

Babe wasn't sure if she should thank him for the compliment or step on him for the insult. "So, what do I got to do as this Magnifica? What's she queen of again?"

"Amazons."

"What're them?"

"Big, bad women." He tried to puff himself out and made a mean face.

Babe winced at that. "I ain't bad."

"Well, when you're in the ring, you have to be," Renoir said.

She hated to ask another question. "Ring?"

"We're having a sparring ring built," he said, exhaling his exasperation. "Haven't you ever seen a boxing match?"

"Just men beating the sap outa each other. Usual, it ain't much of a match."

"Well, this is perfect for you! It's called a grunt-and-groan act. You'll just stand on the stage and lift these fake weights, grunt and groan and pretend you're breaking your back lifting these things. Here, I'll show you."

He took the two weights and placed them on the ground. He strutted around them and then finally, with great drama, attempted to lift them. "Now, there's got to be a lot of growling and squatting and wobbling, and be sure to scare the children and spit at the men and howl at the women. Go ahead. Let me see you do it."

"How come I got to pretend I'm strong when I really am strong?"

"Look, the crowd knows it's a fake. That's what they pay their money for. Who wants to see the real thing when the fake is so much fun? They're not paying to see how strong a giant girl is. They're paying to see the giant girl give everyone a real case of the horrors. Think of it as a ham fat . . . you know . . . a razzmatazz, a comedy act. Not a strong act."

Babe blinked. It made no sense. She was hired to be strong—something she was—not something she wasn't. "Maybe my ol' man'd like to know you're making me a laughingstock, a whatcha call it, a fat ham?"

Renoir laughed so hard, tears came to his eyes. Finally, he looked up at her. "How many girls do you know can make money looking like you do? I mean, isn't that what this is all about? You earning your way in the world, which, do I have to remind you, is hardly a *normal* world?"

"Wish you'd let me work with Euclid some more. I think I can get him back on the stage."

"No, Euclid's time has come and gone. But I'll find something else for him, don't you worry. Now, back to you. Magnifica. We're going to have a big finale."

"What's that?"

"The end of the act. You know, the best part. We are going to invite men to plunk down two dollars and climb into the ring for a chance."

"Chance for what?" she asked, narrowing her eyes at him, recalling Serena's warnings.

"A chance to knock you out of this circle we'll paint on the floor, of course! Your pa said you used to rassle men in his store and not a one could even knock you over. It'll be great! They'll pay two bucks, and you'll get fifty cents. I tell you, it's a gold mine! How's that sound?"

"Do I got a choice?" she asked, fiddling with the tips of the rabbit skins dangling down, tickling her side.

"Nope," Renoir stated flatly. "Oh, here. Read this." He pulled a book out from his pocket.

Babe took the book and squinted at the title.

"Your father said you know how to read."

"Only words I know," Babe said.

Renoir snatched the book, popped in his monocle, and read the title.

"*Proper Boxing Technique for the Sporting Young Man.*" He looked up at Babe. He put up two fists and circled them around. "Read that book so you'll know all the poses. Here, see? Oh, forget the words and just look at the pictures." He shook his head, muttering to himself as he turned to leave.

"Now what do I do?" she asked his back, holding the fake barbells in one hand and the book in the other hand.

But he didn't hear her and kept walking.

For the next two days, Babe practiced grimacing, growling, and groaning. She figured out how to dry-spit, how to bobble under the weights, and most of all, how to pose like the pictures in Renoir's boxing book.

Posing in front of the long mirror in the costume tent, Babe consulted the book, then stood, fists balled and held up, feet apart in a stance, challenging snarl on her face. Another glance at the book, another fighting pose. She was learning how to move in her constricting costume without popping too many seams and risking Serena's wrath.

She heard them before she saw them. High-pitched laughter from the back of the tent. She dropped the weights and squinted. "Come on out from there! You got something to say to me, come out and say it! Won't be nothing

I ain't never heard before!"

First Ina, then Tina, and finally Mina stepped out and stood, swaying as one and facing Babe. She'd been warned by Rosa and Serena to steer clear of this dangerous trio. Called them "fast company."

"I know you're them dancing girls, but which is which?" Babe said.

"I'm Tina. She's Mina, and that chubby one is Ina. She's been putting on the feedbag a lot lately."

"Drop dead!" Ina barked.

They came forward and walked around Babe, taking in her smelly costume, inspecting her up and down. They may not have been related, but they sure acted identically.

"Well, dog my cats, Renoir's outdone himself this time!" one said. Probably Mina.

"Well, what else can you do with a giant girl?" another asked. "Can you do anything real? I mean, your monkey act bombed. Can't you do anything, I mean besides grunt with those fake weights?"

Babe's face went blank. "Do anything?"

"You know! Entertain! Sing, dance, tell jokes? Recite poetry. Anything?" Tina asked.

"I'm strong."

"Yes, but smell ain't everything!" another said, swishing the air. They all three laughed.

"Ignore Ina," Tina said. "She thinks she's a real joke-smith."

"I'm sorry, honey," Ina said, offering a small box to Babe. "Cigarette?"

"No, thanks. It'll stunt my growth," Babe said.

Silence. Then, bursting forth as one, the three women set their heads back in laughter, this time in a discordant harmony.

"Now, *that's* a jokesmith!" Tina said.

"Look, dearie," another said. "Don't let Renoir make a fool out of you. The sooner you find a real act, the better off you'll be. Mina gives singing and dancing lessons. Only a few bucks. Give it a thought."

"Come on, ladies. Let's leave this girl to her fisticuffs," another said.

One by one, they shook her hand and offered a curtsy. Then, they locked arms, struck a pose, and sang as they walked backward and offered their curtain-call song:

We're sad we have to go,
We know you liked our show.
But we'll be back at ten,
Be sure to see us then!

Babe reckoned she'd never be able to tell which one was which.

Finally, it was time for Magnifica, Queen of the Amazons, to make her debut to the world.

"You ready?" Renoir asked, pulling Babe aside backstage while the crowd filled in for her first performance as Magnifica. Babe peeked out between the curtains, watching the crowd take their seats.

"Must be twenty, thirty folk out there," she said.

"Ten cents just to watch, Babe. I tell you, you're heading toward the big top big-time. We'll make a mint!" he said, also peeking at the crowd.

"What town we in again?"

Renoir's face went blank. "Just some two-bit Podunk. What does it matter?"

"Don't sound like any big top big-time to me."

"You just wait. The world's in love with pugilism and . . ." He stopped. "Boxing, Babe, boxing! Didn't you read that book?"

"Not the words I didn't know."

"Sssh! Good. There's Billy and Sol. Just like we rehearsed. They challenge you first. Now don't make it look too easy, and, for God's sake, when you toss them into the straw pit, be careful! Not like you kept doing in rehearsal. They both have to help tonight's takedown."

Babe looked again at the crowd. "You reckon any prizefighters're out there?"

"No, just country yokels. Now remember, just take a swing or two! Don't hit anyone! Don't need any lawsuits! It's showtime. Give 'em hell." He stopped, came back, and added, "Don't really give them hell."

"No lawsuits," she said.

Renoir went on the stage for his ballyhoo.

"Ladies and gentlemen! Boys and girls!" Renoir called out over the hushed crowd. "It is with great pride that we bring to you our latest discovery, Magnifica, Queen of the Amazons and the world's strongest girl. She has the strength of four men! Oh, you ladies in front might want to sit farther back. Sometimes Magnifica forgets her manners. Then, as an added attraction, we've invited challengers to come forward and try to move Magnifica out of this circle before the gong goes off. Two dollars for two minutes, and if you succeed, it's fifty dollars in your pocket! And now . . . Magnifica!"

He stepped aside while the curtains opened for Magnifica. She stood, arms folded, around her shoulders a long cape, which Renoir took off with a dramatic flourish and respectful bow. Since the orchestra played for Carlotta, Babe's musical accompaniment was performed by This 'n' That Ernie, now a one-man band. While she paced the platform, growled, flexed her biceps, and made threatening gestures, Ernie banged this, tooted that, dinged a bell or honked a horn. The crowd reacted with oohs and aahs as Babe stepped easily over the ropes of the fighting ring where her fake weights were ready for her amazing feats of strength. She lifted them with dramatic grunting and groaning, just as they had rehearsed.

Then the crowd started to get restless, boo, hiss, and a

few called out, "Fake! Fake!" The mockery wasn't a part of the rehearsal. Then, it came to her.

She lifted the large barbell dramatically, nearly faltering, grunting and groaning under the weight, just like Renoir said. Then, she contorted her face, twitched her mouth and nose as though the sneeze to champion all sneezes was coming on her.

"Accch acchhh achhhh . . ." The more people laughed, the more she wound up her sneeze. Then, she put the barbell under her arm and "sneezed" loud and musically over the crowd. Ernie was onto her business and clanged the cymbals attached to the insides of his knees. The audience roared. Fine, Babe thought. If folks were going to laugh at her, then it would be because *she made* them laugh! She ran her arm under her nose and pretended to blow her nose out over the crowd. Then, back into the character of Magnifica, she took the barbell from under her arm and commenced to struggle under its weight over her head.

More funny business came to her—balancing the barbell on her nose, hitting the cotton-filled medicine balls up high with her knee, hitting them again with her foot behind her. All the while trying to keep a straight, strained face.

Renoir watched from the side as he took the money from the three challengers, lining up behind the two fakes, Billy and Sol, waiting for their chance to knock Babe out of the circle and go home fifty bucks richer.

As rehearsed, Billy and Sol went over fast and easy,

including limping dramatically, rubbing body parts after landing into the straw pit. The first real challenger hopped onto the stage to the egging on of his pals.

Bong! the gong rang out. The young man put up his fists, circled Babe, and took a few swipes. She held him off with her long arm on his forehead as he swatted the air. The crowd laughed, applauded, whistled. Ernie did his best to punctuate the swings and blows with toots, bangs, and clangs.

Finally, Babe picked him up and tossed him—*plunk!*—over the ropes and into the straw pit. It wasn't the *ching ching* in her head of fifty cents going into her pocket. It wasn't even the clapping and the cheering of the crowd. It wasn't Ernie's comical accompaniment. But Babe felt something different and strange deep inside that grew as she tossed each man out that night and every night thereafter. Each time she would stand, put her head back, and roar her victories.

Babe knew, with each challenger, it was the roar of her beast inside the beast, coming to life. Magnifica was coming to life.

The late May air was hot, and Babe kept her cattle car door open for the cross breeze. She fed Jupiter and Euclid from the scraps she had squirreled away throughout the day, including food from her own plate. Still, the animals were getting thinner and restless.

"Reckon you boys is bored and smelling spring," she said, handing out sections of oranges she'd stolen from Renoir's table. Jupiter just sniffed his and turned his head away. But when Euclid made a reach across to steal the bear's treat, Jupiter gave a gruff growl and licked it.

Babe went to her bed and kicked the stuffing in her straw mattress and, using the rope noose she'd hung in the rafters overhead, eased herself down with a gentle plop. She sat back against the side of the car and looked down at her nightgown of pillow ticking Serena had made her.

Ugly as sin, but so much cooler than her holey BVDs and much more generous in the bust. Serena was right about one thing—when her lady parts started coming in, they came in fast and all over. Babe's body seemed to have changed overnight. Once again.

"Chests galore," she muttered. "Ain't as though I ain't already suffered enough change. Spent my life lettin' out seams."

ARPPP! Euclid called out across the car.

"I ain't talking to you, and my lady parts ain't none of your never mind!"

She picked up her silver mirror and inspected her face. Three giant pimples adorned her giant chin. Babe looked up, watching the flickering light from her lantern and thought back on what Rosa had told her about being smart and keeping her eyes wide but not innocent.

"Babe," Rosa had said, her voice kind, her eyes soft. "I know you didn't have a mother, but didn't anyone tell you all this?"

Babe's face still reddened at the memory. "Butch Nance. He locked me in a outhouse. I was twelve. Said he'd let me out if I give him a kiss."

Rosa had asked, "Well, what did you do?"

Babe had smiled as Rosa's eyes widened when she replied, "Did the only thing a girl can do. Started rocking the privy back and forth till it crashed down. Pieces went everywheres. 'Course, Butch'd run off by then."

"Did you ever get even with him?"

"Sure did. See, it was his own pa's outhouse." Rosa had laughed and Babe had to join her.

"That's what I call a growing pain!" Rosa said.

"I know all about growing pains. Been getting them my whole life."

"Well, there's a big difference between growing up, growing confident, and growing cocky."

Babe had cast her cross-eyed look.

"It means don't be too sure of yourself, just because you're the size you are. You might find yourself riding for a fall. Savvy?"

"What's a savvy?"

Rosa had tapped Babe's forehead. "Smarts. Look, Babe, you best be watching your moves during your act. No swishing, no smiling, no winking to the audience."

"I don't under . . ."

"Just don't be getting too friendly, you know?"

Babe thought hard about Rosa's warning. Come to think of it, Renoir *had* been watching her Magnifica act more and more and mingling in among the crowd, talking to the men, slapping backs, and laughing.

Babe snapped back to the present. "Just what are them laughing at?" she asked out loud.

As though to answer, Jupiter stood up and gave a half-hearted roar. Babe looked toward the sound. "Shush!" she said. "Set down and sleep, Jupiter."

A little flash of white came through the door. A dainty hanky on a long pole—the rod Carlotta used to handle Egypt. She poked her tiny head in. "Truce?"

"What for?"

Carlotta came full in and stood with her hands on her hips. Her purple velvet robe shimmered little flecks of gold in the sparse light. "First say truce."

"Truce. For now."

"May I sit down?"

"Suit yourself," Babe said, nodding to a wooden crate. "Knock them peanuts off it."

Carlotta dusted off the crate, then pulled it closer to Babe. "I don't know about you, but I'm running out of pranks to pull on you." Carlotta smiled slyly at Babe, who couldn't help but smile back.

"Yeah, I reckon if we're down to switching sugar for salt, we've pretty much done all we can," Babe agreed with a nod.

"I know I've been horrible, but maybe it's time for us to look out for each other about some things."

"Like what?"

"Like Renoir and his cheapjack ideas. Look, Babe, I've seen outfits riding low on the hog before, but never like this. Renoir will do just about anything to make a buck, so I thought I'd better warn you."

"About what?"

"He just left my car trying to get me to sign on to this big idea of his."

"He gots lots of them, don't he?" Babe said, remembering how he had told her to put more umph and less grunt into her act.

"This one beats all. I know he'll come to you next."

"What for? What's this new big idea?"

Carlotta looked around the car.

"Don't worry," Babe said, nodding to her animals. "They won't say nothing."

"I know. I just want to make sure Renoir's not outside on the platform." She scooted the box closer. "He wanted me to pose for pictures!"

"Huh?"

"You know! Postcards! Picture postcards."

Babe sat up straighter. "I still don't . . ."

Carlotta pulled a card out of her pocket. "Look. Like this."

Babe's eyes nearly popped out of her head. She squinted to read the writing. "'Jo . . . Jo . . . the As . . . ton . . . ish . . . ing Pinhead Freak.' What's that garb she's got on? That a crown on her head?"

"That's Renoir's idea of a sick joke," Carlotta said. "Dressing her up like she's a queen. See? It says here she is of royal blood. Like Queen Victoria or something. Real funny, ha ha, don't you think?"

Babe couldn't stop staring at the postcard. "Sort of makes me think like he's poking fun at her."

"Of course he's poking fun at her! When doesn't he poke fun at all of us?" She took the card. Babe noticed how angry Carlotta's pretty little face grew hard as she looked at JoJo's royal getup.

"Ain't never seed such a thing," Babe said.

"Oh, I have. And I've seen worse, believe you me." She came closer and lowered her voice. "Even one of a famous opera singer who was darn near naked."

Babe couldn't help but gasp. "Never seed me a naked woman before."

"Not even your mother?"

"She died when I was still on the spigot. Townswomen nursed me up . . . till I run 'em dry, then my ol' man took over finding me vittles. Ain't funny, so stop laughing."

"No, I've just never heard these things referred to as spigots!" Carlotta said, puffing out her chest. Babe joined her with a small smirk.

"And Renoir thinks I'd take to such a notion? Getting my picture tooken like this for all the world to see?" Babe had been putting the pieces together, using her smarts, thinking savvy.

"Anyway," Carlotta went on, "that's why I wanted a truce to our war. To tell you about Renoir and his picture postcards. No telling what else he has up his sleeve. I figure we'll make a better army as friends, not enemies."

"What do we do after the truce?" Babe asked as Carlotta stood up and took her white hanky off the rod.

"I don't know. I've never done one before."

"Thought maybe, since you was so mad about your size and all, you done plenty of 'one of these'!"

Carlotta smiled at Babe's huge fist, then looked down at the lace hanky in her hands. "Well, when you're small you have to have crust. You, you're big, you don't need crust, but I do and . . . I guess that's . . . you know, what keeps me safe. Or thinking I'm safe."

Babe had never considered size and crust and keeping someone safe. "Reckon it wouldn't hurt to shake hands. Don't wars end that way?"

Carlotta smiled again. "Yeah, after they bury and honor all the dead. Peace?"

"Peace. Speaking of peace, you want a piece of orange? I swiped some from Renoir."

"I love oranges!"

"Show me that card again, Lotty. . . . Can I just call you that? Lotty's funner to say."

"Sure. But first, we have to shake hands. You know, to make it official."

Babe wiped her hand on her skirt, then offered it to Carlotta. "Okay, put 'er there!"

It was the oddest feeling. She had never shook a hand so small, so delicate and yet so determined in its up, down, up, down grip.

Two stops later, Babe was fashioning her long hair, making it a mess of rats and tangles, wild-woman-like. She did her own makeup now.

Renoir walked into the dressing tent.

"Maybe you could knock next time," Babe said, tightening her dressing gown over her one-piece and tights.

"Got a straw house for the last show tonight, Babe," he said, gazing in the mirror and using Babe's silver-handled brush to run through his hair, leaving shoe polish tips on her brush.

"What's a straw house? Something the wolf blows over?" Babe asked. She was in no mood to be chatty with Renoir, especially after what Lotty had told her about picture postcards.

"Means sold out. Got some special guests tonight. So,

listen, I want you to put a little—shall we say—*finesse* into your act," he went on, adjusting his tie, snipping some tips off his goatee, and inspecting himself side to side in the mirror.

"Is there extry finesse in my pay?"

He reached up and tried to pinch her huge cheek, but she batted his hand away. "Could be, kiddo. You know how I'm always thinking of ways to . . . well, help your act."

"What's finesse anyhows?" She knew what he was getting at but wanted him to show her. "Show me some finesse."

He put one hand to his ear, the other on his hip, and glided around the tent. "You know. Like this. Finesse."

Babe tried to keep a straight face as she watched Renoir finesse his way around the tent.

"I have this sensational idea and there's big money to be made," Renoir said, coming to a stop in front of Babe.

"If this has something to do with them postcards . . ."

He stopped and looked at her. "You know?"

"Lotty told me."

"Thought you two weren't talking to each other."

"We got a truce."

"Now, Babe, think! Feature this—" He put his hands up to form a big square shape. "The world's biggest girl! No! Bigger than life, Babe the Giant!"

"Me being that in real life is one thing. Me being that

in a photograph for the whole dang world to poke fun at is another! My ol' man used to invite folk to take my photograph. Didn't see me one dime of that."

"Well, we're partners, aren't we? Look, you can get paid by the pose or get a royalty on all the postcards I sell or . . ."

Babe narrowed her eyes. "What's a royalty?"

"A piece of the action."

"You ever talk plain?"

Ernie stuck his head into the tent. "Five minutes."

"I got to climb into my getup," Babe said, rising.

"You know, I could make you do it," Renoir said, his voice hardening.

Babe smiled at him. "How?" She stood with her legs apart and her arms folded—a pose she'd perfected as Magnifica.

He flinched a bit. "But, Babe, this could be fun! You could pose looking mad like you do so well in your act. Oh, I know! Lifting the tail end of a wagon and saving a baby's life, maybe wrestling a stuffed lion, holding back a breaking dike and saving a whole town! The possibilities are endless!"

He pointed out toward the main stage and shouted, "You've been a carnie for over four months now, Babe! Get wise to the money you could make!"

"Ain't got the time; ain't got the notion!"

"Well, that's the beauty part, Babe! You don't have to

do anything or go anywhere! I think your very own cattle car would be a great studio."

"What's a studio?"

"It's where they take the photographs," he stated flatly.

"I think you ought to go so's I can get dressed."

No sooner had he left the tent than Lotty came dashing in.

"I saw them! There's two men out there. I know who they are! One has a camera outfit and everything! You told Renoir to go to hell, didn't you?"

"Told him I wasn't posing for no camera."

"Good! You know . . ." She paused and looked at Babe. "It would be sort of fun to, uh, teach Renoir a lesson."

Their eyes met. "How?"

"I don't know. If I was big enough, I'd pitch a fit or start throwing things or something. Scare the holy bejesus out of them. Just because we're different doesn't mean we'll be made laughingstocks like JoJo."

Renoir's voice reached them. He was doing the come-on pitch for Babe's act on the megaphone. "I got to go."

"Think about what I said!"

Before leaving the tent, Babe took the grease pencil and drew another long, ugly scar down the other side of her face and crossed it with crude "stitches." "There. That's finesse!"

It wasn't hard to pick the two men out of the crowd

immediately—dressed in suits rather than the usual garb men wore in these small, hick towns. When it came time for men to challenge her in the ring, she tossed them out, one, two, three, four. Easy as pie. All the while she was thinking about what Lotty had said.

She didn't even take her bows, but jumped off the stage as soon as the last challenger was limping away. Lotty was just putting Egypt back into her car when Babe rushed up. "Come with me! Hurry!"

Babe lifted Lotty into her train car. Both Euclid and Jupiter were already back in their travel cages. "Light them lamps," Babe ordered, pointing to the lanterns hanging on the walls.

"What are we going to do?"

"Like you said, 'teach 'em a lesson!'"

"How?"

"Gonna scare the bejesus out of them. By the way, what's a bejesus?" Babe said, pulling the bear's cage over toward the center of the room.

"I'm not sure."

Babe pushed Euclid's cage next to Jupiter. The chimp and the bear seemed to sense something was up and paced in their cages, restless and growling to each other.

"They can't get out, can they?" Lotty asked. "I mean, the sign says Jupiter's a man-eating bear. I'd be a snack for him."

"No, they can't get out," Babe said, scrunching her lips

while she thought. Then it hit her. "That is, not until I let 'em get out!" Babe placed the cage openings close to the cattle car door.

Lotty had her ear to the door. "I hear footsteps! Someone's coming!"

The footsteps stopped on the train platform. *Knock knock knock.* "Magnifica? Are you in there?" Renoir called out in a sugary sweet voice.

Babe whispered, "Slip that latch when I open the door. I'll do this one and we'll give them boys the scare of their lifes!"

"Some men here want to make you world-famous," Renoir called out. "Just like we talked about. It's just a few photographs. Come on, open the door. All the famous freaks are getting photographed these days!"

The girls heard their laughter as the men tried to open the door, but Babe leaned into it so they couldn't budge it.

"Come on, Magnifica," Renoir said sternly. "If you want to hit the big pinnacle you need better publicity. No! Don't go, gentlemen! I promise, she'll be willing. She's just a little shy!"

Babe and Lotty looked at each other. Babe nodded her head, yanked back the door, and as the three men approached the car, Babe said, "Now!"

"Look out! The bear escaped!" Babe hollered. Lotty's high-pitched scream added to the instant panic.

Euclid screeched when he was face-to-face with his

enemy, Renoir. Renoir screeched back, and Jupiter roared to support them both. One man, face-to-face with Jupiter, turned and ran back down the platform.

"Killer bear! Killer bear!" the other hollered, losing his hat and the tripod camera stand.

Euclid climbed out of his cage and headed for Renoir, who held the ape off with the fake 250-pound weight. "Get him! Get him, Babe! Get that beast before . . ."

Babe easily grabbed Euclid's chain and pulled him up short, then scooped him up. His screech was deafening. She placed her hand over his head and calmed him.

"I see you're in on this, too!" Renoir screamed down at Lotty, who was doubled over in laughter. "I expect this sort of thing from her, but not you!"

Babe grabbed him by his lapels and pulled him up to her face and hollered, "I said no picture postcards. You pull a stunt like that again and I'll snap you in half like a Chinee chopstick."

She dropped him. He buckled and struggled to stand back straight.

"That goes for me, too!" Lotty piped up.

Renoir dusted the sleeves of his coat. "I'm not going to forget this, Mag-ni-fi-ca! You just ruined any chance of being anything more than what you are. A stupid, ugly giant!" He turned and stomped off.

"Dang, too bad we couldn't take a picture postcard of

them two men, screaming and running like scaredy old ladies!" Babe said. That brought them both back to laughter.

Babe stepped onto the platform, snatched up the tripod, snapped the legs in two, then tossed the whole outfit down onto the tracks. Lotty was still laughing so hard, tears streaked her face. "Did you see the look on Renoir's face?" she said, in and out of gasps. "Wish I had a picture of that, too!"

Babe pushed the animal cages back to their end of the car. Lotty helped hand them their treats.

"Got some orange left, Lotty. Want some?"

Just then, the air was pierced with the elephant's long, inquiring roar. "Uh-oh. Duty calls," Lotty said, heading to the platform door. "I have to get Ernie to swipe some hay from the working stock. Egypt's always starving after the last show and I can guarantee Renoir won't sign for more hay! Not now!"

"I can tote a whole bale on my shoulder. 'Case you need help."

"I'll remember that. And I'm going to remember the look on their faces. Feels good, standing up big, for once."

"Ain't no small thing, Lotty. Standing big."

Lotty smiled, waved, and scurried off.

Babe blew out all but one lamp and swished away the smoke from the wicks. She eased herself down on her bed, looking at the smoky shadows the lamp gave the four corners of her home. The noose handle swung back and forth above her. She breathed in the assorted odors—sweat, musk, peanuts, pomade, even a lingering hint of Lotty's perfume.

"Well, boys," she said into the darkness, "reckon that settles that!"

14

"Okay, people!" Renoir called out, standing on a bench, trying to talk over the sounds of hungry people eating fast. The outfit was anxious to get the show on the road after several stops in the sweltering heat of Nebraska. "Attention, everyone! I have an announcement."

The cook crew brought in plates and platters, and the level of chaos and clamor grew louder.

Renoir called for attention again, but food was front and center. Lucretia the Lobster Woman delicately held up a paper-thin slice of ham. "I can see through this thing."

"And lookee here, what sparrow nest did you rob these from?" Ernie asked, showing the two small eggs on his plate.

"Yeah, these are last week's coffee grounds!" Rosa said to the cup in her hand.

From there, it was an anvil chorus of complaints. The noise was broken by the shot of a pistol.

Renoir stood on his bench and shot his pistol high over his head. "*Now* do I have your attention?" Everyone looked up at the gaping hole in the top of the tent. "Thank you. There have been some changes to the schedule."

That was met with moans and groans. "I know! You want us to do ten shows a day, instead of five!" Ina, Mina, or Tina called out.

"Yeah, twice the work for half the pay!" Donny shouted, slipping scraps to one of his doggone dogs under the table.

"We aren't going to head south for the winter," Renoir called out over their heads.

More moans and groans.

"We are turning around and heading back the way we came."

"Play towns we just played?" Serena called out. "No outfit does that!"

"We'll play towns we missed on the way out," Renoir called back.

"Great!" Rosa said. "Even smaller none-horse, played-out, jerk-soup towns!"

Renoir waited for the griping, laughing, and grumbling to die down. "I'm also making a few changes in Oregon. West to Portland, south to Klamath Falls, where we'll jump the tracks. From there . . . well, we'll see what happens then. Your contracts will be honored, of course. And

I'm sure we'll get track clearance down to California for the winter. So, everyone hold tight. It's a minor change."

"Minor? Sounds major to me," Lucretia said.

"Why the change?" Ernie called out.

"Folks, this isn't coming from me," Renoir said, touching his chest with a stab of sincerity in his voice. "This comes from the men at the top. Investors. All on the dead quiet. Johnny Pepito, our advance man, is already on the road, setting things up. He'll wire our new schedule as he gets our bookings. It will be posted as soon as it's ready. Okay, that's all. Go back to your breakfast. Train pulls out at ten."

He hopped down from the bench and left.

The clamor began again.

Too large for the bench, Babe sat on a large wire spool at the end of a long table.

Rosa waited until Renoir was gone, then turned to the ladies. "Investors my foot! If you ask me, we're down to scraps and bits because he doesn't *have* any so-called investors. When was the last time you saw a supply wagon pull up?"

"Oh yes, he does have investors," Serena said, leaning into the conversation. She looked around, then continued. "Mina and me, well, maybe it was Tina, anyway, we were talking a few days ago. Anyway, Mina said she found a telegram on Renoir's desk when he stepped out for something. You know what snoops those girls are."

"And?" Lucretia asked, taking a pull off her cigarette balancing in the cradle of her two large fingers.

"It was from his investors back east and it said, 'No More Cash! Stop!'"

"Is that all it said?" Rosa asked.

"No," Serena went on. "Then it said, 'Profits or else! Stop.' If you ask me, we'll all be working for other outfits in no time."

"Well," Lucretia said, "that Carlotta and her elephant might be the straw that breaks the camel's back. What was Renoir thinking, bringing on that eating machine and that little snip . . . Ow!"

Rosa smiled sweetly as Lotty entered the tent. Lucretia rubbed her shin.

"Well, look who's here. Little Carlotta," Serena said. "On what auspicious occasion do you grace us with your ecumenical presence?"

Babe didn't understand the big words, but she understood the tone of Serena's voice.

"Someone said Renoir made an announcement," Lotty said.

"Yeah, he announced your elephant is eating us off the circuit!" Lucretia said.

"Lu," Rosa said. "Don't be cruel."

"Sorry."

"Here, sit, dear. Join us," Rosa said, patting the bench next to her. Lotty looked at it, then struggled to climb up. Babe recognized the rise of embarrassment in Lotty's expression. "Here. I can help you."

"No, thank you, I can do it. I can . . ." She grasped the bench, pulled herself to her stomach, grunted as she swung her legs around, then sat upright. Her chin barely reached the table.

More laughter, now from the others in the troupe, watching from their tables. Babe looked around, saw a box, and dumped the cans out of it. She placed the box on the bench. "Here, Lotty. You can sit on this."

The snickering stopped. "Thank you." Lotty climbed on it and sat down with as much dignity as she could summon.

"Coffee?" Rosa asked, reaching for a pot in the center of the table. She poured some into a heavy mug. Lotty looked at it.

"Someone get her a little girl's tea party set!" a roustabout said as he walked by.

"Mind your own business!" Rosa said. "I'm sorry, Lotty. I wasn't thinking."

Lotty kept staring at the mug. "You don't have to kid-glove me."

"You mean kiddy-glove?" another wrangler said, laughing with his buddy. Babe stood in front of them, making them walk around her, then took her seat again.

Lotty looked at each woman, her face crushed, and her lip quivering. "Look, I know what you think of me and my Egypt. Why do you think we came so cheap to begin with?" She dotted her eyes with her hanky. "Don't think we haven't been through this before. Egypt might as well be a white elephant."

Babe's face asked the question, which Rosa answered. "A white elephant is something you don't need and can't get rid of."

"That's us. White elephants," Lotty said, fingering the corners of her hanky. "I was hoping things would be different with this carnie. It's not. It's worse."

"Look, Carlotta, I didn't mean to make you cry. But we have big problems in this outfit," Serena said.

"Money problems," Lucretia added. "Might be time for . . ."

"Picture postcards?" Babe said, nodding her head and catching Lotty's eyes.

"What do you think, girls?" Lucretia asked her hands. "Renoir said all the famous freaks are getting photographed these days!"

That eased them into a more gentle laughter. "Same thing he told us," Lotty said.

Rosa looked at Babe. "You too?"

"Don't think he'll be coming around with his photograph men no more," Babe said, taking the loaf of bread off a plate. "Or he'll get this!" She ripped it in half with a twist and a tug.

"Where are we now?" Babe asked, pulling out the revised map and list of stops. She looked out over the countryside from the train window.

Lotty turned the hand-drawn map around and read, "Let's see. June fifteenth. That makes this Cheyenne, Wyoming. It's just a one-night stand."

"I hate those. Nothing but 'hurry up, set up, hurry up, take down.'"

"I know. But back east the towns are so much closer together, they weren't so hard on everyone. But we've been traveling two days just for a one-night stand? What about all those little towns we blew right on through?"

"I think them towns we played don't welcome us back. Renoir says he wants to spread the show around, but Rosa says he's got warrants and debt hot on his tail," Babe said.

The train seemed to list, then lunge, going around a corner. Lotty grabbed the seat armrest.

"It's okay, Lotty."

"I know. It's just I hate it when the train lurches like that."

"These trains stick to the tracks like glue."

"Not always. I was in a train wreck once."

Babe looked at her. "For true? When?"

"It's been, gosh, three years. I was with the Walter H. Main show. We were traveling through Altoona, Pennsylvania. Our train jumped the track and went down an embankment."

"Lotty, no. Was you hurt?"

"Yes, but not bad. What really hurt was seven in our troupe were killed."

"I'm sorry."

"Still worse was . . . Egypt. She was pretty banged up, but more than that, she's never been the same. That's how I know elephants never forget. Any big loud noises and she's reliving that horrible day. And I think she's always been in mourning. You see . . ." She paused and looked outside, a tiny tear visible in the window reflection. "You see, we had to use her to help move the rubble and cars and . . . so many dead horses. So many."

"Don't say no more, Lotty. You don't have to tell me more."

Lotty took a deep sigh and tried to smile.

"You okay?"

"Yes. I just hate remembering but I'll never forget it. Egypt won't, either."

Keeping true to his warnings, Renoir sacked several of the roustabouts, mess-tent workers, vendors, and wranglers, and then asked the performing troupe to pick up the slack and pull together in double duty. Rosa had to work in the mess tent, Serena worked the beer garden, Lotty sold tickets, and Babe put her shoulder to the lifting, moving, and other grunt work. Gossip ran from backstage to mess tent—the outfit was in trouble. Big trouble.

Adding to the strain, Renoir framed new acts for nearly everyone. Roustabouts became barkers, wranglers became candy butchers and slum pitchmen. Madame de la Rosa added a mind-reading act, Lucretia donned an outfit similar to Ina, Mina, and Tina's and the four had a comic dance act.

Lotty and Babe didn't escape Renoir's new schemes:

THE WORLD'S TALLEST
AND SMALLEST GIRLS!
WILL SING AND DANCE THEIR
WAY INTO YOUR HEARTS!

Babe's voice was low, gravelly, off-key, and clashed with Lotty's high soprano. Nothing was more clumsy than a dancing giant with an awkward dwarf ducking in and out of her legs and being tossed in the air. They didn't trick or quip their way into anyone's heart but were the brunt of boos, hisses, mockery, and lettuce heads.

After every last show, Lotty and Babe had a late dinner in the dressing tent, away from the annoying crowds and other carnival folks. Babe opened her sandwich and gingerly lifted something resembling meat pasted down with ooze. "Look there, Lotty. That's shortening, that's lettuce, and who knows what that meat is? We missing a mule in our stock?"

"No, but I saw a wrangler bringing in some rabbits and God knows what else."

"Can't wait to get back to river country. Wait till you taste salmon, Lotty. Indians stand on platforms and spear it right out of the rivers!"

Lotty lifted the corner of her sandwich. "Sure is skimpy. I don't eat so much, but, you, Babe. You must be starving all the time."

"Thought all our extry work and such we'd see a betterment, but this is getting worst."

"I know. I asked for better hay for Egypt, and Renoir just said elephants do better grazing and shouldn't have baled hay. How would he know? My Egypt needs good feed. She's no spring chicken. I'm tired of finding a field for her every stop we make and I'll tell you, farmers don't take kindly to their trees getting trimmed. Remember a few stops ago and she found an orchard? Someday someone's going to take a potshot at her."

They stared into the lantern flame flickering between them on the table. Babe broke the silence. "Sometimes I wonder why the hell I'm doing it, Lotty."

"Doing what?"

"I mean, don't you ever ask yourself? Ain't there more? On display and making fools of ourselfs and . . ."

Lotty sat up a bit straighter. "Well, I don't exactly think of myself a fool, Babe."

"I'm sorry. I just mean me. You're sweet and pretty and dainty and ladylike and all. Folks want to cuddle you and take care of you. But me. Folks want to just take me on."

Lotty stared into the flame. "Well, getting cuddled isn't all it's cracked up to be. I'm more young woman than old child. And yes, sometimes, well, maybe . . ."

"Maybe what?"

"There might be more. But everything, everyone, out there is so . . . big. It scares me, Babe. But you, what's out there to scare you?"

Babe stood up and walked over to the mirror hanging from a pole. She stood there for some time. "This scares me, Lotty," she said. She flexed her biceps, which bulged out the tattoos of a three-mast ship on each bicep. "Why'd I let Renoir talk me into these damn tattoos?"

Lotty walked over and looked in the mirror. "Because he told you how much the kids would love it, and you do make them laugh."

"Yeah, but now I got me a permanent reminder of being Magnifica. And there's something else, Lotty."

"What?"

Babe bent down and showed Lotty the seams of her Magnifica costume. Popped out, mended, patched over. "Everything's hanging tighter. My dress hems is shrunk, too. I've growed. That's what scares me."

"I know. But, Babe, think about it. You're getting famous now that you're Magnifica."

"Sometimes I think about something Madame de la Rosa said to me when I first come to the carnie."

"What was that?"

"She said folks here is all old carnies doing the only thing a old carnie can do. Ever look at their eyes and faces?" She chuckled and pointed at the mirror. "Criminy, looking in mirrors is hard enough for me. Sometimes they crack looking back."

Lotty laughed, then her face became serious. "But we're not old, Babe. We're just kids, and there's lots left to our lives."

"Even my critters. Even your Egypt. There's something in their eyes that's sad and worn down and beat-up. Alls I know, Lotty, is I don't want to ever see them things in my face reflection."

"But where would you go? Trust me, all carnies are the same. You'll only get the same or worse somewhere else."

"My bones is beginning to hurt, Lotty. Being big hurts. Fighting and tossing off men in my act don't help."

"Guess I never thought of it that way."

"Well, when I'm hurting so's I can't sleep I start to thinking. I ain't no little girl." She grunted a little laugh. "I ain't never been a little girl. But I think maybe I best get out and get on with gettin' on."

"I remember thinking that, too. Back when I was in the orphanage."

"I heard once how them orphanages is hard living," Babe said. "Was it? Bad?"

Lotty smiled. "Sure. But not all bad. For a while, I was everyone's baby with my sweet little-girl voice that will never change. A real living doll who'll never grow up. I remember this one girl—well, I remember her face. She'd been in a fire. Oh yes, Andrea was her name! She and I were the only ones different—I mean, *really* different."

She fiddled with a cookie, breaking it into tiny pieces as she talked.

"We had this . . . comedy act. Andrea found some black scarves she draped over her head. Wanted to look like a woman in widow's weeds. Well, it was to cover her face. You know, the burn scars and all."

"How's that funny?"

Lotty's smile became a snicker. "Well, we had this baby carriage. I climbed in and we put a blanket over me. Then, we'd go out walking through the streets. Andrea held a tin cup, weeped up a storm. 'Pennies for the poor! Help my fatherless baby!' she'd cry out. Ha! I can still hear the sound of the coins dropping into that cup! Then, when someone asked to see the poor, fatherless baby, the blanket came off, I sprang up holding a cigar and said, 'Say, lady, got a light?'"

The girls gushed in laughter. "Lotty, no!"

"Andrea sure could run that carriage!"

"Least you had some fun."

"Yeah," Lotty whispered, looking down at the pile of crumbled cookie. "The nuns finally got word of our flimflam. Got me kicked out. I wonder what happened to Andrea."

Laughter from the beer garden reminded them of the hour. Lotty stared past the mirror and out onto the brightly lit carnie. "I've seen this before. Egypt and me. These cheap, two-bit, ragbag outfits can't take us on. We've been through so many owners, I forget where we even started out. Trust me. I know all the signs. Renoir's coasting on his eyelids."

"What's that?"

"Going belly-up. Out of business. Dead in the water. Everyone says so."

"What's that mean for us? Don't it mean we're out of this carnie?" Babe asked, looking down at Lotty, a hopeful smile on her face.

But she didn't smile back. "I don't know. I'm contracted just like you. He can sell our contracts any time. Sometimes I feel more like a slave than a performer. Makes me sick. It really does. But look at us, Babe. We don't have many other choices."

"Sssh. Someone's coming," Babe said.

Babe took off her apron and looked at herself again in the mirror, her Magnifica costume worn, tired, and thin. Just like she was feeling.

"Well, there they are. The stars of the show—from the sublime to the ridiculous. You two can argue which is which," Renoir said, chuckling. "Sit down, both of you. I have something to tell you." He took off his silk hat and spun it upside down on the makeup table. "I want you to know, I've put a lot of thought into this. I've put the call out and no one, not anyone in any outfit on any circuit in these whole United States, wants to buy them." He ran a pocketknife under his fingernails.

"Who's them?" Babe asked.

"The show stock. Well, not the show horses or the baggage stock, but the bear, the chimp, and that damnable elephant."

"Buy them?" Lotty said, setting her jaw and glancing at Babe.

"Simple. I can't afford to feed them any longer." He looked at each girl, shrugging his shoulders. "It's my only option."

"What's your only option?" Lotty asked.

"It's the only solution. I'm going to have them . . . Jupiter, Euclid, and . . . Egypt . . ." He hesitated, took a step back and concluded, "Stuffed."

"Stuffed? As . . . as in . . . taxidermy?" Lotty asked, barely able to get the words out.

"Ding ding! Hand the little girl a dolly!" Renoir said, pointing his knife at Lotty.

She stood on her box and screamed, "No! You just can't!"

"Now, the way I figure it, Jupiter can be made into a nice roaring mode and then I'll have a rolling, fierce bear to put on display. I'll have some long, shiny bright teeth made and some scary eyeballs spitting fear. I know! Maybe let the kiddies sit atop him and get their pictures taken for a buck a pose."

"Like hell you're doing that to my critters!" Babe hollered.

"Or my Egypt!"

"Need I remind you, those animals aren't yours, they're mine. I own every gray hair, every flea, every claw, every ear, every tail and every tooth in their heads. I even own the hide and the holler."

Lotty started weeping into her hands.

"Oh come on, now, Carlotta, don't be sad. Even you have to admit how feeble that old girl is getting. She's got to be, what, thirty, thirty-five? Why, she's old enough to be your mother!" Renoir went on. "What happens if she falls down and dies in the middle of your act or parading through town? What if we had to shoot her right on the spot? How would it be for all the children? What the hell am I to do with a dead elephant in the middle of some one-horse town?"

"Maybe if she got fed proper," Lotty said, her face hot and wet with tears.

"Well, I can't afford to feed her proper. But once she's stuffed and on wheels, she can stay in show business forever. Just like ol' P. T. Barnum's elephant Jumbo. Why, he's been dead, what, a dozen years. Still out and about and getting cheers and still making P. T. a pretty penny."

"It's murder!" Lotty screamed.

"Not to mention Egypt'll be a heck of a lot lighter and easier to get in and out of that railroad car. Push her in, roll her out." Then, he turned to Babe. "And Euclid. Well, that old ape's older than dirt, too! He doesn't even do anything to make himself an amusement anymore. Used to be he'd do his counting trick act and make folks laugh. Now he just makes folks mad—those obscene gestures, spitting, and blowing those raspberries you taught him. And those farts!"

The more Renoir talked the more Babe felt that pang inside her rumble to life. Seeing a beast—any beast—killed made her own beast rise and want to do horrible things.

"You're going to kill and stuff them critters over my dead body!" she said, locking her jaw, standing, and exercising her size over Renoir.

"You're both just children, really, and you don't understand the economic reasons behind this. You'll get over it. This is just one of those tough life lessons you're going to have to learn."

"Murderer!" Lotty screeched, her voice reaching a new timbre.

"Keep your voice down! There're still lot lice out there!" Renoir ticked his head toward all the customers milling around the ten-in-one. "Fact is, I'm doing those animals a favor. They're old, they're sore, they're flea-bitten, and they're . . ."

"All three gots lots of lifes in them, and it ain't up to you to decide they have to die," Babe said. "You ain't God!"

"Well, yes, actually, here I *am* God, and I say it's time to pull their tickets," he said, snapping his knife closed. He pulled out a paper from his coat pocket. "Look at this. I hear this man's the best in the business. Even did some rare birds for a museum in Los Angeles. Not every taxidermist who can do museum-quality work." He put his monocle into his eye socket and read, "'Uncle Dan's Taxidermy. No Job Too Big. No Job Too Small. Free Premium Eyeballs with First Order. Klamath Falls, Oregon.' Right where we're ending our circuit in August! Can't beat that!"

"You ain't doing no such thing!" Babe seized the flier, wadded it up, and tossed it down with a forceful *whap!*

"Just watch me! Look at it this way: they'll live on, only on rollers. They'll be immortal. You ought to think about that when you die, Babe! Get yourself stuffed. With good taxidermy you can live forever!" He chuckled at his little joke.

"You harm those animals, I'll . . . I'll . . ."

"You'll what? Leave? Go where? And do what? What can the likes of you do other than what it is you do now? Face it, Babe, you were born a freak and you'll die a freak. You, too, Carlotta. That's just the sad, bottom facts of your lives. So don't give me any of your threats."

"Without Egypt, I don't even have an act." Lotty wiped her tiny face with her hanky. "What's going to happen to me?"

He looked at her as though seeing her for the very first time. "Ah yes, that brings me to the next issue. You. You see, Carlotta, dwarfs are a dime a dozen. So what can you do besides your elephant act?"

"I can dance. A little."

"Ah yes. Dance. Well, Carlotta, the only thing more common than a dwarf is a dancing dwarf. Now, maybe a dancing dwarf on a postcard . . ." He grinned down at her.

"Go to hell!" Lotty spit. "You may think that's how carnie women end up and maybe even your cheap little dancing girls are that way, but not me and not Babe!"

"Can't say I didn't make you an offer. So, I'm canceling your contract, Carlotta. Our end of the line will be your end of the line. Sorry. Nothing personal. All a matter of economics. You know what they say: that's show biz."

"If I was bigger, I'd slap your face!" Her beautiful face was scarlet with rage.

Babe's jaw tightened rock-hard and her huge hands became rock-harder fists, holding back her own urge to slap Renoir into next week. "If Lotty goes free, I go, too."

"Don't get any fancy ideas, Babe. I have money invested in you and you have eight months left in your contract."

"I got some money set aside," Babe said, remembering her stash of money she kept hidden in her cattle car. "How much you want for my contract and the whole tote?"

He put his head back and laughed heartily. "For the bear, the chimp, and the elephant? Ha! A far sight more than anything you'll ever see."

"Me too! I have some money! We'll buy them off you!" Lotty joined in.

Renoir ignored her. "If you don't mind, I have important

business to see to." He picked up the flier. "Need to send Uncle Dan a down payment." The girls glared at him as he disappeared, whistling, into the darkness.

Lotty blew her nose. "We're fighting this, Babe."

"Dang right we are!"

"Between my brain and your brawn, we'll fight this!"

They agreed. They would pool their money, save every penny, pick up odd jobs, perform double shows—beg, borrow, or steal the money they'd need to get free from Renoir and his big plans for the end of the line, Klamath Falls, and Uncle Dan the taxidermist.

17

"I'm getting a vision," Madame de la Rosa said dramatically, closing her eyes and putting her hand to her temples. The audience was meager, but the attention she commanded was rapt. She had already told three audience members shocking events in their lives. Those three being Ernie, Sol, and Serena, conveniently costumed in case some suspicious person recognized them from other carnie jobs. This trio, seasoned carnies each, could lie and emote among the best of them.

But this "vision" was for a member of the audience. "Yes, yes, and I'm getting a number. I think, no, I'm sure, the number is fourteen. Strange, this number. Visions are seldom numbers." She swayed, trancelike, onstage. Her robe was black with silver beads sewn here and there to give the effect of stars upon a veil of night.

The audience looked around, wondering which person might react to the number fourteen. Rosa opened her eyes and searched the faces in front of her. Babe was careful when she peeked through the backstage curtains but could barely resist watching Rosa's new act. She thrilled to the applause and the astonished audience. Nothing like the cheering and jeering she got for her physical abilities, but something altogether different—applause for Rosa's mental abilities. Rosa confided to Babe that it wasn't the power of mental abilities but the power of observation. Watch a person's reaction, watch their lips, watch their eyes. Say the key word—the "vision"—over and over and someone will unknowingly react. The fact that Rosa sent Lotty, a tiny sneak, out to eavesdrop on people as they stood in line helped form the "visions."

"Fourteen? It's such a strong image," Rosa continued, walking now to the edge of the stage. "It's important, I know it is. Don't be shy. Perhaps I can help with your concerns, your worries."

Finally, a woman in the back row timidly raised her hand. Rosa pointed to her. "Yes! I knew it was a woman! Please stand up!"

When she did, Rosa smiled. "Fourteen." Again, her hand went to her forehead. "You are going to give birth to your fourteenth child."

All eyes were on the woman whose face immediately

flushed. "Yes," she said, touching her stomach. The audience applauded.

"Wait! I'm getting a name . . ." Rosa said, going back into a trancelike state. "This is a boy. You must call him James. He will be your pride and joy. When he arrives, place this under his bedding for spiritual protection." She handed down a juju fresh off her necklace of horsehair charms used in her palm-reading act. People admired it as they handed it back to the pregnant woman.

Rosa ended her mind-reading act inviting people to come to her tent for a private reading and to get their own juju for health and luck.

"Sure had them going tonight, Rosa," Babe said, helping her friend out of her mind-reading robe and into her palm-reading robe. Rosa lit the various candles around her palm-reading tent, which reflected eerily through the crystal ball on the table.

"I learned from the best. I'll tell you about it someday."

"Now, tell me now." Babe pulled over a large leather trunk and sat down.

Rosa lit a cigarette and sighed out the smoke. "Well, in a nutshell, which is where we all belong, by the way, I worked with the great Alberto on the Clark and Clark circuit. Big-time outfit. I'm an old hand at this. I can read minds in my sleep."

"How come you don't get back to the big time, then?"

"I weary of the road and you will, too, someday, Babe."

"Still ain't use to moving this fast."

"And it gets faster as you get older." Rosa sat down and smiled into her crystal ball.

"Look in that future ball and tell me what you see for your own self."

Rosa kept staring. "I see Madame de la Rosa making a lot of money. Then I see her being Cora Epstein, taking that money and building a big house. The only palms I see are my own making money hand over fist."

"Big houses sound like big work."

Rosa smiled wistfully, looking down at the smoke rising from her cigarette. "Oh, I'll need help."

"Lotty and me, we been thinking . . ." Babe stopped, remembering they were keeping their own escape plans secret. "I mean, maybe, someday, I could," Babe said, swallowing the shyness in her voice. "You know . . . help. 'Course, it'd have to be a dang big house. I can tote and learn to cook and maybe even . . ." She stopped. Rosa seemed far away, maybe envisioning that big house. "Anyhow, tell me what's in the ball for me." Babe leaned down and gazed into the ball, seeing only misshapen reflections of herself.

"Oh, Babe, so much in your future! But now . . ." She leaned into the ball, her voice became low, her eyes squinting into Babe's future. "Beware! I see Renoir coming for you. He's so angry he's fit to freeze! He's . . ."

Just then, the flap to her tent whipped open and there stood Renoir. "Magnifica! If you don't mind! You are late for your entrance! Now move your giant hindquarters out there!"

Babe stood erect, hitting her head on the tent top. She glared down at Rosa. "You seed that?"

She leaned back. "No, I *heard* that. Heard Renoir introduce you twice."

"Now!" Renoir barked, turning and letting the flaps of the tent swoosh closed.

"Hey! You okay? It's the third time I've asked you," Lotty said, tapping Babe's shoulder with her handler's rod. The girls had walked Egypt to a stream to water her.

"What?"

"You've been so quiet. Penny for your thoughts."

Babe smiled vaguely. "You think we got a penny to spare?"

"Well, at least you're smiling. Come on. You've been quiet all day."

"It's nothing," Babe said, looking down into the stream.

"I saw those hicks lining up to take you on last night, Babe. You should tell Renoir you don't want to take on more than two. Someday someone's going to really hurt you."

"I don't mind taking on more. Fifty cent each, remember. We need the money."

"Did that old miner hurt you? He kept coming back for more. Renoir should have stopped it."

"I'm fine," Babe said, rubbing her shoulder.

"I heard you came close to falling."

"Oh, that's mostly for show. Folks get a kick out of a body my size whirling around like I'm a falling tree. Someone always calls out 'timber!' But I worry sometimes. What if I'm looking at the line of challengers and see me another giant?"

"I'll tell you 'what if'! Renoir would sign him on the spot and bill you both as the brawl of the century!" She sat straighter and called out, "'Come one! Come all! See the world's biggest battle of the sexes!' Renoir would book Madison Square Garden in New York City and get himself out of debt with that one, that's 'what if'!"

Babe's thoughts were as far away as Madison Square Garden.

"Babe, that was supposed to be funny. How come you're so quiet?"

"Did you see the new schedule tacked up in the mess tent? We're playing outside of Boise next week."

"So? Oh, isn't that where you came on board?"

"Wasn't original on the schedule. We was going to just blast through to Oregon where folks ain't seed our carnie. I don't want to go back there, Lotty. Too close to where I was broughten up."

"Oh." Lotty's voice softened. "Your father."

"Don't know if I'm scared I'll see him or if I'm scared I won't see him." She pet Egypt's trunk with long, gentle strokes.

"Have you written? Has he?"

"'Course not. Think him and me lost all use for each other. Hell, I tried running off once with a traveling drummer. Said he was going to make me a big star in Chicago. But my ol' man hauled me back. Thought maybe he wanted me back. Nope, turns out he was waiting for a better offer. Renoir's offer. You don't know what it was like, him and Renoir bargaining over me like I was a prize milk cow."

Lotty looked down at her handler's rod, the leather strap wrapped around her tiny wrist. "I know what it's like, Babe. I don't think there's a freak on earth who doesn't know what it's like."

"You think you're a freak, too?"

"It's just a word," Lotty answered, low, almost to herself.

"Ah, who cares about my ol' man! We get by just fine without each other. But wouldn't break my heart if our train just kept on going and didn't stop in Boise. It's mighty close for comfort. 'Course, since when does ol' Babe get her some comforts?"

The stop outside Boise was on the same siding as before. The muddy pasture they'd left behind in February was now a field of ankle-high grass in late June. There was no sweet scent of "home sweet home" in these hills, so close to where Babe was raised, so close to her father. She convinced herself this was just one more stop and to quit looking over her shoulder.

Instead, she thought about escape—what Rosa said she wanted—a big house someplace. What she wanted and what Lotty wanted—to get away with their critters and the planning, money, and courage that would take.

"You have five men," Renoir announced when he found Babe backstage, awaiting her entrance for the last show.

"Five?" She used her fingers to cipher how much money would be coming to her. "Any he-men?"

"Well, there might be some surprises out there waiting for you," he said, arranging the dollar bills so they all faced the same direction, then tucking them into his jacket pocket.

She snapped her fingers and held out her hand. He sighed heavily and handed her two dollars. She put the money down her chest, where it could rest safe and sound. Her face went blank as her lips counted. "Wait. You said five. Give me another fifty cent."

"Oh, I don't think you're going to want to win *all* your matches," Renoir said, giving her a shady grin.

"How come?" She took another peek through the curtain.

"Well, I'm willing to bet good cash money you won't throw your own daddy out of the ring."

Her heart flipped hard. "My ol' man? Out there?" She ran through the possibilities: Coming to see me? Coming to rescue me, bring me home, and make up for his wrong? Save me from all this I become? Then she let it sink in . . . *No, he ain't come to save me. He come to fight me.* "My ol' man?" she muttered again. She felt that beast way down deep inside claw its way past her pounding heart.

"Yes. I just love reunions!" Renoir said, bright and cheery. "Especially when there's money involved. You see, I never made my last payment to him for your contract.

So, naturally, when he showed up demanding his money, I had this sensational idea!"

"What?"

"He has some fun, you get to see your father, he gets his fifty bucks when you take a fall, and I'm off the hook. God is in his heaven and all is right with the world."

Babe shook her head, trying to understand his grand plan. "Sham a fall?"

"Yeah. You know. You lose, he wins, he collects money, and walks away happy."

"Money he wins ain't money you owe him."

"Oh, we have it all worked out."

Babe spoke between clenched teeth. "If I kill him you don't owe him nothing."

"Oh come now, Babe. You know you won't hurt him. He's family. He's your father, for crissakes. Show a little respect. Just take a fall and be done with it. Now, come on! The show must go on!"

He dashed out between the curtains and began his introduction.

"Ladies and gentlemen! It's with great pride and some trepidation that I now offer you Magnifica, Queen of the Amazons, the strongest girl in the world, here tonight to take on all challengers. Any man"—Babe closed her eyes, knowing his spiel by heart. Now he would be pointing out an elderly woman—"or perhaps *lady* who topples Magnifica will win fifty dollars! Tonight five brave men have put their manhood on the line and will attempt to bring fame and fortune to their town. Now, ladies, you might want to step back. You don't want to get blood splattered on your clothes. Please stand back, folks, stand back. Trust me, you won't miss seeing Magnifica. After all, she's all-alligator mean and a bona fide *giant*!"

The curtain parted, she entered and stood center stage to the wide-eyed stares of nearly fifty people. Renoir removed her robe as the usual boos, oohs, aahs, taunts, and whistles began. Her warm-up was now perfected and dramatic: arms up, flexing her sailing-ship tattoos, deep knee bends using the rope of the ring. One-Man-Band Ernie punctuated her every movement. *Boom* here, *bang* there, drumroll when she struggled to lift the big barbell . . . higher, higher—uff—and then, *TAAA DAAA!* when it's over her head and *BOOM!* as she dropped it. All a part of her routine. Magnifica on the outside, Babe on the inside, no idea how normal girls lived. She finally stood, arms folded, her stare cold and snarl mean as her challengers lined up, flashing bold faces, flexing their muscles.

She loved handling her first two challengers—friends Billy and Sol—now seasoned with fake moves and dramatic howls, grunts, groans, and acrobatic landings in the straw pit. The first was Billy, who delivered a few stage hits, but when she sent up a roar to the heavens, the audience silenced and uttered a low, communal *oooohhh*. Like all good beasts must, she growled and spit and let Magnifica's rage grow. The referee tonight was Vern Barrett, borrowed from his roustabout gang. With great, over-the-top flair, he tried to calm her down, so she chased after him while Sol climbed into the ring. The crowd loved it.

"Got a lady friend waiting back in town," Sol whispered up to her while circling her, fists raised. "So hurry it up, will ya, Babe?"

"Sure thing, Sol. I'm in a hurry myownself," Babe said. "Hang on." She picked him up, circled around, then tossed him into the straw pit before he'd landed even one punch. He quickly bounced back up and winked his thanks before running off.

Now for the five real challengers. It was easy to pick out the young rubes right off the farm, the just-paid cowboys on the town, the drunk lumberjacks, and the occasional dude, out to impress his lady friend. She ducked their fists, turned and kicked them in their behinds, and held them at arm's length, leaving them helpless to reach her with their wild swings. The more the crowd laughed, the madder and madder her challengers got. Babe looked bored, yawned, looked at her nails, as though wondering what to do with this helpless pest.

Out they went, one, two, three, four.

Then, there he was. Next in line. "Pa," she whispered. He grinned up at her. *He must know I could kill him easy as look at him*, she thought, glaring back down at him.

"Our last challenger is somewhat of a local celebrity! Arthur Killingsworth, mayor of Neal, Idaho. Lucky you, Mayor. I can tell Magnifica is tiring. So, Magnifica, how do you feel about politicians?" The crowd laughed. He gave Babe a threatening glance, then said down to Killingsworth as he stepped forward, "Perhaps you will be the one to topple the great Magnifica!"

Babe's thoughts ran wild. Why should the fifty dollars Renoir owed this Mayor Killingsworth have anything to do with her? Maybe she should pull a double-cross and let them both square off in their own fight. Did she want to throw her old man down and squarsh him flat? Or throw him clear out of the ring? Or just pick him up by the neck and watch the daylights drain out of him? Whatever she did, she'd best do it now. Her father was stepping forward.

He climbed the platform and slipped through the ropes to great applause. He bowed to the crowd, then took off his suit coat and handed it to Renoir. With great deliberation, he rolled up his shirtsleeves, loosened his tie, and tossed off his celluloid collar. The referee introduced them and gave the usual rules. They didn't shake hands, speak, or take their eyes off each other.

He raised his fists and approached her. She backed away, the crowd hissed and booed, emboldening him. His smile widened and he danced around her, then slapped her arm, and swatted toward her face, which was still head and shoulders above his. More boos from the crowd.

"Babe," Vern whispered up at her. "Put him away!"

Killingsworth punched her hard and she grabbed her side, looking down at her father with disbelief. "Come on, girl!" he taunted, delivering more hits. "You know you've wanted to land a good one on me all your life!"

Still, she didn't fight back, and his courage grew. Was she going to take the fall or was she not able to hit her father? One! Just one solid hit! Put him away! But each time her fists rose, he'd slap her again and her fists came down. Could she? Would she? Several times she nearly stepped out of the circle on the mat. The crowd booed her and cheered her father. Agony!

"One minute!" Renoir called out with the ring of the bell.

More swipes, more kicks, more humiliation. Around and around the ring.

"Thirty seconds!"

"This ain't like you, Babe!" Vern muttered beneath his breath. "Do something! Rib-roast him!"

The spectators now crowded around the ring, calling out bets, cheering, booing, cheering.

Another hard blow to her side. It was as though the hit knocked an idea into her! She knew what to do with only seconds to go! She reeled back like she'd been shot, then twirled about. Another hit. She roared and fell backward, as only a giant can fall. The crowd went wild. She stayed down outside the circle and rolled like she'd been thunderstruck.

Vern knelt down. "Babe! Show him what for! What are you doing? Get up!"

The spectators were pointing and laughing at her. Her father, like the biblical David declaring victory over Goliath, took a tour of the ring, his hands clasped high and wagging back and forth.

Others in their troupe watched, mouths open, eyes wide, shaking heads in disbelief.

The final bell gonged. Renoir flew into the ring and held the victor's hand high. He shouted above the noise of the crowd, "This man! This man is the first, the only man, to have knocked down Magnifica, Queen of the Amazons!"

Renoir counted ten . . . twenty . . . thirty . . . forty . . . fifty dollars into her father's hand. The crowd counted with him, delighting in Babe's defeat. She remained still but opened her eyes. Lotty was standing on a chair, her tiny nose just over the boxing-ring floor.

"Babe!"

Babe gave her a small smile, followed by a big wink.

Killingsworth and Renoir helped each other out of the ring like they were old chums, laughing and slapping each other's backs. The crowd dispersed, the torches doused, leaving Babe in the dark. Lotty scrambled into the ring. "Babe, are you hurt?"

"Feel right as rain," she answered, sitting up.

"But you went down so hard."

"Never felt better."

"Renoir's going to take that fifty dollars out of your pay, you know! Just when we need the money more than ever!"

"How come if you're the brains of our outfit you never once thought of this?" Babe said, rubbing her side.

"What?" Lotty's face was a puzzle.

"Sure, I take a fall with a challenger, then we split the prize money." Her smile grew wider. "Ain't nothing wrong with taking this act a little sideways."

"A con? But that would be . . ."

"A flimflam!" Babe said, breaking her off. "Just like you in a baby carriage, only I'm the baby and this here ring is the carriage!" Babe said, putting her head back and laughing.

Lotty stepped back and scrunched her face. "Huh?"

"Sure! Find us our own fakers each coupla shows. Any yokel'd love twenty-five dollar! And he can brag the rest of his life what he done!"

"You're crazy!"

"Wait and see the kind of crazy your ol' Babe is." She grabbed the ropes and pulled herself up.

"Wait a minute, Babe!" Lotty followed her out of the ring. "I don't get it."

"You will."

"Where are you going?"

"Right now I got me one more round coming."

"Babe . . ."

But she disappeared into the smoky, steamy night. She figured her father would be celebrating his big win in the beer gardens.

"So, Babe, I see you're doing damn good for yourself," her father said, stepping out of the shadows.

Babe whirled around.

"I got to say, when I heard this chintzy show was coming again, I was just tickled to death. Renoir and me had some old business to settle. You remember."

"I remember."

"So, I thought why not just take a trip and see ol' Babe? Or do you want to be called Magnifica?"

"You forgot my given name is Fern?"

He stood back and took her in full. "God, I could swear you've grown, and it's been, what? Only five months? Yessir, I'd say this life agrees with you." He pointed to her hands. "Look at the size of those meat hooks!"

Babe thought of the Big Bad Wolf's line to Little Red Riding Hood—*All the better to choke you with.*

She spotted his winnings sticking out of his shirt pocket, like five green tongues taunting *nah-nah nah-nah-nah* at her. She walked closer. He took a step back. There were stacks of baled straw behind him. He took another step back but stopped when he hit the bales.

"Now, Babe," he warned. "You don't look at me that way, girl!"

Putting her arm against his chest and pinning him easy, she one, two, three, four, five, plucked out the fifty dollars he thought he'd just won.

"Oh, come on, daughter."

If there was one thing she could read, it was fear in someone's eyes. "Don't you never call me daughter." She felt that bubbling rage inside and clamped her jaw to keep it down. "And gimme your wallet."

"Babe!"

She pushed him again. Did he realize if she brought her arm up sharp, fast, and hard, she could snap his neck like a chicken wing? "Wallet!"

Slowly, his hand went down to his pants pocket. He pulled out a tattered but fat wallet.

"I reckon this'll cover my expenses." She slipped the wallet into her belt.

"You can't . . . rob your own father!" he tried, reaching for breath under the pressure of her arm.

"You ain't no father to me any more'n I'm queen of the Amazons!" she said, stepping back and staring down at him. He made a grab for his wallet, and before she could get her calm back, she gave him a hard shove, sending him back and *crash!* Heels over the hay bales!

She walked away, smiling, knowing there was nothing he could do. No man alive would admit he'd been robbed, then "put away" by his own daughter. Even a daughter who's a giant.

"Okay, Babe. What's this all about? I haven't seen you grin like that since . . . well, since never!" Lotty said as Babe climbed into her cattle car.

"Saving things makes me smile," she said, tossing peanuts into Jupiter's and Euclid's cages.

"Huh? Who did you save?"

"Us. You, me, Euclid, Egypt, and Jupiter. I saved *us*." She pulled out the wallet and let the bills swish down where they piled up on the floor.

"Babe! Tell me you didn't rob someone! That man? That old man who floored you in the fight?"

"I just got back what was owed me." She ran a wet towel over her face, pulling off makeup and smearing her long, dramatic "scar."

"That man? He owed you? You knew him? What? How?"

"Yep. But we're square now."

Lotty picked up the money and began counting it. "Babe! There's over three hundred dollars here!"

"Oh. I forgot." She pulled out five moist tens she'd stashed in her outfit. "Sorry they're so whiffy. I sure work up a sweat these days."

"I still can't believe it, Babe. How did that man owe *you* money?"

"It's money he don't never have to spend on my schooling, my clothes, my comforts, and . . ." Her loud laughter caused Euclid to imitate it back. "And my wedding, if I can ever find a man big enough to marry me!"

Lotty stared at Babe, her mouth and eyes wide-open. "Babe, are you saying that man was your . . ."

"My ol' man," Babe said for her. Then, grinning to beat the band, she added, "We don't look alike."

With the cattle car doors open to the stifling, midmorning heat, Babe stood marveling at the two colors passing by—ripe yellow fields under the bright blue of a cloudless sky. The train slowed down, switched to a siding, and came to a halt. In the distance, she could make out the town . . . the redbrick of the buildings, stark white of the church steeples, and the sparkle of a river meandering through. The latest schedule of stops was tacked to the wall.

"Pen-dle-ton, Or-e-gon," she sounded out. "In-de-pen-dence Day . . . What do you think of that, Jupiter?" she asked the bear. He leaned into his cage for his ritual ear-scruffing. Euclid leaned into his cage for some attention. "I see you, Euclid," Babe whispered, handing him some peanuts and cracking a few herself. "Maybe someday we'll get us some of that independence. You think? Could be. Maybe."

"Babe!" Lotty called up from the track below. Egypt stood next to her, swaying, ears flapping. "Are you up?"

"Been up all night. Hard to sleep in this heat."

"I know." Lotty fanned her face. "Can you come with me? Poor Egypt needs some water. She's parched and sure could use a bath."

"I can see a stream over there, in town," Babe said, pointing. "Long walk in this heat."

"There's a water tower on the other side of the train. Hurry. People are already arriving."

Babe quickly tossed some apples and a handful of oats to Jupiter and Euclid, then jumped down to help Lotty with Egypt, who seemed to sense water was in her future. People were already lining the track to see what wonders the carnival had brought to their town. They were rewarded with the odd sight of a dwarf, a giant, and an elephant walking toward the water tower.

It wasn't the first time the girls had arranged a shower for the elephant. Water towers for trains were always perched high up on stilts and had a glorious long waterspout that could swing back and forth, creating a waterfall of pleasure for the elephant.

"That's some tower," Lotty said, shading her eyes as she looked up. "Looks brand-new."

"Bet it holds a million gallon," Babe said. The waterspout

was shiny and glistened in the sun.

"Look at that." Lotty pointed to the crowd of people walking from the station toward them. "It's like they can smell an elephant coming!"

"Well, how often do them folk get to see the likes of us and a elephant taking a bath?"

"Say," a man called out, approaching them. "What's going on here?"

"Oh. Do you work here?" Lotty asked.

"I'm the yardmaster and . . ." His words trailed off. "Say now, that's an elephant!"

"Thought we'd give the folks a little show," Lotty said. "How about you let us water the elephant?"

He took his cap off, looked up at Babe, down at Lotty, and then over to Egypt. "Sure, I guess, I mean, yeah why not? Don't get folks like you in these parts very often!"

Lotty pointed to the large iron cuff around Egypt's back leg. "Babe, watch that rope on her cuff. It's getting tangled," she said.

Babe pulled the rope clear of the tracks where it had caught on something. "Ready?" the yardmaster called, his hand on a lever. The spout swung around and the water began to flow into a holding pond at the side of the tracks. Kids sat on fences and baggage carts to get a closer look. People ran from the station and lined the tracks.

"Woodrow! Get down from there!" a woman called

out from the distance. She stepped forward, her parasol bobbing over her head.

Egypt stood under the pouring water, her eyes closed, her tail twitching with joy. The holding pond filled under her and she pulled in a trunkful of water and showered her back, sending muddy splatters over Lotty and Babe. The crowd laughed and clapped.

"Woodrow!" the woman called out again, her voice rising above the sound of water gushing and people laughing. "Get down from there this instant!" She snapped her parasol closed and pointed it up to her son. "I said *now*!"

Babe looked up. The boy had climbed onto the top of the water tower. The distinctive smell of a sulfur match hit both girls at the same time.

"Babe!" Lotty screamed, pointing up. Woodrow was lighting a string of firecrackers. He tossed them down and they exploded midair. *Bangbangbang!* right above Egypt's head.

"Hold, girl!" Babe called out. Egypt pulled back and *bangbangbang!* More fireworks rained down.

People must have thought it was part of the act, and they applauded. Then the crowd silenced when Egypt let out a deafening trumpet of fear.

"Whoa, Egypt!" Lotty screamed, as though her tiny voice and stance could stop the elephant, pulling against the rope. "Babe! Help!"

Even Babe was helpless against a frightened elephant.

The rope grew taut, then caught on something.

"Get her free!" Lotty called out, pointing to Egypt's cuff.

"The rope's stuck! We need a ax! Someone get a ax!" Babe hollered, following the rope under the water. She pulled but it was stuck around one of the pillars holding the water tower.

People edged back; parents pulled children closer to them; a few men came forward; Woodrow's mother screamed louder.

"Easy, Egypt!" Babe whispered. The tauter the rope, the more the elephant protested, screeched, and pulled back. More fireworks in the background added to the chaos; people screaming added to the fear. "Let ol' Babe help you," Babe said, her face close to Egypt's eye, her voice low and calming. But she recognized that look, that fear in Egypt's eye. "I'm here. Your Babe's got you. Easy, girl, easy."

A train whistle screeched in the distance. Egypt cried out again and pulled even harder. *Crack!* The pillar snapped in two and the water tower began to lean.

"Mama!" the boy cried out, trying to grab on to something, anything, as the tower tilted even more.

Finally, the rope snapped off and Egypt ran free toward the safety of her railroad car.

Another deafening *crack!* Babe stepped back. Woodrow was now dangling off the top of the tower. People screamed, but no one did anything as the water began to spill out and over Woodrow.

With a final groan of surrender, the tower shifted—the gush of water, the crack of wood, the crunch of metal! The water cascaded, spilling wood and Woodrow twenty feet below. Babe and Lotty ran back as the water flooded down.

"Woodrow!" the mother screamed, coming to the wreckage and wading through the filled-up gully. "Help! Help!" Her skirts quickly weighed her down and she struggled to stand. "My boy is under there!"

Babe looked around. A frantic search through the planks of wood, the water, the beams, the crushed metal. Then, a little hand popped up from under the water.

"Here!" someone called. "He's pinned! Over here! Help!"

"Oh God, someone help!" the mother called out.

Babe rushed into the water, feeling below the surface for the beam. She found it, stood astride, leaned down, gripped it, and grunted. The boy's hand flailed.

Babe held her breath. *Legs, Babe, use your legs!*

With all her strength, with all her heart, she tossed the beam aside and Woodrow popped to the surface! His gasps for breath made her fit to kill for what he'd done, yet leap for joy he hadn't drowned. She picked him up and stepped away from the crowd, holding him high over her head to hand him to his mother. Woodrow spit out mud and water and screamed through his choking. Finally, he looked down at Babe and his face spread in terror.

"Help! The giant's got me! The giant's got me!" he screamed. He kicked and pounded Babe's head. "Help! Mama!"

Babe held him at arm's length and glared at him, then tried to shake the screaming out of him.

"Babe! Stop! Babe!" Lotty cried, pulling at Babe's skirt. "What are you doing?"

Babe shook her head to bring her to her senses. Then, she cradled him in her arms, hushing him. But he was still stiff with fright.

"Give him to me!" the drenched mother screamed, now batting Babe's side with her muddy parasol. "Give him!"

"Hesh, hesh, hesh, child. I got you," Babe said soothingly. "You're okay. Babe's got you." Looking into his face, she knew she frightened him. "Here's your mama." Gently, she wiped some mud from his face. "Shhhh."

She handed him, carefully as she could, down to his crying mother. "He's okay, ma'am. He's okay."

But the mother had no words for Babe. She turned and carried her Woodrow away, leaving Babe standing in the water, the broken pillar knocking against her knees, the sting of the parasol along her side.

The carnage around her, the damage, and with the gossip sure to follow, Babe knew, just knew, she would get blamed for the whole thing. Within two hours, Renoir received a bill of damages from the stationmaster. Adding salt to her wounds, Woodrow and his mother sat in the front row center at the evening show, tickets compliments of Renoir. The boy's face was now free of mud and full of candy. His bright red tongue *nah-nah*ed up at her.

Babe couldn't bear to look at him or his prim mother, dressed now in a fresh clean dress, a matching parasol over her head. No respect. Carnies never deserve respect. Only the blame.

On the road again and sleepless in the stuffy railroad car, Babe sat, her legs dangling out the door, thinking about the day, watching the shadowy landscape of eastern Oregon roll by. She still heard the blast of the firecrackers, the screams of that brat Woodrow, the *whap whap whap* of the mother's parasol. She felt the chill of the rising water, the strength of the pillar, and the eyes of the thankless woman. But what bothered her the most was—for an instant—the beast nearly escaped.

Babe shook her head to scare away those thoughts, pulled herself up, and lumbered to her bed. Her joints ached more than usual. Fourteen and she had the pains of an old woman.

A doctor once told her giants usually don't live much past thirty, maybe forty, tops. "Nope, a giant's heart has a lot of territory to pump all that blood through," he'd said, showing her the drawing of a giant's skeleton in a medical book. At first Babe didn't understand it, being only half a giant at the time. But now, rubbing her aching knees, rolling the stiffness out of her shoulders, massaging her fingers and hands, she began to understand.

"Thirty year," Babe said into the dusky car. She used her fingers in the air to cipher the years. "Criminy, Babe, you're near half done." Her eyes landed on the ghostly gray of her Magnifica costume, hanging on a nail across the car. It swayed to and fro mockingly with the rhythm of the tracks. "You just think on that, girl. One-half the way to dying."

She smiled over at Jupiter, who was snoring as only an elderly bear can. It was music to her. Euclid slept in his cage curled up, childlike, in his favorite blanket.

Lying down with a grunt, she pulled a light sheet over her, brought her knees to her chest, and held herself.

"One-half . . ." she whispered, closing her eyes, seeing that medical-book skeleton, thinking, hearing those firecrackers, thinking.

"You got that book to read us, Lotty?" Babe asked, two nights later and after the last show. She felt too tired, too achy to sleep. "The one about Alice."

"Oh, yes!" she said, jumping up and heading to her train car. "I'll be right back!"

Babe loved it when Lotty read out loud, especially on warm nights such as this, around a cook fire.

Lotty bounded back, carrying a book almost too heavy for her. "Where did we leave off?"

"Do that potion part again." Babe settled back against a log, stretching her legs out. "I like that part."

Lotty read with great drama and booming voice, from *Alice's Adventures in Wonderland* where Alice drinks a potion and *pow!* she's big as a room! Bigger than Babe! Big as a tree! Then, Lotty switched to a whispery, teensy voice when Alice drinks the next potion and *swoosh!* she's teeny-weeny small! Smaller than Lotty! Small as a twig! As she read, the firelight grew smaller and the shadows grew larger.

Lotty set the book on her lap and sighed. "Don't you wish there was such a potion?" She stared, stone-faced, into the embers. "You know. Something you can drink and get smaller? Something I can drink and get bigger?" Her voice had never sounded so small, her wishes so big.

"I'd pay all the money I ever could get for that, Lotty."

"Me too," she whispered. Then, snapping out of it, she added, "Anyway, it's just pretend. Just like Madame de la Rosa's fake mind reading and jujus."

"It's fun to think about, ain't it?" Babe poked the fire with a stick. "We both drink a potion and meet somewheres in the middle and finally see eye to eye. Wouldn't that be something?"

"Yes," she whispered dreamily. Then, "Oh, come on. Let's think about something else."

"Okay. Let's think on our own adventure. Let's think about us getting out of here. Betwixt us we got over four hundred dollar. What we don't got is a plan."

"You know," Lotty said, "I have an aunt." She looked down at her hands in her lap. "She's my mother's sister."

"She a midget, too?"

"How many times do I have to tell you, Babe?" Lotty

snapped. "I'm a dwarf, not a midget!"

"It's only a word. And it's fun to say. *Mid-jit*. What difference does it make?"

"Well, I prefer dwarf. Midget makes me think of those dummies on ventriloquists' laps."

"I seed one of them acts once. You ever seed one?"

"Worse!" she said. "I was *in* one!"

"Which was you?" Babe asked, keeping her smile low.

Lotty cast her eyes to the heavens. "Oh ha ha! Yep, I sat on the lap of the Great Martini for a whole season. I was just ten. I'd make like I wasn't real, you know, made of wood, cranking my neck and flapping my jaw. Fixed my face so it looked like wood. Big dead eyes looking at no one."

"I'd pay cash money to see that!"

Lotty went into her dummy imitation. She lowered her voice and said, "'So, tell me, Minnie'—I was billed as Minnie the Midget—'what's your favorite bird?' I'd look at the audience, blink wide a few times, crank my neck this way and that, and he'd say for me, 'Well, it sure ain't a woodpecker!' Folks'd laugh and I'd crank my shoulders up and down like the dummy—well, me—would laugh. We played music and dance halls. I hated it, but the money was good and Mr. Martini and his wife kept me safe."

"You think just on account of we're different, folk can treat us different?"

"Of course they treat us different! Look, Babe, I've

been with one show or another since I was ten, when I got kicked out of the orphanage."

"Ten's mighty young for"—Babe indicated the carnival world around them—"for all this."

"Well, they let me take the eighth-grade exam, and I passed with flying colors. No one was going to adopt a peewee runt like me, they couldn't teach me any longer, so why not get on with being this? What I am?"

"I remember when I was about ten," Babe began, staring into the fire. "One little girl said she'd give me a sandwich if she could take me to her Sunday school to show me off."

Lotty laughed. "And did you?"

"It was ham and cheese, Lotty. 'Course I did it! Think that was the first time ever I went on display for commerce."

Their laughter melted into silence. Babe broke it. "We was talking about your aunt. You never answered. Is your aunt a midg—dwarf, too?"

"Oh, I doubt it. Neither of my parents were small." She sighed, staring into the fire. "If they had been, maybe they wouldn't have died."

Lotty had told Babe about how it was she'd come to be orphaned when she was three. House fire, pushed out through a tiny windowpane, too tiny for her parents to follow her.

"Wait. If you got kin, how come you didn't you go live with her?"

"No one knew. Everything was destroyed in the fire. I don't even have a birth certificate. Who cares? Some people think I was hatched anyway!"

"Ha! I been handed that line, too!" Babe said, snapping a branch in half and tossing it onto the fire.

"Anyway, I was in two different orphanages. After a few years, news caught up and they learned I had an aunt. Here. In Oregon."

"Did they write her about you?"

"Yes. No answer. Least, that's what they told me. Probably she didn't see any good in raising a dwarf." Lotty sighed. "After all, what do you do with a dwarf once the luster wears off?"

"You got luster? What's luster?" Babe asked, trying to joggle her friend out of her blue mood.

"Well, you know, making like I'm a baby for five or six years. By the time I was a year old, they knew I was going to always be small. So, I went out on a free trial three different times but they always sent me back after a few months."

"Why'd they take you back?"

"Maybe they got tired of telling people I wasn't a baby but a child. Who cares? I've always found some carnie work, and even a traveling home is a home. Sure makes you grow up fast, though."

"I reckon," Babe said, her voice now low like Lotty's.

"But it makes me mad as hell I can be a wooden dummy,

dance a jig on an elephant's back, and that's about all. I can't be anyone's pretend baby."

"Well, look at me. What am I fit for? Sure as hell I ain't going to be no highfalutin lady of leisure or gal about town. Ain't no man willing to take on feeding and dressing me."

"But, Babe, you're stronger than any man. You'll always find a job."

"Men's jobs. They don't let women. Besides"—she tapped her forehead—"I'm pretty dang weak here." Babe lowered her voice. "There's something else."

"What?"

"Never told anyone before, but I got this thing inside me." Now she tapped her stomach. "It's a . . . a beast. She tries to get out and I have to work like grim death to keep her hid."

"I think I have one, too," Lotty said. "My beast is pretty tiny, but she's there."

Babe lit a lantern with a stick from the fire. "What about you? If things was different? If you was . . . normal? What would you be?"

"Me? Don't laugh."

"I ain't laughing."

"I've always wanted to be a nurse."

"Nurse? Don't that take schooling?"

She sighed. "Yes. And schooling takes money, if I could even find a school that would take me. After all, how could I even—" She stopped.

Babe envisioned her, all white and crisp and fast, working around a hospital bed. Then it hit her—what Lotty had probably been seeing her whole life, which wasn't the top of anything. She couldn't reach the top of a bed or an operating table or even a bedpan. She was too small to do work so big.

Lotty's pretty face glowed in the firelight. "Anyhows," Babe said, "what's you having a aunt got to do with anything? You thinking about going to her instead of us striking out together?"

"No! No, Babe! Nothing like that! I was going through the papers they gave me when I left the orphanage. You know, the death papers, my release, graduation certificate. Got to thinking about where we might go, once we get free from Renoir."

"I'm thinking maybe we can buy us a bit of land. Just us and our critters. Maybe farm something."

Lotty pulled out a folded paper from the book at her side. "This is the last address of my aunt. See here? Miss Valerie Logan. General Delivery, John's Town, Oregon. I never thought I'd need an aunt until . . . Uncle Dan's Taxidermy."

"What makes you think she's still there, or, heck, Lotty, even alive?"

"Must you always look on the dark side? It's really a very unpleasant feature."

"I'm sorry. Go on."

"I found out John's Town is in southern Oregon, close to Medford. Right where we're heading. And we can get mail in care of this train."

"Mail from who?"

"From my aunt! Aren't you listening?"

"Why for?"

"Because," she sighed, "maybe she'll put us up for a bit, until we can figure out what we're going to do. I mean, she owes me that." She held up the paper. "So I've written her a letter."

"Okay, Lotty, I ain't saying this to show 'nother unpleasant feature, but if she didn't write back to the orphanage folk, what makes you think she'll write back now?"

She looked wistfully at the letter. "Well, it was worth a try. I mean, we're going to be so close. Maybe. Maybe she's alive. Maybe she's still there. Maybe she'll answer."

"Them's a lot of 'maybes.'"

"Maybe 'maybe' is all we have, Babe."

"Read to me what you writ."

"Wrote," she corrected.

"Wrote."

"Hold the lantern still. 'Dear Aunt Valerie; How are you? I am fine. I got word from the nuns at Grace of Glory Children's Home that you are my aunt. Maybe you met me when I was very small. I am still small. My mama was your sister, so I am your niece. I am fourteen years old now. I would like to visit you this August. I will be traveling with a friend and it would be nice to meet you. Our train is the Huxley Line. It is private and uses the Southern Pacific tracks, so you can send me a letter in care of the train and I will get it. Your niece, Carlotta Jones.'"

"Jones?"

"It's the name the nuns gave me."

"Good thing you don't mention who we're bringing with us," Babe said.

"Well, like you said, she might even be dead." Lotty folded the letter with her delicate hands and slipped it back into the book. "But, Medford is close to the end of the line for us *and* them." She nodded her head toward Babe's cattle car. "That taxidermy man is in Klamath Falls, and that's close to Medford."

The word *taxidermy* made Babe's heart jump, and she felt that rage rising up again. Lotty was right. This aunt of hers just has to be alive and willing, and, yes, she did owe Lotty at least this.

"That don't give us much time," Babe said.

"Think you can take a few more falls for half the purse?" Lotty asked, giving Babe a sly smile.

"As long as you keep finding me a come-on guy, then sure. That's twenty-five each time I take a fall."

"Renoir's starting to get suspicious, you know."

"I told him I get wearied sometimes. Besides, what can he do?"

"And I can pick up some extra money making those

horsehair jujus and conjure bags for Madame de la Rosa."

"Are them the ones for love or for hate?"

"Neither. They're the ones for fortune. They sell like hotcakes. Who doesn't want fortune?"

"Make a few for us, will you?" Babe said. "Can't never hurt."

"Have you seen JoJo?" Serena asked Babe and Lotty. "You know she's afraid of the dark." The last show in Hermiston, Oregon, had closed, and the train was mostly packed away with track clearance to leave the siding at dawn.

"Did you find her?" Rosa asked urgently as she dashed into the mess tent.

"No, I haven't seen her since my first show," Donny said. "She helped with the dog jumps. Sometimes she crawls in the cage to sleep with my dogs, but she wasn't there, either."

"Not like her to just disappear. Especially after dark," Serena said, looking around the tent.

"She likes to hide then jump out and scare the bejesus out of me," Lotty said. "But she hasn't done that since we became friends."

"She wouldn't just wander off," Lucretia said, setting down a cup of coffee.

The others in the tent circled and offered an explanation or idea. "Did anyone look in her bed?" Vern asked. "Maybe she was just tired and called it a night. She's no spring chicken, you know."

"Nowhere on the train!" This 'n' That Ernie announced, coming into the tent. "We looked everywhere. Tents, cars, even boxes and crates. Now, this wouldn't be the first time she's gone and hid herself."

Voices outside were calling for JoJo. Babe thought back—didn't she see JoJo that night? Where? What? "I remember," she whispered. All eyes were on her. "Yes! During my act! There was some boys. Podunk town rowdies. Didn't see much past my stage lamps, but I heard JoJo laugh."

"You don't think she'd go with a stranger, do you?" Rosa asked the crowd.

"You're the mind reader, you tell us!" one of the cooks called out.

"They got JoJo! They got JoJo!" Ina, Mina, or Tina shouted, as all three ran into the tent. "Us girls were in town after the show!" one said, catching her breath.

"Someone swiped JoJo's doll and made her come after it," another said. "They went into a tavern!"

"We went inside and saw them teasing her about her doll."

"One man was holding it over her head!"

"Then another man teased her with a brand-new doll! Said she had to sing for it!"

"She wouldn't come back with us. Come on, someone! Help!"

"Lotty, you stay here," Babe said.

"But you're still in your Magnifica costume!"

"Babe, come on. Hurry!" Rosa said, pulling Babe by the arm. "Ernie's getting his gun." Ernie had a wagon hitched in no time. He drove, Rosa sat next to him, and Babe rode in the wagon bed, holding on to the rails.

"Ina said a place called Billy Banks Saloon! There! Where all those horses and wagons are!" Rosa pointed down the block.

The saloon was a beacon of gaiety and light in the center of town. Music and laughter spilled out of the open windows and double doors.

Rosa turned to Ernie. "You can't just go in there guns blazing. Maybe we should find the local law and . . ."

"I can handle this," Babe said, jumping down off the wagon.

"Babe, no! Get back here!" Rosa called.

Babe ignored Rosa, brushed some straw off her costume, and approached the open doors. Cigar and cigarette smoke sifted out as she walked in. All talk ceased.

"Well, look here!" someone called out. "We got another visitor from the freak show!"

Rosa and Ernie dashed in and stood on either side of Babe. Rosa stepped forward. "We just want our friend back. We know she's here!"

"Hey you, Madame de la Whoever you are!" another man shouted from across the room. "Your good-luck charm ain't worth a sucked orange! My horse stepped in a hole on the way back to town! He'll be lame for a week!" His story was greeted with laughter and booing.

Babe recognized one of the challengers she'd faced that evening. He stood up, kicking back his chair and weaving toward her. "I want another go 'round," he said, spitting into his hands and circling her.

"Ain't got time for the likes of you," Babe growled. "Alls I want is our JoJo back."

He tap-tap-tapped her shoulder just the way her father had. With a roar, she slapped his arm away. He lost his balance and fell onto a table. He didn't get up.

Ernie stepped forward. "We know y'all got JoJo somewheres, and we want her back."

Just then, the unmistakably shrill sound of JoJo's laughter came from a back room.

People parted as Babe walked through the crowd, toward the sound. "There's a private party going on in there," the bartender said, standing in front of Babe. He looked up at her, then stepped aside. "Guess it ain't all that private." He opened the door for her.

"JoJo? You in here? It's Babe. Come to take you home."

When Babe filled the doorway, everyone stopped mid-sentence, midlaugh, midtease.

JoJo pointed to Babe, grinned, and shouted, "Look, Babe!" She held up a bright, shiny doll, then cradled it as she rocked it.

"Who brung her here?" Babe demanded, looking around the room.

"She brung herself here. She ain't no child," someone defended.

"Come on, JoJo. We're going home."

"No!"

"These folks is making fun of you," Babe said, her voice kind.

"Don't care!"

Babe walked closer. She noticed JoJo's old doll was in a crumpled heap on a table. "We don't let folks do us this way." Babe took the old, tossed-aside doll and offered it to JoJo. "Maybe you should give that doll back. Ain't yours."

"Mine," JoJo yelped, holding the new doll closer to her chest.

"Yeah, who's going to pay for that doll? Two dollars and fifty cents!" a man said, stepping up with a slip of paper in his hand. "Got the receipt right here."

Babe took the paper, wadded it into her mouth, chewed it, then spit it out where the wad landed among peanut shells, chew spit, and cigar butts. "That there's three bucks. Gimme my four bits change!" She held out her huge hand, snapped her fingers, and stepped closer to the man. All eyes on him, he reached a shaking hand into his pocket, extracted two quarters and plunked them into her hand.

She put her hand out to JoJo. "You come with me. Your Babe's taking you home."

"Mine?" JoJo asked, holding the new doll up.

"Bought and paid for," Babe said, putting the old, tattered doll back into JoJo's belt. Babe looked around the room at the silent faces.

"Keep?"

"Now you gots two you can mama."

Ernie scratched his head, and Rosa smiled in amazement as Babe and JoJo walked out, hand in swinging hand.

Two days later, they were parked on a siding near The Dalles, Oregon. The advance man, Pepito, and either Ina, Mina, or Tina had run off to get married, leaving the outfit high and dry for new bookings and minus one dancing girl. There were only a few bookings on the tracks ahead to Portland and then south to Medford. No one to set up notices of Renoir's show coming meant no track clearance or permits to set up the show. No show, no money.

Renoir ordered the troupe to use the delay to oil, clean, repair, and rehearse, while he headed to town to do business and see about track clearance.

"Baaaaaaaabe!"

Babe's head came up out of a deep doze.

"Babe!" cried JoJo's unmistakable voice, full of urgency,

as she ran toward the railcar. There were now two dolls tucked into her belt.

"JoJo! What're you . . ."

JoJo jutted her two hands up toward Babe, standing in the open door of her railcar. "Here!"

"Here what? What you got there?"

JoJo giggled, grinned, and repeated, "Here." Babe reached down and took the small cloth bag JoJo offered up to her. "For you! I like you!"

Babe looked inside the bag, then pulled out an envelope and looked inside. JoJo jumped up and down with joy. "JoJo. Where did you get all this cash money?"

"You! You!"

"What's going on up there?" Lotty asked, coming alongside the tracks. "JoJo, it's too hot for you being out here."

JoJo stuck her tongue out at her.

"Aw, come on. We're friends now, remember? What's in it, Babe? Babe?"

"Money. Cash money. JoJo give it to me."

"You! You!" JoJo chanted, whirling around in a circle.

Lotty looked inside the envelope. "JoJo, where did you get this?"

JoJo pointed far off down the tracks. "Found it!"

"Where?" Babe asked.

Now JoJo pointed to the scrub brush in the opposite direction. "Found it!"

"But I don't understand," Lotty said. "Where did you find it?"

JoJo looked down at Lotty and gave her a mean look. "For Babe!"

"JoJo, I can't take this money. Ain't yours, ain't mine."

"Can you show us where you found it?" Lotty asked, opening the envelope and fanning the tops of the bills. "There must be over two hundred dollars in here. It has to belong to somebody."

JoJo grabbed the envelope and held it to her chest. "Found it!" She handed it back to Babe. "You saved JoJo! You! You!"

Babe jumped down and bent down to talk to JoJo face-to-face, eye to eye. "JoJo, show us where you got this." She offered her hand. "Come. Show us."

"You. Not her!"

"Okay. Just you and me. Come on. Show me."

Lotty was sitting in the shade under the railcar, fanning herself with a hanky when Babe came back alone, holding the fat envelope.

"Well?"

"Beats me. She showed me where she found it, only I don't think she found it. You know JoJo. She don't always see truths the same way we do."

"You mean she stole it? From who? There's no writing on the envelope," Lotty said.

"She showed me a place in the tracks."

"Well, maybe someone dropped it from a train. Who knows? Finders keepers, losers weepers, right? I say God love Madame de la Rosa and her juju conjure bags!"

Babe's hand went to the horsehair juju. "But what about the weeper out there? Maybe the weeper needs it more'n we do. Criminy, Lotty, what if it's money from one of our own?"

"Who in this cheap outfit has money like that?"

"But . . ."

"But nothing! There isn't anyone around. No hobo jungle, no campfires, no shacks, no nothing. We're almost in the middle of nowhere! I tell you, it fell off a train and the weeper is long down the line!"

"What if it's bank or train-robber money, Lotty? What if they come looking for it?"

"Pishposh!"

"Shouldn't we turn it in or something?" Babe asked, looking down at the envelope.

"Babe, sometimes you make me crazy! We go into town, give it to the local sheriff and guess what? Pretty soon his wife is sporting a new diamond necklace and matching earbobs!"

"And here I thought *I* was the shifty thinker in this outfit," Babe said, coming around.

"And we don't tell anyone! Hide it with the rest of our stash." She ticked her head toward her railcar. "Hurry and hide it! I have to go tend Egypt."

Lotty ran off down the tracks, and Babe pulled herself back into her cattle car. "Look here." Babe fanned the bills toward Euclid. "We got us a grubstake. Wait. What's this?" She pulled out a white piece of paper in the middle of the bills. She read the printing on the top. "De-pos-it ticket. Cal-i-for-ni-a State Bank." She held the ticket to the light and read the handwriting aloud. "Please de-pos-it into the per-son-al account of . . ." She looked at Euclid. "Phillipe Renoir, Number Three-Three-Four. Two hundred twenty-seven dollar. How do you reckon a broke showman gets all this cash money?" She stared across the car, thinking. "Must be carnie money." She looked down at the ticket. "All going into Renoir's bank." She scrunched her face and looked at the chimp. "From our till to his? No wonder we're flat broke all the time." She ran her theory around mentally one more time. "Let's keep this betwixt just us, boys. Got that, Jupiter? Understand, Euclid?"

She added the cash into a secret bin under Jupiter's cage with the rest of their getaway stash, took the deposit ticket—evidence about Renoir and evidence about JoJo— and stared at it. She took a match, struck it and held it to the ticket. "Wait," she whispered. She thought carefully. Maybe she should hang on to this. Babe thought as the match burned down. The flame hit her fingers. "Ouch!" She swished the match out.

She rolled the deposit ticket and put it where no person would ever try to find it—inside the horsehair conjure bag hanging down the front of her shirt, where all things were safe and sound.

Renoir made no mention of the missing money, which made Babe even more nervous and suspicious. Why wouldn't he tell the troupe, why wouldn't he ask if anyone had found the money or accuse someone of stealing it? Well, she thought, if he wasn't going to mention it, neither was she. Is it theft if it's stealing from a thief?

Babe now knew why the rations were skimpy, the soup watery, the stops for the horses to graze more frequent, the stolen fruit from orchards along the river more brazen, and the promise of the taxidermist at the end of the line more threatening. Renoir was skimming the carnival's money.

"Plain and simple," she muttered.

"Babe!" Madame de la Rosa signaled to Babe, who was helping wash dishes behind the mess tent. "Here, dear, look at this."

"What's this?"

"It's the proof for a new flier. You know, an advertisement. Renoir was passing it around the smoking car. Getting a good laugh."

Babe looked at the poster. "I don't read so good."

Rosa squinted her eyes and read, "'Euclid, the world's smartest ape! A mathematical genius! His brain was sent to Vienna for study. Be photographed with him! Ten cents a pose!'"

"What's that . . . ?"

"There's more. 'Jupiter, world-famous dancing bear! The toast of Europe! Dance with him now!'"

Babe dried her hands on her apron. "What this mean?"

"There's one more, Babe. 'Egypt, Rogue Elephant of Borneo! Killed thirty-two people. A dollar a pose.'"

Rosa gave her a gentle smile. "This means he's one hundred percent serious, Babe. Look, something's happened. I don't know what, but I'll tell you, I've never seen Renoir this edgy."

Babe fought the urge to tell her everything—their planned escape after buying the animals and their contracts. Running away and maybe even stealing the animals if they had to. The money JoJo had found—no, stole—and the deposit ticket Babe had found.

"Well, I know what the animals mean to you. I just don't want you two girls getting any more attached than you are. They are Renoir's property and . . ."

"No, they ain't. They belong to them investor men back east, don't they?"

"Maybe legally, but they are Renoir's to do with as he sees fit."

"Rosa, I got to . . ." Babe started, but the sound of Egypt's trumpeting in the distance made her reconsider. She knew she wasn't clever enough to tell Rosa only this and not that. Truth was an all-or-nothing situation with Babe—either come clean or stay dirty.

"Got to what?"

"Go help Lotty with Egypt."

Rosa walked away, and Babe looked beyond her. Renoir

was standing, leaning into a tent pole, staring at her, tapping his riding crop against his boot. She returned his glare, feeling her beast rise again. She wadded the poster into a tight ball then threw it into the cook fire.

If she had any guilt or doubts about keeping Renoir's stolen money, they were as vanished as the poster now curling up into ashes.

25

They traveled along the Columbia River, making stops at a few small towns along their journey. Then, at Portland, they started their final leg south. At each stop along the line, Lotty went to the stationmaster to see if a letter was waiting for her.

No letters. But her own letter hadn't been returned, either, giving the girls a slight glimmer of hope.

"Anything?" Babe asked, as soon as she spotted Lotty on the wagon coming from the stationmaster at the Salem depot. She could tell by her face there was no letter from her aunt Valerie.

"We still have several more stops. Albany, Corvallis, Brownsville," Lotty said, issuing a small sigh of defeat.

Babe lifted her down off the wagon and the driver continued on. Egypt, her huge back foot chained to a tree that she was trimming, rumbled Lotty a welcome as they walked toward her. It was as though the elephant could smell the ripe cantaloupe in her knapsack.

"Look what I found for you," Lotty said. Egypt curled her trunk tip around it, popped it into her mouth, and crunched it open.

"Maybe we got to acknowledge the corn, Lotty," Babe finally said.

"What does that mean? What corn?"

"I mean, we got to plan your aunt ain't going to write, let alone put the likes of us up. So, let's us think on how to get on. Let's make us our last stand with Renoir."

"He'll never let us go until the last stop, Klamath Falls. Why would he?"

"'Cause he can make more money from us buying our freedoms than he can putting us on display. Fact is, he's probably in need of cash about now. Hell, we lost Ina, Mina, or Tina in Portland, leaving him just one dancing girl, and Lucretia says she's jumping track in Corvallis. This outfit's nearly washed-up, Lotty. If we was two-bit before, we're penny-ante now."

"You think we can buy our way off this circuit?"

"You got our total ciphered up?"

She pulled out a piece of paper. "Counting our Portland take, tips, and what I sold some shoes and clothes for, we have a grand total of six hundred sixty-two dollars and twenty-two cents."

"That's a mighty amount," Babe said.

"What should we offer? If he knows how much we have, he'll want it all, you know."

"Then we don't let him know. We'll offer three hundred dollar for the tote. See what he says."

"When? I'm scared, Babe. This is . . . this is scary for me. I've never been on my own."

"You won't be on your own. You'll have me and . . ."

"All those mouths to feed," Lotty said, breaking her off.

"I got me plenty of worries, too, but being on my own ain't one of them."

Lotty's big green eyes landed on Babe. "No. No," she said, setting her jaw defiantly. "I am on board one hundred percent. If I don't jump this life now while I can, then I'll never do it!"

They agreed—with or without a letter from Aunt Valerie or anyone else, they were jumping Professor Renoir's Collection of Oddities, Curiosities, and Delights. Critters and all.

26

"Where the hell did you two dodunks get all that money?" Renoir said, pointing to the three hundred dollars in cash Lotty and Babe had plunked down on his desk.

"Ain't none of your never mind," Babe said. The girls had been rehearsing this scene since Salem.

He crossed his arms, leaned back in his chair, and said, "Oh, it *ain't?* Well, I think it is."

Babe felt her blood pounding through every inch of her body. But she set her jaw just like Lotty. "Three hundred for our contracts, Egypt, Euclid, and Jupiter, and our gear. Per each that comes to . . ."

"Sixty dollars each," Lotty spoke up, a small squeak in her already small voice.

"Fair commerce," Babe added.

"Not by a long shot." Renoir lit a cigar and blew the

smoke out into his once-sumptuous but now faded rail-road car.

Babe waved away the smoke. "Three hundred is fair commerce."

He looked at Lotty, then at Babe, grinned around his cigar, and said, "Well, now that I see the color of your coin, I have to hand it to you nitwits. Saving up that much must have been a real challenge. Either that, or you ran into a sudden . . . streak of luck." He raised his eyebrows inquisitively, stroked his goatee, looking from girl to girl.

"We've been saving for months!" Lotty barked, her prairie dog voice piercing the railroad car. "Picking up cherry pie work, washing, mending! Selling personal belongings! Filling in for anyone who needed filling in! Playing the crowd for tips!"

"So I see. Too bad you didn't save enough," Renoir said.

"Then how much do you want?" Babe asked. They came prepared for dickering.

He puffed his cigar while he wrote a sum on a piece of paper and handed it over to Babe. Lotty popped off the settee and looked at the amount.

"Five?" Babe asked. "So, how much was you going to pay for the taxi-dermy man?"

Renoir took out his cigar and scowled while he thought. "Three hundred, and that's just for the elephant."

Babe let that statement hang out in the air with the cigar smoke. She'd played enough poker to know when someone had tipped his hand. "So, we're going to *save* you money, in the long run," Lotty said. She took his paper, wrote four, zero, zero and handed it back to him.

"You're telling me you chuckleheads have *four* hundred dollars?"

"Cash and carry," Babe said. "And what we want to carry is a wagon, two horses, the cages, the feed what's left, and anything else what goes with our acts."

"And the vet medicines, potions, and liniments," Lotty added. "Egypt's been sneezing, and it might be that horrible Asian croup coming on her again."

Lotty turned around so he couldn't see her pocketbook tied to her belt and from it, she pulled out another bundle and plopped it on top of the three hundred dollars already on his desk.

Renoir's eyes landed on it. "I'll draw up a bill of sale."

"And something that ends our contracts," Lotty was quick to add. "We'll play to Medford. Not a step farther. Then we're leaving."

"And we keep our wages and tips up till then," Babe added.

"We'll want a full accounting of it all up to our last day," Lotty stated officially.

"Fine. Fine. I'll be happy to get rid of the lot of you. Cheesy acts like yours, Babe, strictly *de passé*. Folks nowadays are sick of phony fakes like you and want real talent. Rope walkers, trapeze artists, bareback riders. Not . . ."

He gave her a sad smile. "Not the likes of you." Then he pointed his cigar to Lotty. "Or you. I'll bring the paperwork over to you when it's ready."

"You just get to writing it all up and we'll sit here and wait," Lotty said, climbing back onto the settee.

He pulled some forms out from his desk and started to fill in the blanks. He blew on the paper, then handed the contract to Babe.

"Give it to Lotty."

Lotty read it over, nodding her head. "You sign first, Renoir." She pointed to the inkwell.

"So much for trust," he said, taking the pen and scratching his signature. Babe recalled the same sound in her father's store, a lifetime ago.

"Now, you girls go ahead and sign." He re-dipped the pen and handed it to Lotty. "On the back page. Just your John Hancocks and we're officially no longer associated. As of closing in Medford, Oregon."

"Make sure he didn't fudge the money part," Babe mumbled to Lotty.

"No, I think this is fine." Lotty's lips moved as she glanced over the contract again.

Lotty's signature was as small and dainty as she was. Babe's mouth contorted as she fumbled with the pen in her huge hand.

Renoir fanned the papers to dry the ink, smiled at them, opened a desk drawer, and slid the cash in. "Well, then that's that," he said, standing. "They are all yours. Body, boots, and britches."

The girls were halfway out of the car when Lotty stopped. "Wait. Don't we get a copy?"

"Oh, of course. I'll have this taken into Eugene and get a copy written and notarized. That usually costs fifty cents, but I'll swallow that expense." He stood up. "You two balloon-heads have no idea what you're getting yourselves into."

"No, but we know what we're getting ourselfs out of," Babe said.

Once they were outside his car and well out of his eye- and earshots, Babe looked down at Lotty. "He sure didn't waffle much, did he?"

"No, as soon as you said the word 'taxidermy,' he couldn't sign fast enough!" Lotty said. "That was real smart of you, Babe."

Babe grinned at the compliment as they walked a little further. Then Babe stopped again. "You don't think he said yes too fast, do you?"

"What's the matter with you, Babe? We got what we wanted, when we wanted, where we wanted and for two hundred dollars less than we were prepared to pay."

"But Renoir's crooked as a barrel of snakes. I won't rest easy till I see them papers so's we have proof of sale and all."

"And our canceled contracts, don't forget," Lotty

said, waving to Madame de la Rosa, heading toward her fortune-telling tent. "Oh, Rosa! Wait! I have to ask a favor of you!"

Babe smiled, watching Lotty scurry like a little child and wished she could move that fast and gracefully. But Lotty was the hare, Babe the tortoise.

With only a few more stops to the end of the line, Babe and Lotty were packing their personal belongings into boxes and stacking them into a corner of Babe's cattle car. Everything in the "take" pile had to be necessary. The "don't take" pile grew on the other side of the car. They decided to sell what they could, give away what they couldn't, and burn the rest. On the top of the "burn this" pile was Babe's Magnifica costume.

"Knock, knock!" came a call up from the railroad bed. "Anybody home?"

"We're back here, Rosa!" Lotty called, wiping her hands on a rag and coming to the door. "Well, anything?" she asked, looking down at Rosa.

"Yes, indeed! You got a letter! The stationmaster said you have to sign for it."

Lotty looked at Babe, her face bright with expectations. She headed for the door.

"Hold it," Rosa said, pulling her juju necklace out. "You know what to do." Each girl did the same. "Eyes closed. Now, one, two, three . . . wish!"

Babe knew what each was wishing for.

Rosa winked up at Babe, helped Lotty down from the car, then walked off toward the mess tent while Lotty dashed down the tracks ahead of her, toward the station.

Euclid let out a short, urgent chirp from his cage. "You ever pray, ol' man?" Babe asked the ape, handing him some peanuts. "Then you best pray Lotty's letter is good news." He raised his lips and showed his fangs. "No, that ain't a good prayer face." The chimp screeched, looking past her as Renoir hauled himself into the cattle car.

He pointed to the boxes and crates stacked inside. "See to it you don't take anything belonging to me."

"Ain't taking nothing that ain't rightly ours and listed in what Lotty writ down." She walked to the "burn" pile and threw the Magnifica costume at him. "This is yours."

He dodged it and kept looking around the car. "You know, Babe, I got to thinking."

Babe's jaw tensed. She recognized that tone in Renoir's voice. "About what?"

"You two girls sure came up with an astonishing amount of money, considering the whole country is in a financial depression, people out of work, banks closing."

"You ask anyone how hard we been working. Making things, selling things, taking in work, and playing extry shows," Babe said, looking down the track hoping to see Lotty coming back. She didn't want to discuss anything alone with Renoir.

"Fact is, I happen to know exactly how, maybe not where, but how, some of that cash got into your grubby, fat hands."

"Everything's fair commerce." Her heart raced double-time.

"JoJo maybe can't add two plus two, but she knows a thing or two about stealing."

"JoJo don't have nothing to do with our fair commerce."

"I think she does. You know, there's a way we can call things even Steven."

"Even Steven happened with our boughten contracts," Babe said, carefully choosing her words. She felt a rise of panic and her hand went to her throat. She touched her conjure bag, holding the proof of Renoir's shady dealings—the rolled-up deposit ticket.

"Thing is, everyone *thinks* JoJo is too feebleminded to steal. They think she's as innocent as a babe. But you and me know different, don't we? So, I'll convince the authorities *you* stole it. Everyone knows giants can't be trusted."

Once again, Babe looked down the tracks for any sign of Lotty, or maybe Rosa, even JoJo. No one. Time to make a stand, hold her ground. She folded her arms and said,

"You reckon the California State Bank has closed up yet? You know, on account of that there depression thing?"

He narrowed his eyes, then snarled, "That's what I thought."

"You think them back-east investor folk might want to know about you and stoled money and banks?" She glared down at Renoir. "Besides, you got your money back. It just came through the back door."

The silence between them was broken by Euclid throwing peanut shells toward Renoir. "Well, Babe, this is what they call a Mexican standoff. I have a gun aimed at you and you have a gun aimed at me."

"What's Mexicans and guns got to do with this?"

"Think of it as 'you scratch my back, I'll scratch yours.'"

"You touch my back and I'll squeeze the stuffings out of you!"

"Fine. But just remember this, Miss Killingsworth: a girl the likes of you, the size of you, can never hide anywhere for very long."

Babe wasn't sure how to respond. "Yep, hiding's always been a problem. It's easier to hide cash money, though, ain't it?"

"I knew you'd be trouble," he said, shaking his head and walking away. "First time I saw you, I knew you'd be hell-with-the-hide-off trouble."

Inside, she was trembling like a cornered rabbit, but

outside she was standing tall. Maybe not all power came from being big and strong.

"Babe! Babe!" Lotty shouted. Babe pulled her up and into the cattle car with a playful side-to-side swing. "Put me down! I got my letter! It's from her! There's an Aunt Valerie and she's alive!" She sat down, the letter falling on her lap. Her eyes filled with tears. "She says we're welcome and can stay as long as we want. We're to come as soon as we can! She's drawn a map to her house."

"For truth?"

"For truth." Then her face scrunched up a bit. "She's calling me a godsend. To come as soon as I can!"

"What's that?"

"Well, a godsend is someone, or something, you know, that God sends."

"Like a plague or a flood? Oh no, I ain't going in for anything churchy, Lotty. You know I ain't."

"No, I don't think she means it that way. I think she means we're coming at a good time for her," Lotty said, looking back down at the letter.

"What'd you reckon that means?"

"Who knows? But at least we have a barn or maybe even a real house to sleep in!" She looked out over the trees on their siding. "And an aunt. We have an aunt!"

"Babe, Renoir's raging about something. Says he wants you and Lotty in the mess tent pronto!" Rosa called up to the girls as she passed Babe's cattle car. "This may be the end of the line for you, but we're busy as hell taking down! Hurry it up! We have to get this show on the road!"

"Uh-oh," Lotty said. "You don't suppose he's going back on his word, do you? Leopards don't change their spots."

"Unless them spots is painted on rabbit fur."

"I mean it, Babe. If he . . ."

"I know." Babe held up her clenched fist. "It'll be one of these."

The mess tent, always the last tent to be taken down and packed away, still had lingering aromas. The night's last meal had been short on meat and long on cabbage, and the odor was a piquant reminder of Babe's first day on the train.

"Where is everybody? Where's Renoir?" Lotty said, looking around.

"Maybe in the cook tent." Babe opened the adjoining curtains and again, no one.

Just then the tent flaps behind them swished open as voices called out "Surprise!" The girls were enveloped by nearly all their fellow performers and some of the road crew. Not Renoir.

The cooks brought in a huge cake, festooned with lit candles. The crew broke into a chorus of "For they're the jolly good carnies, for they're the jolly good carnies!" Ernie, in his one-man-band getup, pounded, tooted, banged, and whistled in accompaniment.

Scrolled across the cake was a bright red, gooey:

Good Luck!
B-L-E-E-J

Rosa pointed to the letters on the icing and said, "Cook didn't have enough time to spell out your names!"

No sooner had they cut the cake than a tent flap whipped open. Renoir, hands on hips, shouted above the din of the crowd, "Did you freaks hear that train whistle? Everyone, get this tent down and loaded!"

The roustabouts snapped to it, grabbing handfuls of

cake and tossing goodbyes and good lucks toward the girls.

Lucretia held a teacup painted with tiny, purple violets and handed it to Lotty, the matching saucer to Babe. "I know it's not much, but this was my mother's and I'd like the two of you to have the set. Maybe you'll think of me when you sip your tea. I wish I had one for each, but . . . years on the road . . . you know."

"It's the prettiest thing I ever seed!" Babe said, holding up the saucer to the light. "Why, so dainty I can see the light shine right through it."

"Thank you, Lu. You've been sweet. Even when I wasn't," Lotty said.

"Here. I've been stockpiling these since I knew you were leaving us," Ernie said, climbing out of his band rig and holding up a large burlap bag. "Peanuts. Oh, and here, I requisitioned you some stuff from the medical tent. Reckon with those poor old critters, you'll be needing this."

Babe took the bags, nearly speechless. "Thank you, Ernie. You been a good friend to me and my critters."

"Aw, ain't nothing." He cast his gap-toothed smile to the girls and backed away. "Got to go see to your wagon and team. Been an honor, ladies." He winked, picked up his portable orchestra and left.

Serena stepped up and swished two beautiful sashes, one purple, one gold. "One for each. Remember, ain't no costume complete without a splash of color."

Babe took the gold, Lotty the purple. They swirled them around their necks. "Thank you, Serena. I'll think of you when I wear this," Lotty said.

"Sorry it's so long on you," Serena said.

"Me too. I'll remember you," Babe said.

"Sorry it's so short on you," Serena said. "Face it, you girls are just plain hard to costume!" She gave each an awkward hug, then dashed off.

Donny carried Babe's rescued pup in the crook of his arm. "I know you might want your pup back, but . . ."

"Heck no, Donny. That pup spends so much time in your arm it's like you two is attached." As though the pup agreed with Babe's decision, he gave a little chirp and bounced up to offer Donny a kiss.

The last two came up—Rosa holding JoJo's hand. "Sorry to see you leave, girls," Rosa said. "But I know it's what's best for all of you. Babe, here's the address to my brother's place down in 'Frisco. He'll know where I am. You know. Just in case you want to write."

JoJo tugged on Rosa's robe. "I will, JoJo dear, be patient." She bobbed up and down, giggling in excitement as Rosa pulled something from her robe pocket. She held up a scroll of paper. "Here, JoJo made this for you."

Babe held up what looked like a crude painting of a humpbacked two-legged creature sporting a top hat, a long, curlicue tail, a huge face with jagged teeth. JoJo screeched with delight.

"It's Renoir," Rosa explained. "I think it's a remarkable resemblance. Except the tail. Can't explain the tail."

"Ren-or! Ren-or!" JoJo said, twirling around with joy.

"Ain't you sweet?" Babe said. "Going to keep this special."

JoJo peeked around Rosa's robe, smiled shyly, and gave Babe the *okay* sign with her hand—something she'd never known JoJo to do. And was that a wink or just something in her eye?

"You girls still have your good-luck conjure bags and jujus?" Rosa asked. Each girl's hand went to her throat, where the charms hung on leather tongs. "Good. Well, I guess this is goodbye."

A gentle hug and a bear hug and Rosa left, JoJo trailing.

Babe ran after her. "Rosa?"

She turned.

"I hope you get your dream someday. You know. The big house and all. Hope it's big enough for a girl the likes of me. So's I can come visit maybe."

"I would look forward to that, Babe."

Lotty joined Babe, watching Rosa and JoJo disappear into the darkness. Behind them four men's voices called to each other, "Ready!" and the mess tent collapsed onto itself and was quickly rolled away.

Not ten minutes later, the train tooted its angry warning into the night. "Come on, Babe. We have a lot to do!" Lotty said, leading the way back to the siding and their belongings, stacked and ready to go.

Babe hesitated, listening to the sounds of their last night, the last time they'd hear the carnival being packed up and put away. In the distance, horses snorted, dogs barked, and Egypt trumpeted.

Renoir had sent some men over to unload the girls' gear and set it alongside the tracks. Lotty immediately started giving orders: Take this! No, not that! That stays! Careful there!

"Babe, I have to make sure they got everything for Egypt." She dashed off to inspect the trunks.

Finally, a wagon came rumbling up. The laughter of

the wranglers added to the shouting. One look and Babe understood what was so funny. Renoir held the lead rein, having a last laugh on the dwarf and the giant.

"Ajax and Honeycomb?" Babe asked, pointing to the span of horses. "This is what you give us for a team?"

"I think they fit you to a T," Renoir said, chuckling. "I agreed to two horses. Didn't state which ones. And that's the long and the short of it." He laughed, then strolled off, shouting more obscenities to the crew.

Babe went to the horses. Ajax, an old, gentle draft horse, stood nervously next to Honeycomb, nicknamed the Holy Terror. She was the Shetland pony used for kiddie pony-cart rides. Babe could tell neither horse was happy about the arrangement. Honeycomb had old Ajax in a state of flusteration already, nipping at his massive chest and side-kicking a back leg. Babe had come to think of Ajax as a peace pipe, and Honeycomb as a tomahawk, so night and day were they.

"I'm sorry, Babe," Ernie said, looking down. "Renoir insisted. I'll unhitch Honeycomb and put Ajax in a single harness. Got to be honest. I'm glad to be rid of that little savage pony."

"She's a pretty thing, but she's mean as cut snakes," Babe said. Even she didn't like Honeycomb, but there was no way she would just set her free to fend for herself. "But poor Ajax? You think he can haul the wagon and all that?"

"Well, you might have to help. And Egypt can do her

share. Here, look. I crooked the pony cart. Renoir'll never be the wiser. It's loaded with more stuff I swiped for y'all."

"Thank you, Ernie."

"Well, it's just as well," Ernie went on, giving Ajax a farewell pat on his big, grand nose. "Vern told me on the q.t. that Ajax and Honeycomb were heading for the slaughterhouse down in K Falls."

It all made sense.

It was chaos in the dark while the horses got reharnessed, and the boxes and cages got loaded onto the rickety wagon Renoir had graced them with. Babe had made sure the tarps over Euclid's and Jupiter's cages were secure while they were still in her cattle car. They didn't need to worry about this sudden arrangement. They would be the last taken out and loaded onto the wagon.

The train engine chugged to life, puffing out steam. Three long toots warned everyone to get onboard and now.

The torches were doused and taken away, and only two lanterns remained on the siding. Babe could barely see what was where.

Lotty came up behind Babe and pulled on her shirttail.

"She's scared, Babe. Egypt is scared. She's tapping her trunk along her face. That means she's scared."

"Where is she?"

"Down there by those willows. One of the boys helped me with her chain. She's too frightened to even eat. Oh

Babe, I hope we're doing the right thing."

"You two women of the world have everything?" Renoir asked, appearing out of the shadows of the train.

"No, we don't," Lotty said. "Our copy of the contract, if you please. You've been promising it since Eugene, and we want it!"

He reached into his vest pocket and pulled out an envelope. "Of course. Here you are. And your last wages are inside. To the penny, as of ten o'clock tonight, July eighteenth, 1896."

Lotty shook the envelope.

"Go ahead, count it, if you don't trust me," Renoir said. "But hurry. We're late already."

"No, just as long as we got our signed contract," Lotty said. She held the papers to the lantern and glanced at them. "Okay. Thank you."

"I give you both a hale and hearty farewell and a good riddance," he said, taking off his hat and giving them a gallant, deep bow. "And good luck. You're going to need it. Oh, and when you track me down to beg me to take you all back, make sure those flea-bitten animals have glass eyes and are on wheels."

Babe had never heard Lotty swear. Her blue streak of cuss words must have shocked even Renoir, by the way his eyebrows shot up to his hairline. "You just keep that up, Carlotta. You're going to need that grit. And so, without any further ado, I bid you adieu."

It was the same tired line he used at the end of every show.

He backed away into the shadows and signaled a lantern to the train engineer to take his cars from the siding to hook up with the main line.

Lotty and Babe stood back and watched the train chug by. Friends waved from the train cars. As each car passed, Babe felt a deeper, more troubling feeling. Then Renoir pulled himself up into Babe's old cattle car.

"Look there, Lotty," Babe said, pointing down the line. "Renoir's climbing into my car. Why's he riding there instead of his cushy car?"

The car chugged closer, and the lantern swinging from the rafter lit the car, casting odd shadows as it approached.

"What's that . . . ?" Lotty said, pointing. "Babe! Look!"

The car chugged by and there was Renoir sitting in the doorway, giving the girls a wave goodbye. And next to him was Euclid, standing in his display cage. Around the ape's neck was the rope-noose handle Babe used to pull herself up with.

"Euclid!" Babe screamed, running to catch the car. The train picked up speed and she ran clumsily along the track, nearly tripping in the thick, sharp gravel. "Euclid!" she hollered again. He saw her and started to jump up and down, screaming. But Renoir gave the rope a mean yank and the screaming stopped.

"Euclid!" Babe felt her chest about to burst as she tried

to keep pace with the train. It was no good. She stopped
and the train picked up speed as it rounded the bend and it
was . . . gone.

"Euclid," Babe whispered into the darkness.

"He's a no-good, low-down crook! I get aholt of him, I'll kill him; I tell you, Lotty, I'll kill him!" Babe was spitting fire. That beast she worked so hard to keep inside was raging up and clawing to get out. And for the first time ever, Babe wanted to let her out.

Lotty coaxed Babe back to their encampment by the tracks and tried to settle her down. She offered her a swig of whiskey Ernie had squirreled away for them. "It'll only make me madder," Babe said, sitting down and taking in deep breaths.

Lotty sat next to Babe. "Hold the lantern. Let me read this," she said, pulling out their contract. "We'll just take this bill of sale to the authorities once we get settled and get Euclid back, that's all. You know that Renoir. He's just getting our hackles up like he always does. Don't worry."

She turned over a page. Her head came up. "Worry," she said, looking at Babe with a tight face.

"Huh?"

"He's a no-good, low-down crook!"

"Huh?"

She flashed the papers in front of Babe. "That snake in the grass! He didn't put Euclid in our copy of the contract!"

"What? No, we agreed! On the bill o' sale. We agreed!"

"How could I trust that low-down mucker? That no-good foister cheated us!"

Babe looked down at the papers but had no idea what Lotty was talking about.

"Look, on page two where it lists all the inventory we bought. There's no mention of a chimp or Euclid or even a fake pygmy gorilla!"

"I'll kill Renoir. He touches a hair on my Euclid's head, I'll kill him."

"Oh, Babe! What are we going to do?"

Babe stood up. "I'm getting him back, that's what!"

"That train is miles away by now. How are you going to get him?"

Babe circled their campfire, thinking. Lotty was right. She couldn't just leave her friend and the animals to fend for themselves. Lotty couldn't even reach Ajax's head to harness him. They had to stick together, because they couldn't manage alone. It was going to take two of them, working together, to even get a few feet down the road.

"There's nothing we can do now, Babe. Let's check on the animals and get some sleep."

"Quit looking down those tracks, Babe," Lotty said at first light the next morning. "We'll think of something. Let's just go find my aunt and we can figure out about Euclid later." She reached for Babe's hand and tried to urge her away from the tracks.

Babe looked down at her. "Okay. But we got to do something before Renoir finds that taxi-dermy man." She felt Lotty's grip on her hand grow tighter.

They pulled together something to eat and made sure the animals were fed a ration of oats, watered, and ready to move on. While Lotty doused the fire, Babe loaded the rest of their belongings onto the wagon.

"You're feeling cramped, huh, Jupiter?" Babe asked, passing through some apples. "You're gonna just have to wait to stretch your legs, boy."

Babe pulled the tarp off Euclid's empty cage and felt her rage begin to build again, cursing herself over and over. Why didn't she make sure things got loaded right? Why didn't she keep an eye on her animals?

The girls decided to follow the trail close to the rail line and head toward the train station in Medford and from there, follow Aunt Valerie's map.

Babe stopped the wagon where the road split into two directions.

Lotty looked at Aunt Valerie's map. "She says stay right and take the back roads."

The road was well used but dusty and made for easy going. As they walked, Babe noticed it was handsome territory, displaying more shades of green than she'd ever seen, so cool and welcoming after their summer in sunparched towns. She took in a long breath, trying to decide if what she smelled was pine or maybe blackberries. She glanced over to Jupiter, whose nose was also high and curious.

By early afternoon, the road divided once again. To the left, a road was closed by a rickety wood gate, and a faded, painted sign above.

"I can't read it so good. What's it say, Lotty?"

Lotty stood up and shaded her eyes from the sunlight stabbing between the tree branches. "'Logan Logging—Proprietor, V. M. Logan. Main Entrance. No Trespassing. No Solicitors.'" She looked down at Babe, smiled, and added, "'And No Bible Salesmen!'"

"I like your aunt Valerie already!"

"Well, we're here," Lotty said tentatively. "Now what?"

"Think maybe you better go in alone? Meet her and, you know, maybe spring us on her one at a time?"

"Yes, I've been thinking about that, too."

"That road ain't too well traveled," Babe said, noticing the overgrown bushes and low-hanging branches.

Lotty consulted the map. "The map stops here at the gate. What should we do?"

"You want to drive Honeycomb in?"

"Not on your tintype! That would be suicide."

"Well, I think you should just walk on in then. You're here on invite. You ain't trespassing, and sure as shootin' you ain't selling no Bibles. Go on!"

Lotty straightened her belt and fanned dust off her skirt, then stuffed a wisp of her long black hair into her straw bonnet. "How do I look?" she asked, plastering a nervous smile on her face.

"Hell, Lotty, you're so pretty. Everyone falls in love with you first sight."

She rubbed her tummy. "Feeling a little like I'm sick. I mean, I've never met family before. You know what they say. We only get one chance to make a good first impression."

"She must know you're small."

"I know. I just . . . What do I say? Here we are! Elephant and all! A bear to boot! Oh, and that's a giant! Stay away from that pony, she's a man-killer and we're all starving!"

She took a deep breath of determination and sighed it out. She started for the gate, stopped, then turned back around. "Nope."

"Nope what?"

"It's all of us or nothing! Come on. Open this gate, I'll drive the team in, and dang it all, Babe, we're in this together. None of this one-at-a-time business."

Babe gave her friend her widest grin.

31

The gate groaned as Babe hauled it open. Lotty scrambled back up into the wagon. She tapped the whip over Ajax's head. He started up, groaned, and leaned against his harness.

Babe pushed, Ajax pulled, but Egypt was too busy, trunk held high, inhaling the new scents, to help out. Honeycomb trotted behind, objecting with snorts and pony bucks.

"Look at Ajax," Babe said, pointing to the horse's flicking ears and slow, easy steps. "He looks like he's just as jumpity as we are."

"I know," Lotty agreed. "Egypt's had her trunk high and sniffing this whole way. Wonder if she can smell what's around that bend."

"I smell cookstove fire, I can tell you that." Her stomach agreed with one of its loud, long growls.

Finally, the road widened with trails and paths springing off in both directions. Babe felt her heartbeat pick up as they approached a clearing. On the right, a large red barn was visible between a stand of evergreens. Then on the left, a log building, and soon more and more small buildings and yet another barn. One last bend and there was the house.

Babe stopped, holding up Ajax and their parade. "Look at the size of that house, Lotty!"

Lotty shaded her eyes. "Lord, it's *giant-size!*" Then down to Babe, "No offense."

"I've seed log cabins, but nothing this grand!"

"Sure is quiet," Lotty said, standing and looking around. "It's early. Maybe no one's up yet."

"This here's a farm, Lotty. 'Course everyone's up."

Just then, Egypt issued a long, deafening trumpet announcing their grand arrival and causing instant pandemonium. The screen door crashed open as a child ran through it, followed by a woman in an apron holding a broom. Terrified horses screeched and bolted in their pasture; Jupiter roared back; Honeycomb snapped her tether and ran off; Egypt snorted again and ran toward the house, her leg cuff clanking.

"Lotty! What's . . . ?" Babe started, but Lotty had shot down and run after Egypt. What was happening? Babe walked toward the house and there, standing, eye to crying eye, was Lotty and a woman, a dwarf woman. Between them was Egypt's trunk, searching, sniffing them both.

"Reckon we're here," Babe muttered, trying to make sense of the chaotic scene. Then, to the woman, she said, "Why, you ain't no youngin. You're . . ."

"A dwarf," the woman replied, looking at Lotty. "I'm Aunt Valerie!" Babe was struck by how very similar their faces were.

"And you're small! Like me!" Lotty cried. "And Egypt! It's like she knows you!"

Her aunt touched the tip of Egypt's trunk, which went slowly, gently along her tiny face. The woman closed her eyes, smiling fearlessly. "Oh my God, Egypt!" she whispered, holding the elephant's trunk to her face. "I heard you died in the Walter Main train wreck!"

"Wait! I'm confused. You and Egypt know each other?" Lotty asked.

Her aunt smiled and wiped her face with a large hanky. "Yes. We're old friends. Don't tell me you've never heard of Valerie the Valentine and Her Dancing Elephant."

"No, ma'am," Lotty said.

"Well, that was years ago." Egypt's trunk began to sniff Aunt Valerie's pockets. "Look there. She remembers."

"I don't understand," Lotty said, pulling Egypt's trunk back toward her.

"Egypt's always worked with small people. After all, in the elephant world, she's small, too. What else do people like us do?"

"All they told me was she was well trained and we'd hit it off. I never even knew you were small—like me. That you had an act, let alone an elephant act! I never knew anything," Lotty said.

"I was praying I'd find you someday. We heard some cheap carnie was coming down from Portland. Wasn't much but had a dwarf elephant act. Then I got your letter and . . . well, let's tend to these animals and get you girls settled. All this can wait."

She put her hanky on top of her hair, done up prim, proper, and fashionable. Egypt, on cue, raised her trunk and gave a mighty puff and off flew the hanky—*swoosh!* It floated down and landed ten feet away.

"Look, Babe!" Lotty laughed. "So *that's* why Egypt is always blowing my hats off!"

"Uh . . ." the woman in the apron interrupted. "How about some introductions?"

Babe thought this might be the homeliest woman she'd ever seen—maybe even uglier than herself. So walleyed she didn't know which eyeball was looking at her. But her voice and smile were warm and welcoming, even if her eyes weren't.

"Oh, of course!" Aunt Valerie said. "Sarah Franklin, this is my niece, Carlotta Bradshaw."

"Bradshaw? The orphanage said it was Jones."

"It's Bradshaw, dear." She lightly touched her niece's shoulder. "We'll have a nice, long chat over lunch."

"I'm happy to meet you," Sarah said. "I'm the head cook and bottle washer in this circus. See that tall stretch of water over there? He's my better half. Cleve! Get over here! Come meet family!"

Babe stepped away as the man approached to meet "family."

"And this is Cleve Franklin, head tree wrangler," Aunt Valerie said. The man was shoulder-high to Babe, and he bent down with an elegant bow to shake Lotty's hand. Egypt investigated him with caution, and he was careful to keep his distance.

"Say, don't mean to be nosy, but isn't that a bear you have in that cage?" he said.

"He's a bear, all right," Babe said.

"Carlotta, aren't you going to introduce your friend?" Valerie said.

"Oh, sure! Sorry. Babe, these are, well, you heard their names. They're family! This is Babe, the world's strongest girl!"

Babe smiled awkwardly, deciding a curtsy would be too laughable.

"Well, come on. Now that we're all old friends, let's get these animals put up and taken care of," Valerie said. They walked off toward the house, arm in arm, followed by Sarah.

"So, how do I 'put up' an elephant?" Cleve asked Babe.

Within a few minutes, Cleve Franklin had moved his live-stock into what he called "the bug barn" so Babe could move Egypt and Jupiter into the main barn, where they wouldn't spook the stock. Ajax and Honeycomb got turned out into a small pasture.

"Look at 'em," Babe said, watching them tentatively inspect the area. "Don't know when them critters ever had pasture. Big one's Ajax. The pony is Honeycomb."

"Look there," Cleve said, pointing to Ajax, who, with a great huff, dropped to his front knees, then leaned over and *umph!* rolled, kicking his legs joyously in the air.

"Uh-oh, there goes that dang little Honeycomb, taking after poor ol' Ajax." The pony nipped Ajax's neck, making him pop up and trot off. "She's hell on wheels."

Inside the barn, Cleve opened up six box stalls so Egypt

could have the roam of the whole area. He stood well back while Babe unhooked the elephant's leg cuff.

"She'll be happy here," Babe said, smiling at Egypt's joyous chirp and swishing tail.

"Now, how about that bear?" Cleve asked, pointing outside. "Can't let him just wander around." Babe wondered how a voice so deep could come out of a body so slim.

"He's a bit spun about. I'll haul the wagon in and he can stay in his cage. He don't like change."

"I'll help," he said. "That's one heavy wagon."

"Ain't nothing for me," Babe said.

Cleve pushed while Babe picked up the shafts and pulled. Jupiter growled as the wagon entered the dark barn.

A familiar clanging rang out. "Lunch is on," Cleve said, grabbing his hat off a nail. He headed toward the barn door. "You coming?"

"Let me feed Jupiter, then I'll be there. Critter is first."

"Jupiter, huh?"

"He was God of something. I forget what."

"King o' the gods," Cleve said, his fine voice pleasing to Babe's ears. "Hurry now! Let's not keep the ladies waiting." He trotted toward the house.

Babe fed her bear, then dusted off her skirts and pulled stray hairs away from her sweaty face. "Well, Jupiter, reckon I can't keep the *ladies* waiting."

Babe stooped on the front porch and tap-tap-tapped gently on the glass door. "Hello again," Sarah Franklin said, opening the door wide. The smell of home cooking nearly dragged Babe inside. "Come in. Oh! Watch that . . ."

The crystal chandelier hanging from the ceiling set to swinging. Babe carefully stilled it. "I'm sorry. Now I remember why me and houses ain't such a good match."

"It's nothing. Come on. They're in the dining room. Follow me." She led her down a hallway. Babe was careful not to sway into the walls and risk upsetting the pictures and mirrors hanging. She stopped.

"Is that there a telephone?" Babe asked, pointing to a contraption hooked low on the wall in an alcove.

"Yes."

"Ain't never seed one in a house. What a world!"

They passed through a sitting area with wall-to-wall bookshelves, and in the corner was an elegant fireplace made of stone. A bearskin rug anchored the center of the room and Babe figured Jupiter didn't need to know about that. But something was strange here, something different. The rooms appeared so large, but what was it? Then it hit her. The chairs, the tables, and even the bookcases. All small. It was just like a big dollhouse, making Babe feel twice her size and three times more awkward.

"Oh, Babe, come in, come in," Aunt Valerie said.

"Thank you, ma'am."

"Oh, call her Miss V. She says everyone does," Lotty chirped from across the table.

"Thank you, Miss V."

Now here, the dining room furniture was regular size. Miss V sat at the end of the table in a small chair atop a carpeted platform with steps up, just her size. Lotty didn't have it nearly as good as she balanced herself on a stack of pillows. Cleve sat across and there were still three places set at the table.

Sarah showed Babe a chair. They both looked down at the elegant cane weaving.

"That chair, there," Miss V said, pointing out a sturdy chair in the corner. Babe picked it up and moved it to the table, then carefully eased herself down, testing the strength of the chair. She wondered if she looked as out of place as she felt, sitting across from Lotty, who looked as though she was born to such a house.

"Sorry I'm late," Babe said lowly. "I ain't often late for vittles and—" She was interrupted by a growling noise. Eyes landed on her. "Excuse me, please." Babe turned bright red. "Don't know why that always happens. My ol' man used to hear my stummy rumble, grab his hunting rifle and poke it out the window looking for game."

Silence, then laughter.

Sarah left through swinging doors and they hardly came to a stop before she was back carrying a tray full of sandwiches. Next a plate of steaming corn on the cob, next thick sliced tomatoes, next potato salad!

"That's cherry pie cooling on the sideboard," Sarah said.

Once the table was laden with food, Cleve stood up, pulled back a chair for his wife, and she joined them at the table. That left one empty place.

The silverware arrangement confused Babe. Two forks, two spoons, small and large knives. Lotty noticed, and picked up her larger fork, and Babe followed suit.

Once everyone was comfortable, Miss V cleared her throat and said, "Well, I guess it's time to explain about . . . us."

"By 'us' she means Cleve and myself," Sarah said. "Pass the potato salad, will you?" Babe hesitated because Sarah appeared to be eyeing the corn.

"Our hey-hey days are over, thank God," Cleve said, passing her the plate.

"Well, I think the girls can certainly understand things," Miss V said. "After all, from what Carlotta told me, they're no strangers to strangers like us."

"You ain't so strange. Hell, you should meet JoJo and Lucretia and some—"

"Babe," Lotty said, cutting her off with a warning smile.

"Well, like you know now, I was a carnie, just like Carlotta," Miss V went on. "Me and Egypt played the best towns back east. Big shows. Toast of the coast! And the Franklins here were with the show, too. Go ahead, Sarah. Show them."

Slowly, Sarah unbuttoned the top three buttons of her dress, then rolled up her sleeves. "I was the first tattooed lady to wow 'em in New York City. Sweet and Walleyed Sadie, the Famous Tattooed Lady!" Her chest, neck, and arms were a swirl of intricate, faded tattoos. "Don't ask me how many or where I got them or even what they are. I swear I bleed ink when I cut myself."

"But your face ain't touched," Babe said. "We had a tattooed man, and even his face was a map of England with ol' Queen Vic setting on his forehead!"

"I might be dumb, but I'm not stupid," she said, laughing. "I know my face is my fortune. I hennaed the tattoos on my face every few weeks."

Cleve took her hand and said, "Your ugly mug is beautiful to me, with or without henna."

She gave him a playful slap and passed the plate of tomatoes around the table. "And who doesn't fall in love with a man with three arms?"

Babe and Lotty stopped chewing and stared at Cleve as he rose from his chair and announced dramatically, "Curious Cleveland, the Three-Armed Man!" He began to unbutton his shirt.

"Cleve, not at the table," his wife warned.

"Oh, yes, of course." At that, he stepped away from the table and took a stance in the corner and continued to unbutton his shirt.

"Thank you, dear," Sarah said.

There, protruding from the middle of his chest, was an appendage. Babe and Lotty both silenced their gasps of surprise.

"Who couldn't use a third hand now and then?" he said jovially. "But unfortunately this little thing can't do much. Mostly just gets in the way. So my other stage moniker was Clever Cleve—Soft Shoe, Snappy Songs, Witty Quips." He tapped a few steps, took a bow, rebuttoned his shirt, sat back down, and attacked his meal.

"You see," Miss V said, delicately peeling the crust off a sandwich, "we're all carnies here. Between the three of us, we've played everywhere, seen it all, and hated it all."

"That month with Barnum wasn't so bad," Sarah said.

"Until he welched us our pay," Cleve barked.

"Well, if you'd gotten our contracts signed," Sarah snapped back.

"If maybe you didn't bat those pretty eyes both directions at ol' P. T. . . . ."

"You don't need to air your dirty linen," Miss V said, breaking him off. Then, to the girls, "Don't *ever* mention P. T. Barnum around these two old troupers. It'll only bring on a fight!" The adults chuckled in agreement.

"Speaking of dirty linen," Lotty said, voice serious. All eyes landed on her. "I have to ask, Miss V . . ." She hesitated and cleared her throat. "How come, after the fire, after I lost my parents, how come you didn't come and find me?"

"Well, I was always on the road, so when I finally got word about the fire . . ." She reached over and touched Lotty's hand. "You'd already been adopted. I thought anyone good enough to take on a girl . . . well, a girl like me, I should leave well enough alone. Besides, I was just a cheap burlesque act back then. Not the best way to raise a young lady."

Babe remembered the "free trial" adoptions Lotty had suffered and added, "She was adopted out on the wait-and-see plan."

"The what?" Miss V asked.

"You know," Lotty began. Babe noticed the tremor in her voice. "We'll take this tiny little girl, then 'wait and see' how she works out. It never worked out."

"Three time out and three time back," Babe added.

"Oh Lord, no. If I'd only known," Miss V whispered. She dotted her eyes with her napkin, then smiled. "Well, anyway, we're all together now. Babe, bring over that pie!"

Whack! The sound came from the kitchen. Sarah said, "Well, if the door slams, that's our Denny."

Babe stopped chewing and felt a pain that jabbed her palms, ran up her arms, and through to her ears, where there it pounded like war drums when "our Denny" came in. *Oh, God help me. God help Babe!*, her thoughts raged. Her face and ears burned hot and glowed scarlet. She figured he was fifteen, maybe sixteen, gawky, lean, tall like his father, and the good looks Sarah didn't get were heaped on Denny.

The boy stopped, letting the swinging doors hit his backside. He stared at Babe, eyes wide, mouth open. "Wow," he muttered.

Miss V said, "Denny, this is my niece, Carlotta. And this is her friend, Babe."

Babe finally swallowed, leaned across the table, and tried to make her paw of a hand seem smaller by offering him just her fingers. Horny-knuckled, cracked, and any-thing but delicate. "Glad to——" She stopped, cleared her voice and began again, a bit higher. "Glad to meet you."

His face was still full of awe and surprise. He grinned and took Babe's hand and pumped it up and down. "Uh . . . hello."

She would pass out cold if her heart didn't settle down. Denny was the most beautiful boy she'd ever seen. She could barely keep from staring.

He broke his stare and turned to Lotty, as small as Babe was big, as pretty as Babe was ugly. "Wow," he said again, as he shook her tiny, delicate hand. "Hello. You're the spitting image of Miss V!" Sitting there, pert and petite and pretty, more like a doll perched on a doll's throne of pillows, it wouldn't have surprised Babe if the handsome prince kissed the little princess's hand.

"Is it true? What Pa said? You have an elephant and bear locked up in the barn?" he asked, taking his seat and loading his plate. "Pa said I couldn't go into the barn. Is it true? You're from a circus and everything? I mean, you're a dwarf and a real giant! Man! I wish school was in! A bear and an elephant, too! Wow! The guys will never believe this! Ma, can Hank come over? He never believes anything I tell him, and . . ."

"Why don't we wait until our guests get settled?" Miss V said.

"Oh, yeah. Sure," he said. "When can I see them?"

"They're a bit antsy and goosey right now. Best wait till they cool their heads a bit," Babe said, suddenly aware of how even her speech was out of place in this elegant room.

"So what do you do? In the circus, I mean?" he asked Lotty. "My folks don't let me see geek shows, being, you know, retired freaks and all."

"Denny . . ." his mother warned. "Grab your plate and help me in the kitchen." She stood up, taking her plate.

Plate in hand, Denny stared at Babe. "Did you do those contests where the horses pull one way and you pull another? Wish I could see that! Man!"

"Denny!"

"Coming, Ma." Then halfway into the kitchen, he looked back, first at Lotty, then Babe. "Wait till the guys hear this!"

When he left he pulled some of the life out of the room, just like life seemed to gush in when he entered. Babe glanced at Lotty and she knew she was thinking the same thing; that Lotty's tiny heart was beating faster than the fandango Ina, Mina, and Tina danced to, just like her own big heart was beating.

Babe wasn't one to think back or ahead, knowing a girl like her best stay in the here and now, but she thought this had to be the best day of Lotty's life. She watched her on her pillowed throne, like a fairy princess. But Babe? This was the worst day of her life—because it was perfectly clear—the giant always gets croaked by the handsome young prince, while the princess always lives happily ever after.

No sooner had the room recuperated from Denny's absence than he came dashing back in. "Something's out there! Howling! Come on!" He tossed a rifle to his father, and Cleve ran out the door, followed by the others.

Babe clumsily pushed back the heavy chair and looked around the empty dining room. Then she heard it, too. Another screech. She dashed through the swinging door, not looking back to see what it had crashed into.

Another screech. Babe loped into the clearing, kicking up dust. When she got to Cleve, he was just aiming his rifle toward the sound. She slapped it out of his hands and screamed, "Don't shoot! It's Euclid! Euclid!"

When the ape saw Babe, he picked up the pace, cantering on all fours. Babe knelt down on a knee, arms out. The ape's speed and weight were enough to knock her flat on her back as he leaped into her arms.

He wrapped his legs around Babe as she grasped him, rocking him. He whimpered like a lost child found. "Hesh, hesh. Your Babe's got you," she whispered to him.

"Hesh." The noose was tight around his neck and the rope was unraveled and frayed on the end. Babe gently pulled it off and tossed it high into the treetops.

Lotty ran to them. "Euclid!"

The others stood, staring at the reunion. Egypt sent muffled trumps from the barn, Jupiter roared. Even Ajax and Honeycomb trotted to the fence, eyes and ears transfixed.

"Babe, how do you think . . . ," Lotty began.

"Dang, I wisht he could talk! Dang, I wisht I knew how he done it—how he got away from Renoir."

"It's a miracle he found us!" Lotty said, reaching to touch the ape's shoulder. He jumped at her light touch.

"Reckon he sniffed out Egypt's calling cards alongst the road. I don't care about nothing, 'cept I got my Euclid back! If Euclid killed Renoir, I don't care. Saves me the trouble. He ain't going to no taxi-dermy man now, Lotty."

Babe carried Euclid back toward the house with Lotty alongside. Denny came running up, eyes popping. "A monkey! Wow!"

But Euclid shrank deeper into Babe's arms. "He's had a big day. You best stay back."

"No closer, Denny," Sarah said.

Cleve said to Miss V, "And here we all thought we left carnie life behind." Then, to the girls, "Any more creatures out there you need to spring on us?"

"He don't take much food," Babe said, cradling Euclid's

head in her giant hand. "He's old, and he don't eat much."

"Never mind that," Miss V said. "Let's just get him safe and settled."

Babe carried Euclid into the barn, asking to be alone. She could feel his heart throbbing wildly against her chest. He chirped when he saw Jupiter, reached out toward his own cage, and leaped into it. He went to the farthest side, trembling and blinking back at Babe.

"What have you been through, ol' man?" She sat down next to him and offered him a few peanuts. He looked at them, sniffed indifferently, then looked away. She left a handful in the corner of his cage, scrunched his tiny, trimmed ears. "Your Babe's got you now," she whispered.

She ran her hand against the grain of his hair and tried to work out some of the mats. When she pulled up a few stuck-together hairs and rolled them between her fingers, they left a rust-colored stain. Blood. He pulled his arm back and bared his teeth.

"Don't you give me that look. You know I'm stronger'n you, so gimme your arm." She took back his arm. "Gonna need iodine."

She found their first aid box, took his arm again, and touched the glass applicator to his cut. She blew on it to ease the sting. Euclid pulled away, then imitated Babe's lips as she blew. "What the hell happened to you, Euclid?" She inspected his other arm and found scrapes and scratches and more matted blood. She handed him her silver hairbrush to keep him distracted while she ran her hands up and down his arms and legs.

Then she set the cages so Jupiter and Euclid were side by side, just like they had been in their cattle car. There was an open space above the walls between this room and Egypt's stalls, and every so often, the tip of her curious trunk sniffed over the top.

"I see you, Egypt girl," Babe said. "We're all right over here. Euclid's home."

"And look, Babe," Lotty said as she showed off her bedroom after dinner that night. "Everything is just my size!
Miss V had a lot of furniture in the attic, and Denny helped
me arrange it all. Took all afternoon. I'm exhausted! Oh,
how's Euclid?"

"He's a bit spun about, but he'll be all right. Glad to be
with his old friends." Babe stooped under the threshold
and scanned the dollhouse room. Perfect and petite.

Lotty swirled around the room. "Isn't this beautiful?
I just love the curtains, and look at that lamp! Have you
ever seen anything so pretty? Hand-painted flowers on
the shade! It'll be great to read by."

"It's a nice room, Lotty."

"Oh there you are, Babe," Sarah said, passing by the

room. "If you're done in the barn, then let me show you your room."

For a minute, Babe's face lit. Her own room?

"Here you are," Sarah said, opening a bedroom door down the hall.

"Dainty," Babe whispered, taking in the size of the guest room.

"Sorry?"

"I mean it's, well, small."

"I'm afraid it's the best we can do, under the circumstances. Maybe Cleve can make you a bigger bed or something. Here's your pitcher and washbowl. But you can also wash up in the bathroom across the hall."

"A necessary? Here in the house?" She felt her face heat up just remembering her past experiences. "No privy out back?"

"Heavens no. We might be in the forests of Oregon, but we're civilized."

"I reckon your necessary is fit for a little person?"

Sarah's hand went to her mouth. "Oh. Oh. Yes. Oh dear. Well, there is an outhouse behind the barn. The hands use that. Used to, that is, when we still had hands."

Babe edged herself into the tiny room. "Can't hardly catch my breath in here."

Sarah opened the window. "There. Is that better? Babe, I know what it's like. Being a carnie. Living out of a trunk.

We just make the best with whatever we have." She pulled back the coverlet. "You know from carnie life we just grow where we're planted."

Babe cocked a half smile as she imagined herself growing, a giant sequoia, erupting like Alice in Wonderland, right up through the roof. "I'll try. Thank you."

"Well, good night," she said, closing the door behind her.

Babe sighed, looking around. She'd have to remember not to hit the electric light overhead, and to be careful with the porcelain pitcher and washbowl, stay away from that dinky rocking chair and footstool. "Dainty," she muttered. She switched the light on and off, on and off, trundled to the bed, cringing at the creaks in the wood floor. She gently tested the strength of the bed before sitting down.

The bed sagged under her, tossing her off-balance, the sound of springs and ropes protesting under the strain of her weight.

But it had been a long, hard day filled with enough surprises and changes to last her for quite some time. She fell asleep, folded nearly in half.

She'd barely been asleep when she sat upright, awakened by the muffled, familiar roar of a bear. The roar was answered by Euclid's screech, then Egypt's grumble. She groped for the light switch, picked up her valise, and tried to ease herself out of the house without upsetting or breaking anything.

The gush of fresh night air welcomed her. She made her way back to the barn, back to her critters.

"Back to sleep, everyone," Babe said. "Your Babe's here now."

There was a bunkhouse off the barn. Perfect! She pushed together some bunks, found an ancient horse blanket in a trunk, then curled up.

She closed her eyes, pulled the blanket up to her chin, and saw her Euclid running toward her, the large log house, the pastures, the trees, the barn, and the comforts for her animals. Then she tried to remember what Cleve, Sarah, and Miss V looked like, but all she could remember was Denny Franklin.

"You know, Babe, we can't just live here and take her hos-
pitality and not *do* something," Lotty said as they sat alone
having breakfast on their second day. Babe looked down
at her third helping of a half-dozen eggs and two more
slices of ham.

"Way I eat, I'll wear out my welcome real fast," Babe
said. She looked around. "Where is everybody?"

"Sarah said Cleve and Denny go every day to the logging mill down the hill a piece."

"And your aunt? She still asleep?"

"No, Sarah said they *all* start out every morning and go
work at the mill."

"That tiny little lady goes to work in a lumber mill?"
Babe asked. She'd never seen a lumber mill, but had met
plenty of timber savages—all hale and hearty men.

"I guess. All I know is, we have to pull our own weight. All of them up there working and us down here living like the queens of Sheba."

"You girls have enough?" Sarah asked, sticking her head in from the kitchen.

"Yes, thanks," Lotty said. "And don't worry, we'll clear and clean up. Don't do anything special for us."

"And, ma'am?" Babe said. "Thanks again for them nice blankets and curtains and fixings for my room over to the barn. Looks like a real home to me."

"My pleasure. I should have realized you'd get cabin fever in that tiny little guest room. Still, I hate to think of you sleeping in a barn."

"It's home to me." Babe winked at Lotty.

"Oh, Sarah . . . ," Lotty started, "um, can you tell me . . . I mean, when Miss V wrote me, she called me a godsend. But why? Seems like she has everything she needs here and good help to boot."

"I'm not sure what I should tell you and what I shouldn't. After all, you only got here yesterday. We're all just getting acquainted. But I can tell you this, she needs all the help she can get."

"And we want to help. Just not sure how," Lotty said. "I mean, I'm not much help with big things."

"But I can help! I can drive a team, tote just about anything, swing a ax like any he-man."

"Oh dear," Sarah said, cutting Babe off. "Maybe not

that sort of help. Well, she'll never say anything, but I will. Well, she's nearly forty, and her health isn't the greatest."

"Why? What's wrong?" Lotty asked.

"Her heart. They told her it was from birth. You know, a part of her condition, being small and all."

"She setting for a heart attack?" Babe asked. "Seed one once. Man fell over splat-dead just standing in line for a beer."

"She's had a few, oh, they call them episodes," Sarah said, fiddling with a napkin.

"Her heart?" Lotty's hand went to her own heart.

"We women get older, we get to thinking about our lives," Sarah went on. "What's past and what's future. We think about family. But Miss V has such a difficult road ahead. And *you* are a godsend. And you, too, Babe, and maybe even that menagerie you brought with you. She's needing family now, and we've been needing new life blowing into this place for a long time."

Babe recalled how Denny had blown life into this very dining room.

Sarah reached to touch Lotty's hand. "When Miss V got your letter, she started to cry. She was so happy she found you. Well, *you* found *her*."

"Why?" Lotty asked.

"And she didn't even cry when she came back from that heart specialist in Portland. Or when the county assessor sent his judgment about the property lines. Well, I'm saying too much."

"How come if she's doing so poorly she's out working? Shouldn't she be here, resting and taking care of herself?" Babe asked.

"Lay in bed and wait for a heart attack that may never happen or work to keep your land, your business, everything you've worked hard at for nine years?" Sarah said.

Lotty began, "That sounds like she's—"

"Angry!" a voice snapped as Miss V eased herself through the kitchen door. She glared at Sarah, who popped up from the chair.

"Oh, weren't you down at the mill?" Sarah asked.

"We forgot the lunch hamper, so Denny drove me back. Now, if you don't mind, I will do my own explaining from now on and you can make sure that hamper is full!"

Babe wondered if all small people could shout such big orders.

Miss V turned to Lotty. "I suppose she told you about my health."

"Yes, ma'am. I'm sorry. About your heart, I mean."

"No pity, please. Fact of the matter is, doctors have been wrong before, and I feel just fine. Now, if you two want to stay on here—and you can surely change your mind when I tell you what we're up against—and my weak heart is the least of it. Fact of the matter is," she repeated, then stopped, thinking. "Well, I'm in the middle of a conflict here. But I didn't invite you here to fight my battles for me."

Babe asked, "You mean like a war?"

Miss V walked to a wall with several hanging photographs. She pointed up to one. "That was Logan Lumber, just last year. Babe, could you hand that down to me?"

Babe got it, pleased to put her size to good use and set the framed photo on the table. "We had a crew of fifty-three men, four women. Full-time, two shifts. Putting out enough lumber to ship all around the state."

Babe blinked, making sure she was seeing what she was seeing. "Youngins make good lumberjacks?"

"Look closer," Miss V said.

Both Babe and Lotty leaned into the photo, then looked at each other.

In unison, they said, "Dwarfs!"

Lotty pointed to the photo. "And that man there! He looks familiar!"

"The Great Harry Harlequin," Miss V said, "World-Famous Rubber Man. Contortionist, actually. Quite an act in his day."

Babe and Lotty looked at Miss V, the same question on their faces.

"No, carnies don't make the best lumberjacks. But, what else could they do?"

"All thems're carnies?" Babe asked.

"No, of course not. But many. I always had a job for any performer who needed to get off the road. Or was forced off the road."

"You said last year. What about this year?" Lotty asked.

"Had to close the mill. Lay everyone off."

"Tell them the rest," Sarah said, standing next to the sideboard.

"Sarah!"

"I'll tell them if you won't, Miss V. Several of those carnies, old and out of work and hardly able to lift a nail let alone a hammer, are set up in the county charity home and guess who sends them a wagonload of food and supplies once a month?"

"Sarah, do you mind?" Miss V said.

"Yep. Donation Day, we call it here. Just so you know and, okay, *now* I'll see to that hamper!" She pushed the door open and let it *whap whap whap* after her.

"What happened to the mill?" Lotty asked. "Fire?"

"No, no. At least I would have had insurance to cover fire. No, this conflict is with Mother Nature."

Babe stayed silent but knew from her own life, Mother Nature won every time.

Miss V climbed up her steps and sat, breathless, in her chair. "Are you all right, Miss V?" Lotty asked, jumping down off her perch and coming to her side.

"I'm fine. I have my nitroglycerin if it gets bad."

"Nitroglycerin!" Babe boomed. "Don't that blow things up?"

Miss V chuckled. "No, it's all right. My pills won't blow anyone up, least of all me. It's just medicine for my angina."

The kitchen door swung open again. "Excuse me, Miss V," Denny said, his hat in his hand, "did you want me to keep waiting?"

There he was again . . . maybe the nitroglycerin would calm down Babe's *own* rampaging heart.

"Oh, yes, Denny," Miss V said. "Coming. Well, girls, do you want to come with me down to the mill? I can explain things better there. Denny, you stay here and help your mother."

Babe stood aside to let the small ones go through the door, which Denny held open.

Babe smiled at him, hating her huge red lips, her crooked piano-key teeth. She tried to edge through the door, but bumped into Denny, sending him off-balance. Babe grabbed his arm and pulled him back up with an easy tug.

"Oh. Excuse me," Babe said. "You okay?"

He rubbed his arm and looked up at her, his face full of wonder. "Man, you're strong!" He gave her bicep a squeeze—something Babe usually hated, but this was new, different; this was Denny.

Lotty had seen the whole awkward moment from the kitchen. "Babe. Can't you try to be a little more careful?"

It was only a short but steep wagon ride down to the mill.
Babe walked, matching her strides to the turn of the wagon
wheels. Miss V handled the reins and Lotty sat next to her
on the small bench, just their size.

Babe kept glancing over at Lotty and thought there was
something different in her face, in her manner. She wondered what it must have felt like—finding not just an aunt,
but an aunt she could, in every sense, see eye to eye with.
Ol' Babe ain't never going to see eye to eye with no one,
she thought, looking down at her boots. Never.

They tied off the horse, then walked through a yard
with dozens of empty slots for holding lumber. They
went through two huge doors on rollers and entered the
mill itself. A gush of damp, chilly air greeted them. Babe
looked around . . . sawdust, cobwebs, a long, half-cut

board in the middle of a huge round saw. It was almost as though a witch had cast a spell and everything stopped working right in the middle of a job.

Their footsteps echoed as they walked through. "The office is over here," Miss V said, pointing to a room. Cleve sat at the desk, doing paperwork. There were maps and charts and photographs spread out along a long, low counter that ran the length of the room.

Babe stood back, looking over everyone's shoulders.

"Cleve, bring those photos over, will you?" Miss V asked, pointing. "The girls need to know what we're up against. Here's a photo I had taken of the Heartbreak Creek, which my property borders, when I first bought this place."

"Didn't know they could make photographs that big," Babe said. "We've only seed postcard-size!" She gave Lotty's leg a small nudge, but she got a rude *shuush!* back.

"That's a swimming hole big enough for six Egypts," Lotty said. "That a rope swing?"

"Yes, it was great having all the local kids come swim and play. Picnic. We all loved it," Miss V said.

"Hold up," Cleve said. "That was last summer. This is now." He placed another photo over the first.

"And this is the photo that was taken from the same place. The surveyors for the county took it," Miss V said, her mouth hardening.

"That can't be the same place," Lotty said. "What happened?"

"Landslide," Cleve said. "That creek? Gone way over there. Water's going to go where water's going to go. Over here's swampland. Nothing but a huge mess now."

"And every time it rains—*swoosh!* More hillside fills up the creek," Miss V added. "That's what I meant when I said I was up against Mother Nature."

Cleve took a pencil and used it to point. "This property here belongs to Maynard Luckett. Here, here, and here, along Heartbreak Creek. He's this old lunatic prospector hermit."

"Well, he's not that old," Miss V said. "And he wasn't always a lunatic hermit."

"Miss V," Cleve said, sighing heavily, "he keeps to himself and never figured out why they call it Heartbreak Creek. And what he *was* has nothing to do with what he *is*."

Miss V turned to Lotty. "I told you there was conflict."

"So what's the conflict?" Lotty asked. "What's logging trees have to do with that creek?"

"Come on. I'll show you," Cleve said.

They followed Cleve through the deathly quiet mill and came out into the sun. In front of them loomed a huge swampy area, as though a lake had once been there and the water had simply evaporated into thin air.

"See that? It used to be our holding pond."

"What did it hold? Mud?" Babe asked.

"Logs for the mill," Cleve answered. Then he pointed

toward a high, narrow structure. "That's called a sluice. Think of it as a long, high slide. Heartbreak Creek used to flow into it and that's how we slid our logs down from the hill. Can't even fire up our steam engines without water."

"I don't understand," Lotty said.

"It's like this: no water, no logs, no work, no crew, no lumber, no money," Cleve said. "See, things always come down to money."

"Don't we know it!" Lotty said.

"We've been living on the ragged edge for almost a year now, and then there's all those at the county charity home." He put his hand over his mouth. "Oh, maybe I've spilled too many beans."

"Sarah already spilled those beans," Lotty said.

Babe pulled Lotty's sleeve and whispered, "We got money left."

"Yes! Babe and me have some money. We can help."

"You just try to give that proud woman charity," Cleve said. "She only now agreed to let us stay on for just room and board. And I'm afraid we won't be able to even do that much longer. Might have to take our washed-up acts back on the road. Miss V needs to toss in the towel and sell out. You can't fight Mother Nature."

Babe threw a rock out across the pond, where it *pinged!* off a tree stump, sending splinters flying.

"Maybe you could talk to her, Carlotta," Cleve said. "She won't listen to us. We can winter over, but come next spring . . . we'll have to move on and she should, too. She can't go on fighting without weapons."

As they walked back through the mill, Babe wondered what kind of weapons could ever go against Mother Nature.

"Now can I see 'em?" Denny asked, pointing toward the barn.

"Sure, but don't move fast, or say nothing, or even look 'em in the eye," Babe warned.

Lotty gave Babe's leg a little kick. "Don't listen to her, Denny. These animals are tame as kittens. Especially Egypt. She loves people. You can come pet her, and I'll show you some of her tricks."

Denny's face lit up like the Fourth of July. "Man! Yeah!"

Denny followed Lotty into the barn, and Babe went over to Ajax. She pet his grand, graying nose. "Reckon elephants and pretty little dwarfs is more exciting than ugly giants and worn-out, smelly old critters. No offense, Ajax."

Babe went into the barn, trying to ignore the lilting

laughter and "Man alives!" seeping through the walls from the other side of the barn. The bear and chimp had been snoozing, and both their heads popped up when Babe gently called to them.

Euclid's chirp was more Where have you been? than Hello, Babe ol' girl!

As though to answer him, she said, "Been learning about this place Lotty's landed us in."

"Denny! That's not funny!" Lotty giggled from the other side of the barn.

"Then why are you laughing?"

"Well, I guess maybe it *is* a little funny."

Now more laughter from the other side; each new note of gaiety annoyed Babe. Jealousy? Long ago she decided the green-eyed monster was about the only monster not inside her. Once she'd realized who and what she was and that there would never be any recovery, jealousy made no sense. Yet the sound of Lotty's cheer and Denny's laughter and even Egypt's nose snorting stirred something inside her.

Her jaw clamped down and she tried to swallow her anger and started cleaning Jupiter's cage, working around his water bowl and pan of untouched food. "Tell me, Jupiter, if that boy can fall for a dang midget, then why can't he fall for a dang giant? What's so good about small and what's so bad about—" She stopped. "Never mind. You don't got to answer that. I ain't fooling no one." She'd always realized Lotty was happy, smart, dainty, pretty—all of a perfect lady only in a small package. Carlotta the Dwarf was wheat, Babe the Giant was chaff.

Still grumbling to herself, she tossed the bucket of soapy water out the door. Euclid, free from his cage while it was being cleaned, paced and jabbered to himself, imitating Babe. She smiled, put her hand down and, childlike, he reached up and took it. She swooped him up and cradled him with a gentle rocking. "Look at me, Euclid," she whispered to him. "Look at your ol' Babe."

His old eyes were oozy and starting to cloud over. He pursed his lips and said, "*Tcht tcht tcht.*" She wondered if he knew what she was feeling. He stroked her hand with one of his fingers, finding and fiddling with a stubborn wart on her thumb.

She set him down and opened one of the burlap bags of peanuts. His eyes lit up when she let him take a handful. Jupiter raised his head, but when she handed him some he just sniffed, put his head back down on his paws, sighed, and closed his eyes.

Jupiter hadn't been himself since they'd left the train, and now he was so far off his feed—listless and refusing to eat—she worried about bringing him back around. She doubted there was a veterinarian near, and even if there was, what could he know about black bears? She remembered the pill, potions, and patent medicines This 'n' That Ernie had given them. What were they, though? Which ones? How much?

"Hey, Babe!" Denny called out. "Can I come over now? Is it safe?"

She put Euclid in his cage. "It's safe," she called out, then added under her breath, "But there ain't nothing to laugh about over here."

He stepped lightly in, cautiously looking around. Lotty took his hand and pulled him in. "It's okay, silly. They won't eat you."

Babe's eyes landed on their clasped hands.

"How do you know?" he asked tentatively.

"Euclid's just a love. Hi, Euclid," Lotty said.

"Better let me," Babe said, taking a step in front of Euclid. His cage door was wide-open. "You best step over here, Denny." Oh, how she hated her giant-deep voice!

He edged closer. Babe reached into the cage. "Gimme your hand, Euclid." She took Denny's hand and allowed Euclid to grip it.

"What are we doing, shaking hands?" Denny asked, his face beaming, his hand pumping Euclid's up and down. "What kind of monkey is it?"

"He's a chimpanzee. That's a ape, not a monkey. Monkeys gots tails," Babe said.

"Well, I really can't see what he's sitting on. But man, he ought to wear some undergear or something."

Lotty snickered. "Denny!"

Babe knew what he was looking at. "He can't help how

nature takes its course."

"He gonna let go my hand?" he asked, looking up at Babe.

"Nope, you two is betrothed now." She tried to hold in her smile.

Fast as slick, Denny pulled his hand away. "Let me see the bear. Does he bite?" Denny put his hand up to the cage.

"That's like asking if a horse will kick. All horses kick. Question is, will he kick *you*?"

"Well, will he?" Denny asked again, pulling his hand back.

"Here, see if he'll take this," she said, handing half an apple to Denny. She winked down at Lotty, who didn't wink back.

Tentatively, Denny stuck his hand through the cage bars, then Babe called, "Jupiter, get 'em!"

The bear rose up and let out a roar. Denny leaped back with a holler, and Babe laughed. Lotty didn't.

"It's okay, Denny. Babe trained him to do that. Really, he won't hurt you. Babe, that was cruel!"

"You seed me do that a million time and it wasn't cruel then!" Babe snapped. "But look, Lotty, ol' Jupiter's still got some spunk in him. Look how he roared up."

"Man alive!" Denny rubbed some of the red out of his face. "I thought for sure he was going to take my hand off! Wait'll I tell Hank."

There was a tiny knock on the door. "May we come in?" Miss V called out.

The door opened, and Cleve, Sarah, and Miss V came in. "Come on in, Pa!" Denny said. "The bear almost got me! You should have seen it! It was neat!"

"Good thing you survived. You have chores," Cleve said, ticking his head toward the barnyard.

"Oh, right." He dashed out of the barn.

"Well, I have to say," Cleve said, looking around the barn, "this is the dog-gonedest bunch of livestock I've ever seen."

Babe slid the door open to let Egypt stroll over to Miss V, who offered her a treat. "Egypt can't stay locked up in this barn for very long," Miss V said.

"I thought we could see how she does in the pasture," Cleve said. "Did she ever roam free when you worked with her, Miss V?"

"She'll do fine," Babe said. "She don't know her own strength, and she's gentle as a newborned pup, ain't that so, Lotty? Lotty?"

"She ran after Denny," Sarah said.

Babe followed her gaze outside. Together, Lotty and Denny carried a fence rail, laughing at their lopsided tote.

"And what about these two?" Cleve asked, pointing to the bear and the ape. "Sooner or later, I'm going to need to get my stock out of our old bug barn. It's nearly off its foundation now, what with the termite infestation."

Babe's head came up. "Termites? Hear that, Euclid? You favor termites!"

"This ape eats *termites*?" Cleve's deep voice boomed.

"Like they was peanuts," Babe said, smiling. "He'll put a proper cramp in their style. Him and ol' Mother Nature'll see to that."

"Well, look at you, Babe. Now what have you gotten yourself into?" Lotty asked the next day. There was a sniff of humor—no, mockery—in her voice.

Babe brushed the dust off her overalls. "Working on that pasture fence so's *your* Egypt don't run off. Remember, like you said, earning my keep."

Lotty looked up at Babe, standing on the bottom porch step. "Suggesting I'm not earning my keep?"

"Didn't say that."

"I know that's what you meant."

"Did Madame de la Rosa give you mind-reading lessons?" Babe snorted.

"Some minds are easier to read than others," Lotty snorted right back.

Their tiff was broken up by the screen door opening

and Denny coming through, holding a tiny chair made of sturdy logs and a velvet cushion. He set it down next to Lotty. "Here you go, m'lady! Your own throne!"

"Oh, it's beautiful! Did you make this?"

"Ma made the cushion, but I put the logs together. Go ahead, try it out."

Lotty fluffed her skirts out and sat down in the chair, just her size. "It's very comfortable. Thank you, Denny!"

"Now you and Miss V can chat nose to nose, eye to eye," he said, grinning down at his handiwork and the pretty little thing sitting on it.

"Oh, hi, Babe. Say, Pa wants to know if you can unload those nine-foot peeler logs we brought down from the mill. Gonna use them for Egypt's fence." He grinned down to the chair and added, "And furniture."

"Sure thing," she said, staring right at Lotty. "Gotta earn my keep." But Babe was teeming inside. Lotty gets log thrones; Babe gets logs to haul for *her* elephant's fence. She took three posts out of the wagon, hoisted them to her shoulder, and headed past the storage sheds.

But there was an odd sound, so she stopped to listen.

Whap whap whap.

It came from under the steps of the shed. She tossed the logs down, then, on all fours, took a look under the porch of the shed.

Whap whap whap.

"Well, who're you?" she whispered. She tapped her

leg and the *whaps* became fast *tap tap tap*s. Babe grinned, knowing that sound.

"It's okay. Come on out. I won't hurt you."

She went on her stomach and reached under the steps. "Come on, girl."

"I wouldn't, if I were you."

Startled, Babe's head came up fast, hitting the porch floor. She rubbed her head, looking up. Denny.

"I like dogs. This one yours?" she asked.

"They all are."

She looked again. "How many you got in there?"

"I don't know. She won't let me see." Denny knelt down and snapped his fingers. "Come on out, girl. We won't hurt your pups."

"Pups? She's got some pups?"

"Yep. She's gone and hid them good this time," Denny said.

"Dogs think like wolfs when it comes to babies," Babe said, trying to avert her eyes from Denny's face, so close now she could smell how clean his shirt was.

"Well, she's remembering her last litter."

Babe pushed back and sat on her heels. Both knee joints cracked. "What do you mean?"

"Meaning this isn't any dog kennel, and we don't need any more mouths to feed. Once I get them out, Pa says to get rid of them."

"How come you let her out when she's in season?"

"Oh, some wandering mutt got her. Look, I don't like it any more than you do, Babe."

"How old'r they?"

"Two weeks, I guess. Hard to say. They should be coming out pretty soon."

"What's her name?"

"Aces. Call her that because she's ace-high at bird hunting."

"What's she made of?"

"Who knows? A little of everything, I guess. Anyway, she won't let you get any closer. You better not bother her."

"Okay. I won't."

Babe waited until he'd disappeared into the barn before she flattened herself out again, reaching out to Aces. "Hey, Aces. Look what a pretty girl you are. So's them babies of yours. Come on out, girl."

Slowly, Aces inched forward and licked her hand, then allowed a head pat and an ear scrunch, which she leaned into, groaning with pleasure. "I can clean them ears for you. And I'll get them tangles out of your hair. Say, want a treat?" She had a few cookies she'd taken for Euclid and Jupiter from the plate on the sideboard.

"Thata girl," she said softly. "Here, have another one. Now, you come find your Babe if that Denny comes at you with a gunnysack, hear?"

Babe got up with a grunt, dusted off her skirts, and turned her thoughts to Jupiter. She decided the fence posts could wait and she headed to the barn to check on him. He wasn't coming around like she'd hoped. She let him out of his cage to walk around the barn and stretch his legs. She was building him an outdoor cage so he could sniff the air and roll in the dust. Be a bear again. Start eating like he should.

At least Euclid's wounds were healing, but he also had a sort of restlessness Babe hadn't seen before. He'd started to sway back and forth like caged animals sometimes do, even though she took him out for walks, and gave him termite-hunting excursions in the bug barn. She wondered if he missed the excitement and human contact he got being on the road and on display.

"Well, Jupiter's getting on, Babe," Lotty said. She and Denny had come to the barn to bring her a basket of peaches left over from jam making a few days later. "I mean, how old is he? Thirty? Forty? After all, nothing lives forever."

"Criminy, Lotty, you think I don't know that?"

"Well, you don't have to bite my head off," she snapped back.

"I'm sorry. Didn't mean to holler. Been a week now, and he ain't come around. I just been worried, that's all."

"Want Ma to bring over some castor oil?" Denny asked. "Ma says it cures everything. But stand back, it gives you the . . ."

His eyes landed on Lotty's face. "Uh, sorry, Lotty."

No apology to Babe.

"We have money," Lotty said. "We can maybe find a vet and . . ."

That set Denny to laughing. "We don't have a vet in John's Town, but there's some over in Medford. Man! I want to be here and see some horse doctor's face when he walks in and sees that Jupiter. Bet he's never taken a bear's temperature!"

"Denny, here. Your mother wanted the basket back. Could you, please?" Lotty handed it to him.

"Sure. Don't forget, I'm driving you into town later."

She shot him a glance, and Babe read it right away—suggesting he shut up because Babe hadn't been invited to go to town.

"He can be pretty obtuse sometimes," she said after he'd left. Babe's face went blank and Lotty added, "Stupid."

"Don't call me that, Lotty!"

"No, not you. *Obtuse* means 'stupid,' and that's what Denny is sometimes. Maybe not stupid, more like immature. He hasn't seen the things we have."

"How would I know? Ain't never been around boys my own age."

"Well, me neither, but I'm learning." She took a peach and rolled it around her hand. "I have to say, learning is the fun part."

"Just what are you learning?"

"I don't like the sound of that! You know what I mean!" Lotty said.

"How come you get all in a lather like that?"

"I'm not in a lather. I'm sorry. Really, I didn't mean to be . . . in a lather," Lotty said, not sounding sorry at all. "Besides, I have this gigantic pimple coming in! Nothing's more ugly than—"

Babe cut her off. "You're taking to this place just fine, ain't you, Lotty?"

"Heavens, yes! It's all I could have hoped for! It's . . ." Her voice trailed off. "Babe? Aren't you? Happy here?"

Babe didn't answer right away. She looked around the large barn and the animals it held.

"Babe? Answer me." She scampered on top of a bale of hay to look Babe eye to eye.

Babe hunched and rolled her shoulders, as if easing away stiffness. "I feel sort of itchy, like my skin is too tight. Still getting used to it, I reckon."

"But this is what you wanted. No more Renoir or Magnifica. How did you say it? 'Get on with gettin' on'?"

"This ain't what I want, Lotty," she said, turning away. "What I want is to just be normal. I ain't any more normal here than I been any other place."

"You have to give it time."

"Not sure how much time Euclid and Jupiter got." Her eyes filled. She squeezed them tight and changed the subject. "So, Denny's got a spark for you."

Babe was hoping she would laugh at that notion. Instead, they locked eyes.

"I know," she finally said. "I mean, I guess he does. I think it's just because I'm new and I'm well, you know . . . different."

"No, it's because you're pretty and smart and fun. You've landed plumb in your own promised land. You got your home and you got your family. Maybe a beau. Hell, you even got furniture your own size."

"Babe, you know I had no idea what awaited us here—my aunt Valerie being small. She could just as easily have been a giant and then *I'd* be feeling extra small."

"Denny would still spark after you."

"So, you're upset because why? I fit in here and you don't? Or is it because Denny 'sparks after' me?" Lotty asked, taking a tug at Babe's sleeve.

Babe pulled her sleeve back and thought before replying. "Truth, both. But I ain't upset so much as I'm . . ."

"What? Out with it!"

"I'm just cross as two sticks!"

"Cross at who? Not me!"

"Oh, you know me, Lotty. I'm cross at everything. Maybe it's what I like being. Maybe it's because cross is what I'm good at."

"You're talking nonsense," she said, nudging Babe with her foot.

Babe looked down. "New boots?"

"Yes. Well, new to me. They were Miss V's. We wear the same size. She's got this sensational seamstress down in Medford who's a whiz and has all the latest patterns. Miss V's given me lots of . . ." Their eyes met again. "I'm sorry, Babe. I want you to be happy here. So does Miss V. But being so angry all the time is just . . ."

"There's something else," Babe said, looking at her two dresses hanging from nails.

"What?"

"I growed a half inch, I reckon."

"How can you tell?"

Babe put her leg on the hay bale, lifted her skirt, pushed down her sock. Three ink lines circled above her ankle. "Them's markers I made, so's I can tell I'm on a spurt."

"I don't understand."

"I mark where my hems go. See? There's May, there's June, and now here's today. Half inch, I cipher."

"It's been hot. Maybe your dresses just shrunk. Heat can do that."

"No, I can tell. I'm bigger," she said, holding down a deep, dark sigh.

"Well, so what? Look, you grow bigger and I'll probably shrink some. Miss V says when she turned thirty she got a bit smaller. So what? You just have to cross to the bright side of the street and try to . . ."

"Save it!" Babe barked. "I don't need no lectures about no bright side of the street what I'll never walk on! And I don't need no pity, neither, so get that oh-dearie-me look off your face! Been getting that hogwash my whole life."

Lotty snorted and popped down off the hay bale. "Really, Babe, I would think you'd be a little more grateful! You may not have everything just perfect, but you do have things pretty good. At least you're not tossing country hicks out of a ring or posing for picture postcards!"

"Okay, fine, Lotty. I'm grateful, okay?"

"Sometimes there's just no talking to you!" She folded her arms and set her jaw.

Babe was always the first to break their long silences and starefests. "I'm going to find that Heartbreak Creek tomorrow. Thought I'd take Euclid down and give us both a bath. Tired of just spit baths at the sink."

Lotty pointed to Babe's ankle. "Well, be sure to wash those stupid lines off."

"Wanna come?"

"Ug, won't catch me bathing in the creek! Miss V lets me soak in her tub and it's luscious."

Denny stuck his head into the barn. "Lotty? You coming?"

"Yes!" Lotty dashed through the door, leaving it ajar.

Babe looked around for something—anything—to throw. One, two, three, four, five, six, seven peaches oozed their splattered, ripe pulp down the barn door.

Babe walked to the door, scraped some peach pulp stuck between the cracks, and ate it.

"Stupid Babe!" she growled at herself. "You love peaches!"

Babe took a towel, a bar of lye soap, a set of clean clothes, and stuffed it all into a canvas bag. She took her dirty clothes so she could whack them clean at the creek. She grabbed her silver brush for Euclid's hair and began planning how she was going to wrestle him into his bath.

Euclid sniffed the air as Babe approached. "Yes, that's soap you smell. Come on, you," she said, holding up his collar and leash. "Quit your whining. You know this is a long time coming."

He screamed at her, but she knew it was just jabber. She opened his cage and put a handful of cherries next to the door. He looked at them, then at Babe. Slowly, he put his hand toward the cherries. "Just onaccounta you're moving snail-slow don't mean I don't see you," she said, acting casual and watching him out of the corner of her eye. She slapped the collar on him while he popped the cherries into his mouth. "Come on. Time we see the sights and get our-selfs cleaned up."

Euclid's answer was *ping! ping! ping!* Cherry pits shot up at Babe.

"You're a regular clown, Euclid. Maybe you oughta join a circus."

At first, Euclid walked on all fours, then two-legged. Babe thought he looked like a kid on his way to the first day of school. Little excited, little frightened. He took her hand. They probably looked a sight from behind. A giant lumbering along, duffel slung over her shoulder, walking hand in hand with a chimpanzee.

Euclid stopped, sniffing the air.

"You're smelling water, ain't you? Come on. Don't be a baby." She gently tugged him along. "I seed the creek from the hillside the other day. You'll like it. Cool and pretty and private."

The creek sparkled through the trees below. The trail widened as they got closer. Babe looked around and there it was—the landslide Miss V said had put an end to her logging business. It was easy to tell where the hillside had once been. There were trees, mud, rocks piled into the creek, which had taken another course on the opposite shore. "Miss V says there's a lunatic living over there," she said down to Euclid, pointing across the creek. "So, don't you go wanderin'."

Babe's knees cracked as she crouched down to talk to Euclid. "Now, you been in a creek before." Euclid sat on his haunches, staring at the water as though thinking things over. "I ain't gonna throw you in, if that's what you think." He looked up at her. "Unless you want me to.

"We got to bring Jupiter down here when he's better. See if he's up to smackin' a fish or two out of the creek. Might be just the change he's been needing. Remind him of his wildness.

"Come on now, you first, old man," she said. She took his leash and walked him to the water's edge. He stopped. "I know it's cold." He stepped back. "I seed you swim plenty of time, so don't tell me you can't."

She waded out a few feet. "Come on. It's fun." She whisked water toward him, splashing his face. Babe grinned at his look of insult. He slapped his hand on the water. Babe tried to look insulted right back.

The rest was easy. It had become a game. They kicked, waded, and splashed. He drank his fill and spit water out toward Babe. Back on shore she brushed him, taking extra care around his cuts. She cleaned and patted dry his small ears, forever enraged anyone would cut them off to look like a gorilla. He leaned into her as she massaged his ears dry, and he groaned in delight.

"Now me," Babe said. She found a warm, sandy place to undress. Part of a downed tree jutted out—perfect for hanging out clothes to dry.

She tied Euclid off so he could sit turning over rocks on the shore and look for things to eat underneath. With a great *oooof*, Babe pulled off her boots and placed them on their side in the creek so water could run into them. Next her socks. She hated looking at her bare feet—so huge, red, gnarled, dirty—so she stepped into the water so she didn't have to. Everything else was quickly off. Grabbing her soap, she waded further out.

"Cold as snakes!" she bellowed.

Once she was just over her knees, she dropped down, gasping at the cold, then lay back and let the water run over her.

Finally! Free of clothes and the trappings that made her feel so big and cumbersome. She felt somehow smaller this way, especially out here where there were no bathhouse mirrors. A wide grin covered her face as she took water into her mouth and gushed it out and up, then splashed water all around.

Euclid sent out a screech.

"I'm okay, Euclid! Ain't drowning! This is fun!" She splashed more, making waves. She felt along the bottom and brought up huge scoopfuls of sand, silt, pebbles, and slippery things.

She took the soap and ran it all over, then leaned her head back and let the water pull against her long hair, which streamed past her shoulders and arms.

Freezing now, she splashed her way back, toweled off, and pulled a clean slip over her head.

Euclid started jumping up and down, barking and chirping.

"What are you jabbering at?"

But he wasn't looking at Babe. He was looking at two people across the creek. Babe stood up straight and squinted. "Hesh, Euclid. You stay here and hesh."

She waded back into the creek, fording easily, even as it got deeper and the current stronger. She got a closer look at them. They were boys, she could tell. One held binoculars to his eyes and the other held a small, square box. It wasn't the first time Babe had been spied upon. It wasn't the first time she'd been photographed by those new box cameras.

She scooped up some silt from the creek and let a few rocks stay in her hand. Stalking closer, she doubted they knew what an arm and aim she had or how fast a giant can run, especially free of a heavy skirt.

Their laughter stopped. The closer she got, the bigger she got. Her face felt angry red and her eyes were spitting blue fire. She let a rock fly. *Bonk!* The boy dropped the binoculars around his neck and his hand went to his mouth. Denny! His scream was echoed by Euclid, jumping up and down across the creek. Another rock flew and this time she hit the boy with the camera. She kept walking. They turned tail and tried to scramble back up the rocky hillside toward the woods, screaming curse words behind their backs.

Babe crashed out of the water and grabbed the one with the camera and yanked it out of his hands.

"Hey!" he said, falling down, looking up at the sequoia-tree-tall girl over him. He was covered in her shadow.

"Don't crush me!" he screamed.

She took the camera box between her huge hands and squeezed until the wood snapped apart and the insides fell out. She yanked at the film and flung it far into the creek, then tossed the remains down to the scrawny, redheaded boy.

"We were just having some fun!" Denny shouted, holding his hand to his bleeding lip. "Babe! Don't hurt him! You okay, Hank?"

She glared at the boy on the ground, then at Denny. She felt like her jaw was crushing her teeth into dust. "Don't no one spy on me!"

"We weren't sp-spying!" Denny stuttered, holding his upper lip. "Lotty said you were going to give the monkey a bath and . . ."

"Don't give me that line of gab!" she yelled. "You knew what you was looking at! Up close!" She pointed to Hank. "Taking pictures!"

"We didn't hurt you!" Hank called out.

Denny looked at the blood from his lip. "Bet I'm going to need stitches!"

"You'd need a hearse and a six-foot hole if I had a bigger rock!" She looked around, picked up a large rock, and tossed it up and down in her hand. "You wanna try for that?"

"No!"

She looked down at Hank, who had been trying to backstroke up the sand and rocks. "Not me!"

Babe realized her wet slip was clinging to her body, giving them a detailed image. She figured they'd seen what they came for.

"You're not going to tell, are you?" Denny asked, stepping a bit closer. "Hank just wanted to meet you. After all I told him about . . ."

"You know, that camera was new and cost me five bucks and . . ."

She picked up the crushed camera and tossed it at him. "Ah, it broke," Babe said. "Maybe you can get your money back."

She plucked her slip away from her body and hoped her face wasn't showing as hot as it felt. She gave them one last, threatening Magnifica glare and turned, praying her backside didn't show through.

"Say, are those real tattoos?" Denny asked, pointing to her arms. "Look, she's got tattoos! Man! I'm getting me some of those when I leave home! Did it hurt?"

She turned on him, and he took a step back. "Did 'em myself with a fishhook and lion's blood!" She didn't crack a smile while watching their eyes bulge and mouths drop open. "Stupid rubes," she mumbled under her breath. "Believe anything." She turned again to leave.

"Hey, what's your monkey's name?" Hank called out, pointing to Euclid, still making a racket across the creek.

All Babe had to do was toss and catch the rock in her hand and the two boys ran off like scaredy-cats. She picked up a part of the smashed camera for a souvenir.

"Monkey!" she growled out loud, looking at Euclid across the creek, still pacing on his short leash. "I'm coming, *monkey*!"

Slowly, Babe allowed the smooth current of the stream to calm her. She splashed water on her embarrassed face. "Gonna always be cameras, Babe," she whispered through handfuls of water. "You know that."

She washed her eyes in case there had been tears of anger, and took in a deep breath as she marveled at the greens, the sparkling of the water, and the soft breeze overhead. She turned a complete circle. There, upstream, was an old tree leaning away from the hillside. A long rope dangled, useless and now far above the shallow water.

"Some swimming hole," she muttered, recalling the large photo of this very area before the . . . landslide. She scanned the hillside, wondering how just that small section of it coulda just—*swoosh!*—slipped away. And why didn't Miss V just hire men to clean it all up?

"Hire," she said, continuing across the stream. "That's why. Dope."

The closer she walked toward the slide, the larger the cleanup job looked. She stopped where a tree had fallen into the water. The branches were still sticking out, but the needles and cones were dead and golden. She easily snapped off a few and tossed them across the creek. Sizing up the tree, she bent down and wrapped her arms around it. Touching what she couldn't see was . . . "It's just a tree, Babe. Ain't no sea monsters in that water." She bent down deeper, gripped harder, and *Uuuuuuhhhhhh!*

She gave it a second go, this time pretending the dead tree was just a fake half-ton barbell. *Grrrrrrrr!* Nothing doing. She stood up, rubbing her cramping backside, then stepped back, looked down, and thought the problem over.

A long, deep breath and a third try. One . . . two . . . *Ugggggg!* This time she remembered the boy with the firecrackers named Woodrow, stuck underwater back in Pendleton, and she felt a surge of strength. *Threeee!* Her knees slowly straightened, her legs burned, her face burned, her eyes squeezed tight, and she grunted like no lady ever had before. But, yes! Finally! Babe had the tree in her arms. Now what? Do something before her blood vessels all pop open! She backed up, pulling the tree free of the mud's grip. She dropped it with a splash and a huge crack on the shore of the creek.

"Easy . . . as . . ." she gasped, "pie." She washed the bark, pitch, and sand from her hands and arms.

She washed out some clothes, twisted the water out of them, then began the uphill trek back. They arrived at the barn clean, hungry, and tired.

"Hello, Babe. I see you're all spiffed up," Miss V said as Babe stepped carefully onto the front porch where she, Lotty, and Denny were sitting. Her hair was dry and curly and she let it hang down her back, held with a blue ribbon. She wore a clean shirt and skirt. She couldn't bear climbing into her overalls when she was so clean. Her boots were still drying, and so she wore the stretchy slippers Lucretia the Lobster Woman had knit for her, saying she knew the value of comfortable footwear.

"Had me a good time at the creek this morning." Babe's eyes landed on Denny, sitting on the porch railing, whittling a stick. There was a bright-white dressing on his upper lip.

"Cut yourself shaving, Denny?" she asked, straight-faced.

"Walked into a door," he muttered, not looking at her.

"Babe," Lotty said, "I haven't seen that shirt on you before. Blue is your color!"

"Got this up in Hood River." She didn't add she'd pinched it off a clothesline. Men's size extra large and hard to come by. "Sure's a nice creek, Miss V. Seed the landslide."

"Horrible, isn't it?" she said.

"Well, I seed the problem from the other side."

"I'm sorry?"

"I . . ." Another glance toward Denny. "I waded acrost the creek and took me a good long look at that landslide from over there."

"I hope that horrible Mr. Luckett didn't see you. He's been known to shoot at trespassers," Miss V said.

"I been known to do that myownself," Babe returned. Denny's head popped up. Lotty noticed and Babe wondered if she should snitch—tell her what her sweety-cakes Denny and his ogling friend, Hank, had been up to.

"You know, Miss V," Babe went on, "if we was to plan it right and with enough manpower, we could maybe clean out that landslide and you'd get your creek back."

"Oh yes, we've all thought about that," Miss V said, waving Babe's idea away with her wee hand. "Cleve says it's just too much land in too tricky a place. And what manpower? And with what money to pay them? Then there's that Mr. Luckett. He won't even answer his door, let alone work with us on getting the creek back. How many times did your dad go over there to talk to him, Denny?"

"I dunno. Lots. I guess." His lip was so swollen it slurred his speech.

"Then Luckett's set up that rig for gold mining. Stupid old fool," Miss V snapped.

"He's not so bad," Denny said. "Lets us boys fish and trap there."

"Aren't you forbidden on that side of the creek?" Miss V said.

Finally, Denny looked up at Babe. "Kinda."

"I got a few ideas. We got Cleve, Denny, and maybe a few of his friends to help. Me, of course."

"Well," Miss V said, standing up, putting an end to the conversation. "It's nearly one. Time I got myself down to the mill. Got a small order in for some cordwood. Come along, Denny. Your father's going to need to help splitting wood. Get the wagon."

Denny tossed his stick and jumped down off the porch.

"Denny, wait up!" Lotty said. "You promised to show me how fast you can hitch a horse."

"Ma'am?" Babe said. Miss V stopped and turned. "What do you do down there at the mill besides look at photographs and maps of what used to be?"

"Well, that's a bit impertinent!"

"Sorry, ma'am. I wisht you let me tell you my idea."

"Idea for what?"

"To get you your creek back."

"Were you listening? I'm nearly broke. I'm not a woman of God, but maybe that landslide was God's way of telling me to sell out."

"Oh, you mean that landslide was a *godsend?*" That brought Miss V's eyes back to Babe. "I thought you said *we* was the godsends."

"Babe. I have family now. Real blood family." She tapped her chest. "Now I have a reason for this to keep on beating. If I sell, there'll be some money for her. Keep her safe and away from carnies and circuses and all that humiliation."

Babe felt that pain inside again—the one that started in her toes and shot up through her body and made her eyes and ears throb. *Real blood family.* She crushed down the pain. "But, Miss V, if we was to clear the landslide, get your creek and pond back, could you start up your mill?"

"You're sweet, Babe, but you're just dreaming. Do you know how many tons of rock, dirt, and downed trees are there? We'd need teams of oxen and steam tractors and a crew of dozens and—"

"And Egypt," Babe said, cutting her off.

Miss V stopped midstep and looked up at Babe. "Egypt?"

"'Member how good that ol' girl is at moving things? How she can wrap her trunk around a tent pole and carry it like it was a baseball bat? How she can pull a skid full of hay?"

"I remember," she whispered.

"So, what do you got to lose if it don't cost nothing?"

"Well, I can't spare Cleve. He has to help with some small lumber orders. And Denny, he's about the laziest boy I've ever met."

"Then you won't miss him."

Babe toyed with the piece of broken camera in her skirt pocket, her new good-luck juju. "How about you let me be a godsend for a bit?"

Miss V looked up at Babe's large, grinning face. "You're an odd one."

"All giants is odd. Says so in them fairy tales."

An hour later, Babe, Lotty, and Denny stood next to the creek, taking in Babe's proposed task. "Oh, sure," Lotty said, looking up from the creek at the landslide. "We're going to move all of that there"—she pointed up—"over there. Sure we can do that. Sometimes I worry about you, Babe."

"Not just over there. We have to move it over this way, too," Babe went on, undeterred. "We got to sort of spread it down and back so's the creek there will cut back over here. See?"

"Yeah, someone get me a spoon and I'll start right here," Denny said, picking up a handful of dirt and tossing it downstream.

"Look at the way them trees is just laying half in and half out of the water. We can lift or pull 'em out."

"Impossible!" Denny grumbled.

"Criminy, I moved that one just this morning." She glanced slyly over to Denny. "When I was taking my swim. Easy as pie!"

"Well, easy for you. Not me!" Lotty said.

"You can set atopt Egypt and she'll know just what to do. Denny, you can drive a team. Ol' Ajax's got some pull left in him."

"That wind-broke crow bait? Ha!" Denny said.

"And I reckon that friend of yours will want to help. What's his name? Frank?"

Denny narrowed his eyes on Babe. "Hank."

"Bet he don't got nothing else better to do 'cept"—she dangled the camera part—"go on nature hikes."

Denny's face drained its color. "Well, maybe. He might have some spare time." Babe figured she had him just where she wanted him.

"What's that you have there, Babe?" Lotty asked.

"Something I found acrost the creek," she said, putting it back in her pocket. "Keeping it as a juju."

"Okay, we'll help. But I'm telling you, Babe, it's hopeless," Denny said. Remember, we have our regular chores to do." He turned to Lotty. "I know! Let's you and me drive into town. We'll go find Hank. He's a swell guy. Lots of fun."

"No, I think I'll just stay here. See if I can talk some sense into Babe."

"Lotty, alls we need is a good working plan," Babe said.

"Lord, Babe, when you get the bit between your teeth . . . ," she said, kicking a dirt clod.

"And nobody plans better'n you, Lotty," Babe said. "'Member? You're the brains of the outfit. I'm the brawn?"

"Okay. You two geniuses figure it all out," Denny said, jogging back up the trail. "I got to go help Pa split cordwood."

"Come on, Lotty, let's you and me go get Egypt and see what she thinks about this here creek."

"Babe!" Lotty screamed. "Jupiter's cage door! He's gone!"

"Let him go last night," Babe answered, pulling Egypt's head harness down off a hook.

"You what?"

"Opened his cage, opened that barn door, and watched him stroll hisself on out."

"But . . ."

"Lotty, he was dying in here. I'm going to haul his cage outside so's if he wants to come back, he can."

"But how can he survive out there? Babe, he'll starve!"

Babe tossed Lotty's handler's rod to her. "He was starving in here!" Her words echoed through the barn. "Now come on. You get Egypt and let's get her harnessed."

"What do you think she's thinking?" Babe asked Lotty after they'd put the elephant in her harness.

"She's going to take one look at that landslide and go running away screaming like everyone else has!"

"Look at her eyes. She's thinking she's earning her keep."

"She's thinking she's running out of hay. Well, let's go show her that creek."

They had barely started the path down when Egypt's ears started to flap and she took in big gulps of air. The closer to the water, the livelier Egypt stepped.

"Now what's she thinking?" Babe asked as Egypt dashed headlong into the creek. She took a long pull of water, shot it into her mouth, then dropped to her knees, went on her side, and rolled joyously, sending wavelets onto the shore.

"She's thinking she's a baby again," Lotty said. "We might as well sit down and enjoy the show."

Egypt waded in deeper and sucked up enough water to give her back a shower. Then she pulled up globs of sand and tossed them on her back.

Finally, Egypt came up on the bank, sandy and muddy, flapping her ears to dry herself, and started to browse on the shoreline brush.

"You there! You! Get out of here!"

Across the creek a man, short and squat, stood shaking a large stick.

"Uh-oh," Lotty said. "Bet that's the prospector Miss V warned us about. That Luckett man. We better go."

Babe stood up and stepped closer.

"Babe, no!"

Babe waded into the water. "We ain't doing you no harm!"

"What's that beast doing in my creek?" he demanded.

"Taking a bath, and this ain't all your creek." Babe stood her ground midstream.

"Who the hell are you?"

"Your new neighbor."

"And that thing? An elephant? Here?"

"Also your new neighbor."

"What's that crazy midget woman doing now, starting up a circus?" he yelled.

As Babe approached, he took a few steps back. She used her full size to her full advantage.

"First midgets, then elephants, and now giants," he said, shaking his head. "What next?"

"A trained bear and a chimpanzee."

"All up there at that lady midget's place?"

"Yep, only she's a dwarf, not a midget."

"Dwarf, midget, homunculus. She's small and a woman and the last thing she needs is running another lumber mill circus. Now git! You're trespassing!" He raised his stick in warning. Babe knew she could easily snap it in half.

"You that Luckett gold miner?"

"That's the name. Now, git!"

Babe could tell up close, by his scrappy voice and gray

hair springing out from under his hat, he was maybe fifty or older. His whole body listed on bowed legs, like Euclid.

"I'll go back," she said. "But if you don't like looking at the likes of us, then take you someplace else. We're working Miss V's side of the creek."

His face went stone hard. "Working what?"

"Going to move us a mountain." She ticked her head toward the landslide.

He set his head back and laughed. "And they say *I'm* the one missing some buttons!" He limped away, laughing to himself, and using his stick as a cane.

"Oh, no, you're not," Sarah said, tapping the date on the kitchen calendar. "It's August first. Donation Day. Everything is packed and ready on the front porch."

"But we want to start down at the creek," Lotty said. "I have plans drawn up and everything!"

"Chores first. It's beyond me why Miss V said you kids could mess with that stupid creek in the first place. All the work needing done here."

Babe tried not to laugh, but it seemed like Sarah could glare at two kids on each side of her at once.

"Anyway, Denny has to deliver food and supplies to the county charity home today," she said. "Chores first!"

"But Pa has both wagons and the teams up at the mill," Denny said. "How can—"

"You'll have to go by shank's mare and use the hand-cart."

"On foot? Haul all that by myself?" Denny protested.

"So you better get started," his mother said, taking her bonnet off the hook. "It might even take you two loads. Babe, can you help Denny load the handcart? I have to get lunch to the mill." She tapped Denny's arm. "*On foot*, and you don't see me complaining!"

"Just for the record," Babe said, adding the last package of Donation Day food to the handcart, "bringing Egypt ain't my idea."

"It's okay, Babe," Denny said. "This'll be fun!"

Babe walked next to Egypt and gave a side glance toward Lotty riding atop the elephant with Denny snuggled up right behind her, his long legs dangling down past Egypt's curious and fanning ears.

"Egypt don't look too happy about this, neither." Babe petted Egypt's trunk. "She thinks she's a parade spectacle again."

"Maybe Babe's right, Denny," Lotty said. "Maybe we should leave her . . ."

"Hey, you're the one always spouting how well trained Egypt is," Denny said. "But, if you're afraid . . ."

"No, I'm not afraid. And Egypt always does what I say," Lotty said.

"What you think your folks and Miss V would have to

say about this?" Babe asked, glancing back at the house.

"They're all at the mill," Denny said. "We'll be back in two hours. It's just down the road. You don't have to come, you know."

"Oh? Then who'd be hauling this handcart? Should I round up Honeycomb?"

"No!" Lotty shouted. "Oh come on, Babe!"

Babe weighed the situation. *Go with them, go work on the creek, go back to bed?* She *did* favor a trip to town, see the sights, the sights Denny had already pointed out to Lotty.

"Okay, but for the record . . ."

"We know!" Denny and Lotty said in unison.

"Hey, all those old geezers at the home'll be thrilled to see an elephant. Heck, half of them are old circus folks. They'll get a real kick out of it! And Donation Day is for doing good deeds!" he justified with giving Lotty a squeeze. He put his arm into the air. "Onward!" Lotty tapped Egypt's foreleg and they started out.

Babe picked up the handcart handles and started pulling. The load of smoked hams, fruits, canned goods, and jams wasn't heavy, but she hauled it with long, hesitant steps, mumbling, "For the record."

Denny pointed the way through a winding road, flanked by farms and orchards. "See? Isn't all trees around here. Around that bend is a great view! Wait till you see it down in the valley. Lots of fruit trees and farming. That's where the future is, they say. In fact, that's . . ."

"Stop right where you are!" A man stood in the middle of the road, pointing a rifle straight at Egypt.

Babe held Egypt's trunk. "Whoa, girl."

"Stop, Egypt!" Lotty commanded. "Denny. Who's that?"

"Uh-oh . . ." Denny started. "That's crazy old Preacher-Man Munley."

"He a real man of God?" Babe asked. "Toting him a rifle?"

"I mean it! Not a step closer!" the man yelled, his rifle still aimed high. His black pastor's frock was threadbare and his beard was long and scraggly.

"Hey there, Mr. Munley. It's just me. Denny Franklin."

"Don't care who you are. That elephant is the devil's work!"

"Don't say anything," Denny warned Babe as she moved forward.

Babe ignored him. "Devil's work?"

"And you! Devil's spawn! Like all them devil's imps at the county home! Like that woman up there on that hill! Devil's handmaid!"

"Lotty, just turn this elephant around," Denny said, keeping his voice low and calm. "Babe, come back here. Don't rile him."

"We aren't any devil's handmaids!" Lotty shouted.

"We're leaving," Denny called out.

"Heard about that beast! Devil's work! Folks pay good,

hard-earned cash money to see such a thing! So git and don't you never come back this way!" the man continued, coming even closer.

"Babe, come back," Lotty pleaded. "Please! Why do you always have to . . . ?"

Babe stopped. "Got vittles here. You want vittles? Maybe feed the poor?" Babe stepped aside and showed him the handcart.

The shot rang out, Egypt issued a horrible screech, stumbled, dumping both Lotty and Denny. Babe didn't know whether to go after the running preacher-man, see to her friends, or run after Egypt.

Before finding her way back to Miss V's, Egypt had mowed through several rows of crops, stampeded a herd of terrorized sheep, crashed through three fences, and overturned a field worker's outhouse.

"It's just a graze," Cleve said, inspecting the bloodied streak along Egypt's side. He dabbed it with alcohol on a rag and threw the rag down. "Damn lucky!"

"What were you kids thinking?" Sarah demanded. Babe, Lotty, and Denny stood, dirty and sweaty, in the barn.

"You know that elephant wasn't to go off this property!" Miss V screeched. "I've already gotten three phone calls from neighbors! The sheriff is on his way out here! Do you know how much your little prank is going to cost me?"

"Didn't think about that," Lotty said, following her aunt as she paced the barn. "Honest, Miss V, we just did it thinking your old carnie friends, you know, the ones we were taking the food to, would get a kick out of . . ."

"That's another thing! Where's all the food I sent you with?" Miss V said.

The kids exchanged glances. "Um, I reckon that preacher-man's got it," Babe finally said. She'd never been chewed out by adults she admired, and this first time was humiliating to her and she knew her face showed it.

"That's another thing!" Sarah bellowed. "You should have never gone even close to Preacher-Man Munley! Everyone knows he belongs in the bughouse! What were you doing way over there?"

"Showing them the sights," Denny answered, looking down. "And besides, who knew that old coot would show up out of nowhere? He's the one who . . ." He trailed off.

"Want me to go back? See about that cart and the food?" Babe asked.

"No!" all three adults shouted in unison.

"Denny! Back to the house," Sarah said, leading the way.

"Carlotta, go get cleaned up," Miss V ordered, following.

That left Babe looking at Cleve. "Babe," he said kindly. "I think I know whose idea this was."

"I didn't say nothing."

"Still, I think I know. Egypt best stay in the barn tonight."

"I'll tend her," Babe said, running her hand down the elephant's trunk.

He turned to leave, then said, "You're a good kid, Babe."

"Can you wait here a minute?" Babe went into her room and returned with the envelope of cash, all that was left of their stash. "Will this help? It's over two hundred dollar."

Cleve smiled, looking down at Babe's offering. She placed it in his hand. "Well, I'd be lying if I said all the damage isn't going to hurt us in a big way."

He smiled and left. Babe turned to Egypt, now swaying calmly in the safety of the barn. "Sorry, girl. I'm real sorry. Should have stood my ground. Should have."

It was as though everyone around the table at lunch knew the hard *rap rap rap* on the door meant more trouble.

"I recognize that knock," Miss V said. "Sarah, would you let the sheriff in?"

Lotty looked at Babe, who looked at Denny, who looked down at his lunch, still untouched.

"Sorry to interrupt," the sheriff said. His uniform was nothing more than a dingy gray shirt and black pants, a lopsided necktie and a badge. His slouch hat was in his hands. He nodded to everyone around the table, eyes landing on Babe, sitting head and shoulders above the rest. "Miss V," he said, trying to smile. "Here. What I told you about on the phone."

Miss V smiled and tapped the tablecloth. "Set it here,

Arlo. Have you had your lunch? Sarah, see to an extra plate, will you?"

"No, no. This is far from a social call. Here's the damage estimates," he said, placing several scraps of paper on the table.

"Is there a total?"

"Somewhere in the two hundreds," he said. "You'll have to settle with each person. I think I convinced everyone not to sue. But Miss V, that elephant has to go."

"Go? Why? What for?" Lotty said.

"Lotty, I will handle this," Miss V said sternly. "Our elephant is tame as a kitten. That Munley shot her! What would you expect an elephant to do? I'd sue that lunatic if I thought he had a dime to his name!"

The sheriff pulled another paper out of his shirt pocket. "Well, another concerned citizen sent this in shortly after word got out about that elephant being here. I didn't think much of it at the time."

He placed the newspaper on the table. The headline screamed all the way from Pendleton.

MAD ELEPHANT NEARLY KILLS LOCAL BOY

Miss V's face grew pale. She lowered her glasses and passed the paper to Lotty. "Is this true?"

Lotty scanned the headline with the accompanying

photo of Egypt from the carnie flier. "No! I told you about that! That kid nearly killed Egypt!"

"Now, Arlo," Cleve said, standing up. "I'm sure we can come to some sort of arrangement here. How about we— I know! We'll just keep the elephant chained and promise no escapes."

"Yes!" Miss V said. "We have plenty of room and can easily keep her here. And the children have promised under threat of death never to take her anywhere off this property."

Arlo scratched his chin. "You know what an animal lover I am. But I have a job to do."

Babe wasn't sure when or where or how to jump into the conversation. She sat silent, keeping her beast quiet with deep, steady breaths. But it was too much. "What if that gunshot killed Egypt? Would you be hauling that preacher-man to jail?"

Silence all around the table. "You do have a point, miss," Arlo said. "Look, let me see what I can do. The county vet is out of town, and he'd be the one to decide this."

"I'll sign whatever I have to. I'll pay these debts, and I'll . . . I'll even . . ." Miss V began, then, out of breath, sat back.

"She needs to rest," Sarah said. "This has been all too much."

"Of course," Arlo said, backing away. "Sorry to interrupt. Just doing my job. Look, I'll do what I can to stall all this business. But for God's sake, everyone, keep that elephant under control. I can see myself out."

The room was deathly quiet. Babe and Lotty looked at each other. "We have money," Lotty said. "Not a lot, but Babe and me have money."

"I can't take your money," Miss V said.

"Yes, you can," Cleve said. He stood up and pulled out all the cash Babe had given him. "In fact, you already have."

Babe looked down at the stationery, pen, and inkwell Sarah had given her when she excused herself from lunch after that horrible morning. She'd shown her how to fill the pen with the ink using the delicate glass eyedropper. She examined the dropper and the pen—so small, so delicate—in her large hands, then picked up her stub pencil. She clumsily began to write, sounding out the words as she wrote.

An hour later, she exhaled heavily, stood up and stretched, then took the three pages of large, scribbled writing over to Euclid. "You got a minute?" she asked the ape, reaching in to pet him.

He opened an eye, then went back to sleep.

"Tell me if this is okay," she said. "I don't spell good

but she knows that." She brought the lamp closer and read aloud to Euclid.

> *August 1, 1896*
>
> *Dear Rosa,*
>
> *How are you? I am fine. No I am not fine. I am sad. We are at a nice house. I sleep in a barn. Ha ha. Like home. Lotty is happy with her aunt. They are a like. Small.*
>
> *Guess what? Euclid come back. I do not know how he run from Renoir. He is fine. But Jupiter got sad. He would not eat. Guess what I done. I let him go free. He run off and is happy I hope. It hurt seeing him go, but I done right by him.*
>
> *Lotty and me got in a big mess. Egypt got gun shot so she run wild and we got to pay what she done so we got no money. The law man said she might have to be killt. So me and Lotty are scardt.*
>
> *The people here say I gots to do school come fall. Lotty says she likes learning at school and she is happy. I cannot do the school, Rosa. I am done with school and am scardt to get teased by youngins again. Youngins is the worst teasers. There is a nice man here. His name is Cleve. He was a carnie and says he can teach me my grades but I am dumb so I want to go away.*
>
> *Did you find a big house? I was keeping money so I can come see you but it is gone.*

I do not write so good and I am sorry. I hurt all over. My bones make cracks and they hurt. I am bigger too. Can you write to me? Can I come see you?
Your friend,
Babe Killingsworth

She looked over to Euclid, now vaguely interested. "Wipe that worry off your face, ol' man. Your Babe ain't going nowheres without you."

46

"Well, at least we can still work on the creek," Lotty said, brushing caked mud off Egypt. "But you, my dear," she said into Egypt's eye. "You are hereby confined to quarters. No more out and about for you."

"Don't seem fair, huh?" Babe asked. "Us slipping up, her having to pay for it."

"After looking at the list of damages, we'll be paying for 'us slipping up' for a long time!" She turned and looked up at Babe. "By the way, thank you."

"For what?"

"For never saying 'I told you so.' You were against taking Egypt the whole time."

Babe smiled. Things hadn't been overly friendly between the two girls lately. "Well, I *did* go on record."

Lotty tossed the brush at Babe and laughed. "You can be *so* annoying!"

"What time did Denny say him and his buddy was going to meet us here?" Babe asked, gazing through the barn door.

"Nine. Denny said the only reason Hank was showing up was to see the rampaging elephant."

Babe smiled. Showing up probably had more to do with a broken camera than meeting an elephant. Just then, Denny's dog, Aces, came springing into the barn, full of glee. Babe grinned watching her—tail up, nose down, dashing about the barn, smelling this, smelling that.

Babe knelt down and called out, "Here, Aces girl! Come see your Babe!" Aces bounded into her arms and Babe gave the dog a good tussle about her ears. "Nice to get away from them pups, huh?"

"At least somebody's happy around here." Lotty smirked. "Where's Denny?"

"You *still* talking to him after . . . you know?" Babe asked, nodding her head toward Egypt.

"Well, he didn't shoot Egypt. He had no idea what was going to happen!" she defended.

"Thought you'd be mad and giving him 'one of these,'" Babe said, showing her upraised fist. Babe knew her answer when Lotty's face lit up like Christmas as Denny entered the barn.

"It's safe, Hank," Denny said. "Come on in."

Hank slid into the barn. His eyes landed on Babe and he looked away. Babe walked over to meet him—for the second time.

"Carlotta, this is Henry Hannity. But we call him Hank. And you can call her Lotty," Denny said. "The giant's name is Babe."

Hank stepped delicately over to Lotty. "Why, you're as bitty as that Logan midget!"

"She's bitty and I'm big," Babe said. "Now we got that settled, let's get to work."

"Okay, so where's this elephant everyone's been yammering about?" Hank asked.

"She's on that side of the barn," Lotty said. "We want to keep her quiet."

"You mean I came out here and I can't even see the elephant? My old man wasn't keen on me working out here in the first place. Now I don't even get to see the dang elephant?"

"Maybe in a few days," Lotty said. "Tell him, Denny."

"Quit bellyaching. It's just an elephant. Come on, we're burning daylight. Let's get down to the stream and show these girls just how stupid their idea is."

Denny led the way out of the barn, followed by Hank. Babe raised her fist again, Lotty shook her head and followed the boys out.

★ ★ ★

"How many years do we have to get this done?" Hank asked, shading his eyes, surveying the landslide up and down.

"Miss V says she'll give us one month," Babe replied. "In and out of our own chores."

"That'll be after Labor Day!" Hank ran his hand through his unruly red hair.

"Fitting," Denny mumbled.

"Hey, Franklin, you said just move a few yards of sand and rock," Hank went on. "You didn't say we were moving a whole mountain!"

"Look, these girls have it in their heads that they— we—can do this," Denny said, picking up a shovel and tossing it to Hank. "So let's just dig in and show them how impossible it is. You know women," Denny said, as though the girls weren't standing right there. "They don't understand these things."

Lotty and Babe looked at each other, then both cast eyes to the heavens.

A short time later, Babe and Lotty stood aside, watching the two boys try to outdo each other, digging, loading wheelbarrows, hauling, shouting orders. When the girls had pitched in, they got all sorts of reasons why they shouldn't or how wrong they were going about things.

Babe grinned ear to ear. "Remember that story you read to us, Tom Somebody?"

"Sawyer. Yes, what about it?"

"Remember that part about whitewashing the fence? How ol' Tom made it look like fun and then all them boys wanted in on it?"

"Yes, but . . ." Then Lotty's gloved hand went to her mouth to stifle a giggle. "Oh. Say no more! Just watch this. I'm going to make Tom Sawyer look like a rank amateur."

She fixed her bonnet, then strolled over to Denny, who had a large rock halfway out of its resting place. Babe watched them talk and gesture. Never had she seen Lotty's smile so fetching.

"What did you tell him?"

"Oh, that I thought him being so big and strong and *manly*, that he should be in charge." She fanned her face with her drawn-up plans. "Just used my feminine wiles." She winked at Babe, then raised her fist in the air and added, "For when 'one of these' won't work."

"Where can I get me some of them feminine wiles?"

"Don't ask me. They just showed up." She shrugged her wee shoulders. "Well, I don't know about you, but I could go for some lemonade."

Babe looked after her in amazement. "Feminine wiles, huh?" She looked at Denny and Hank, now working in harmony to unearth Denny's rock.

She grabbed a pickax and found her own rock to unearth.

47

"Say, I better get going! Those newspapermen will be at the gate at ten." Cleve gave himself a look in the dining room mirror, adjusted his tie, and trimmed his hat. "How do I look?"

"They're coming to interview me, not you, Cleve," Miss V said. "I'm still not sure you calling that reporter was a good idea. Not after all the trouble Egypt stirred up."

"That's why I called him, Miss V. We need good publicity and we need it now."

"Well, I hope you're right. Maybe once people know about my problems up here, someone will step up and help."

"And they should, after all the good you've done this community. All the men you employed. Not to mention your Donation Days," Sarah chimed in.

"I better go escort them in," Cleve said.

"Remember, Cleve," Miss V said. "I'll decide what they need to know and what they don't need to know."

"Yes, ma'am. I'll keep my trap shut."

He left and Miss V climbed down off her chair and headed to her room. "Guess I better gin and tidy up myself."

When it was just Babe and Lotty in the dining room, Babe said, "What do you think about it?"

"Well, it isn't as though getting photographed is anything new to us, Babe. After all, we're a curiosity. And trust me, it's not for postcards."

"Handful of kids carving up a hillside. Guess that's pretty dang curious," Babe said, taking cookies off the plate and putting them in her pocket.

"Well, if it can help Miss V, then why not? Face it, Babe, you and me will get articles written about us for the rest of our days. No matter where we are, no matter what we're doing."

"Yeah, but whose business is it we're here?"

"Did you really think you and me could hide an elephant, an ape, and even a bear probably out there someplace stealing pies off of windowsills?"

Babe smiled at the vision of her Jupiter stealing pies. "No. Guess not."

"Denny!" Sarah shouted from the kitchen. "You are not

wearing that sweater! Now get a clean shirt and collar!"

Sarah popped into the dining room. "What do you think? This blue hat with the peacock feather or this yellow that shows my hair better?" She turned around. "Any of my tattoos show?"

Babe, Lotty, Sarah, Denny, and Miss V stood on the front porch as Cleve rode ahead of the reporter's buggy. With great to-do, he introduced everyone. Babe was reminded of Cleve's show-business background, the way he gestured grandly, shouting play-to-the-gallery words.

Babe was used to wide-eyed, wide-mouthed looks of amazement, awe, even fright. She stood, nearly seven feet tall between the two dwarfs, barely six feet tall put together.

"Let's get that," the reporter said to his cameraman. "Those three on the porch."

"Head to toe?" the man with the camera asked.

"Yes, we want to show their full size."

The cameraman shrugged his shoulders, picked up his camera tripod, and went into the center of the yard to get Babe in full frame.

"Good! Now, hold still . . . Wait! You there, yes, you with the fancy hat. Could you . . . ?" He signaled Sarah to stand aside. "And you, son, you! Move aside. Just the giant and the midgets."

"Dwarfs!" everyone on the porch yelled.

Next, they escorted the newspapermen to the barn, Denny leading the way and jabbering about his role in their excavation adventure. Babe was pretty certain the reporter didn't care anything about the creek or Miss V's problems by the questions he wasn't asking. Instead, he wanted a photograph of all of them now standing with the animals—Miss V, Euclid, Egypt, Lotty, and Babe.

"Now, we heard that elephant went on a rampage. What can you tell me about that?" the reporter asked.

Miss V quickly put his mind to rest about that, but to be on the safe side, didn't let the cameraman close with his flash pan.

"And you say there's also a bear?" the reporter man asked, pencil on a notebook. "I was told he was a man-killer and you just let him go out there to ravage the countryside?"

"Worst he's done is stealing pies," Babe said flatly, having never met a reporter she liked.

They took some more photos, then they took the entire troupe down to the creek. Waiting for them was Hank, also cleaned up, hair slicked back, posing between two shovels stuck in the sand.

A few days later, Denny came galloping in from town, a dozen *Medford Mail* newspapers flapping out from his saddlebags. He handed the papers to everyone on the porch. The article's headline read:

CIRCUS FOLKS AND MONKEYSHINES
AT THE OLD LOGAN MILL
ROGUE ELEPHANT SAFELY CONTAINED

Babe didn't bother struggling to read the article. She knew it would poke fun at all of them. But Miss V was satisfied—it accomplished what they hoped it might. Within days, boys from town showed up, sleeves rolled up, shovels and picks over their shoulders, horses, wagons, skids—anxious to help out and gawk at the dwarf and giant working with the elephant.

A few times a week, Babe, Lotty, and Denny showed off their work to Miss V and the Franklins. It was a good time for Babe to bring Euclid out to give him air and let him run and climb. They brought Miss V down in the pony cart, since the walk was too much a strain on her heart. They were all worried about her—the money, the mill, the landslide, and the extra food for the sudden rush of volunteers.

Also each evening, the prospector, Mr. Luckett, walked his side of the creek, measuring the shoreline, sometimes panning for gold or running water through his sluicing rig.

"Look at that crazy old coot," Miss V said, looking down at him, kneeling now, swishing water out of a pan, inspecting it, tossing it out, and doing it all over again.

"Well, he isn't the one trying to move a mountain,"

Sarah said. "Come on, Miss V. It's getting cold. Let's get you back home."

"I'm fine, Sarah, quit fussing! I like coming here, seeing how far the kids have gotten."

Babe looked around for Euclid and called out for him.

"He's just over there," Lotty said, pointing. "I see his head bobbing."

"Don't want him going too far," Babe said. "Denny, call in Aces and maybe they'll both come back."

"Never thought I'd see the day when a chimp and a dog would keep such fast company," Cleve said.

"Euclid's no dummy," Babe said. "He knows carnie dogs. Aces ain't no dummy, neither. Euclid drops her plenty of treats."

"How's that for a carnie act? The ape and his pet dog!" Cleve laughed. "If we ever go back on the road, Sarah, let's remember that one!"

"Aces! Come, girl!" Denny called.

"Euclid! Come on back now!" Babe called.

Two heads popped up from the bushes. Aces barked and Euclid chirped as they raced each other back.

"What's that you got there, Euclid?" Babe asked. She always knew when he was hiding something—sitting off to the side, ignoring her while he inspected what he'd found. He turned it over and over and then tasted it. "Hand that over," Babe said, reaching her hand down to him. "Come on. You know I'll get it one way or t'other."

After a small tussle, Euclid handed it over, then sat, disgruntled, turning his back on her. "Spoilt sport," Babe mumbled down to him. "What you reckon this is?" She held the small, round, metal box, then shook it. "Some sort of candy box?"

Cleve stepped over. "Let me see that."

"Maybe I can jimmy it open," Babe said, running her thumbnail along the seam.

"No!" Cleve shouted, grabbing it from her. "Don't!"

"What is it, Cleve?" Miss V asked.

"Blasting caps! Whole box of them!"

Everyone but Babe took a step back. "What're blasting caps?"

"Dangerous, that's what they are," he said. He placed the tin on a tree stump, away from the gathering. "Miss V, I don't remember us using any blasting caps. Do you?"

"No, never," she said.

Cleve walked carefully, inspecting the brush where Euclid and Aces were sniffing around. He knelt down, tugged at something, then came back holding a couple of feet of wire.

"I think I know what caused the landslide," he said.

"You mean, someone blasted it? On purpose? But why? Who would . . . ?" Miss V said. "Wait a minute! Who else uses those things around here but a prospector?"

She glared down at Luckett on his side of the creek. "You kids take the animals away. No telling what other explosives have been left here," Cleve said.

Miss V stood up in the pony cart, opened the door, and jumped out. She lifted her skirts and started picking her way downhill.

"Miss V, where . . . ?" Sarah said, going after her.

"You know where I'm going!"

Everyone looked at one another, unsure of what to do. "You best come on, Miss V," Cleve said. "I'll go talk to him. You go back."

Miss V ignored him and turned to Babe. "I hate to ask you, Babe, but could you carry me?" Babe looked back at the others. Should she?

"Babe, please!" She leaned down to pick her up. "No, I'll just hold on to your neck."

Babe gingerly took a few steps downhill.

"Thanks for doing this," Miss V said. "My heart's already going like sixty! I'm just so mad!"

Babe picked her way down the hillside and into the creek. Luckett kept swishing water in his pan. Finally, Babe stopped, her shadow darkening Luckett, who still didn't look up.

"Any luck, *Lucky*?" Miss V asked as Babe swung her gently down.

"You're trespassing," Luckett said, running a hand through the sand in the pan. "And you're in my light."

Miss V stood next to Luckett and demanded, "What do you know about blasting caps?"

Still, he kept panning. "I know they go boom."

"And what do you know about 'going boom' over there on *my* side of the creek?" She stood with her hands on her hips.

"Unlike you, I stay on my own side of the creek."

"We found a tin of blasting caps and evidence of dynamite. Someone blew my hillside apart!"

"Looks like," he said.

"Why did you do it?" Miss V demanded.

Babe watched their faces as they talked to—at—each other.

"Better question is why *would* I do that?" Luckett mumbled.

"So, so, you could claim more of this creek! So you could blast out some gold. So you could sit here, panning for something you know you'll never find!" Her voice got higher, louder; her face redder. She added a resounding "For spite!"

Now he looked at her. "Spite? What spite? Good God, Val, you and me pulled the pin years ago!"

Babe turned, feeling like she shouldn't be listening to this.

"Yes, spite! I can't even log now because of your . . . your . . ." She stopped and glowered at him. "Yes, that's it! Every success I ever had made you angry! You broke it off, sir! Not me!" She paused to catch a breath.

"It wasn't because of your success, Val! It was because of that man and you know it!"

"Excuse me, Miss V," Babe broke in, now very uncomfortable. "You want I should just come back for you?"

"No, she's leaving! Kindly get to your own side of the creek and don't you ever come over here accusing me of anything other than being a good and quiet neighbor."

Quite a spiel for a crazy old man of few words. Babe might not have known much about spite, men, and break-ups, but she knew spitfire when it flew back and forth.

"Come on, Babe! Let's go!" She turned on her tiny feet and swished her skirts with a snap. "Take me back and—" She stopped, suddenly unable to speak. Her face froze in pain and she gasped for air.

"Quick!" Mr. Luckett hollered, tossing the pan down and coming to her side. He caught her before she fell and pulled open her high-collared shirt. "Quick!" he said, handing Babe the handkerchief from around his neck. "Wet this."

She quickly did and handed it back. "What is it? Her heart?"

"Do you know where she keeps them?"

"Keeps what?"

"Her nitro!" He looked for something around her neck, then her wrists.

She gasped for air and clutched her chest. She pulled at her broach.

Luckett pulled the broach off, fingered it for the tiny latch, then sprang it open. Babe spied the tiny tablets inside. He took one out. "Come on, Val. Quick. Under your tongue."

Miss V squeezed her eyes tight in pain. He pulled her to his chest, rubbed her back, and whispered in her ear. "Easy, Val, easy. Relax and let it work. Let it dissolve. Easy, easy. Stay with us." He rocked her like she was a child or, no, Babe thought, he rocked her like she was an old and very good friend.

He looked up at Babe and said softly, "I didn't blast her hillside. She's got to know that. God, I've loved this woman. I'd never do that. My shed was broken into and my explosives were taken last summer. That's all I know." Then he said down to Miss V, "Come on, Val. You're okay."

Her eyes finally fluttered and some color returned to her face. Slowly, her breathing steadied and all the while, Luckett dabbed her face and forehead and held her.

"Is that better?" he asked.

"Yes, yes, thank you," she whispered.

"You sure?"

"Things are a little hazy."

He looked at Babe. "All you folks over there need to know where she keeps these pills. You should have them everywhere, all the time. They just saved her life." Then, down at her, he added, "Valerie, these don't do you any good if you don't let people know where you hide them."

"Must you lecture me?"

"How many times do you think you can have these spells? What's that hillside and this creek have to do with your life? Can't you just . . ."

"Stop it! I don't need your advice to run my life!" she gasped out, coming back into her old self. She looked over to Babe. "I told you moving that hillside won't work. He'll just blow it up again."

"Okay, now you're trespassing again," he growled, giving Miss V a gentle hand up.

Babe watched the silence between them, wondering what the heck these two were . . . friends, enemies, lovers? What? Are they going to go three rounds or walk off, hand in hand?

"Come on, Babe. I need to get home and rest."

Once again, Babe got her aboard, but her body felt a bit limp now.

"Careful now," Luckett said, pulling Babe back by the arm. "She's going to have one hell of a headache." To Miss V, he added, "Three days' bed rest. No less."

"All right. All right," Miss V whispered back, all the fight drained out of her. "Doctor."

Babe nearly lost her balance. *Doctor?*

Cleve rushed to meet Babe as she trekked back up the hillside. "Oh my God, what happened over there?" He took Miss V and placed her gently into the pony cart. "Are you all right?"

"I'm fine."

"She had a heart spell. That man, that Luckett, he knew all about it and found her pills."

"Come on, let's get you home, Miss V," Sarah said.

"That Luckett! . . . Makes me so angry I could eat iron and spit nails!" Miss V said, holding her head. "Ow."

"He said you got to rest now, Miss V," Babe said.

"God forbid I don't do what he tells me!"

Babe couldn't tell if she was being snotty or what. Luckett just saved her life. Shouldn't she show a speck of thanks?

Babe watched as they disappeared up the path. She looked back across the river where Luckett was standing, watching. She took the trail back to the barnyard to check on Euclid.

49

Babe knew when she heard Aces's tail *whomp whomp whomp*ing on the wood floor that Denny was in her room.

"Oh!" he said, whipping around. He was holding a photo. "I put Euclid in his cage."

"Thank you."

"Is this you?" he asked. It was a photo of Magnifica lifting a fake five-hundred-pound weight.

"That's John L. Sullivan," she said, setting her jaw.

"Oh, go on! That's you."

"You got a reason to be here in my room?"

"Uh . . ." He held up Euclid's leash. "Just returning this."

"There's a hook on his cage for that."

"Oh. Well, here." He handed her the leash.

"So, which of you boys blasted that hillside?"

His ruddy face went blank. "Huh?"

"Luckett says his blasting caps and dynamite was stold from his storage shed. Sort of queer—him getting things tooken, that hillside blowing up, and then Euclid finding them blasting caps."

"What's it to you? You're just some freak coming here and making like you own the place! Things were fine with all of us until you showed up!"

"Miss V near died thinking Luckett blasted that hillside. You can live with that?"

"She did?" He finally looked her in the eyes.

"Yes, she did."

"Well, she already hates him. Everyone knows he jilted her! Ma's even got newspaper stories about it!"

"You're changing the subject."

"Come on, Aces. Let's get out of this sideshow!"

Babe stepped in front of him.

"You got to tell Miss V what you done. You got to take the blame. And how about you own up to Luckett?"

"Out of my way, you . . ."

She pulled him around by his arm and gave him a Magnifica glare.

"Look! I didn't steal the stuff; I didn't set the explosives! Hank did . . . !"

His voice trailed off. His sandy hair fell down into his bright blue eyes and he smiled up at Babe. She knew what was coming. He was going to try to charm her just like so many other men had tried.

"Babe, look, it was a year ago! It was an accident! Hank found the stuff and we thought it'd be fun to make some noise, that's all! It was an accident! Who knew the whole dang hillside would fall in?"

"You made noise, all right. Didn't your folk wonder what that was?"

"They were all in Medford on business. Aw, come on, Babe. Don't tell. A girl like you must know it's just boys being boys. You know how it is."

"Sure I know how it is. And here's how it's going to be: you keep working, dawn till dusk, till we get that big cedar tree moved and I don't say nothing what I know."

"Why, sure, Babe. I'll keep working. But there is no way we can get that huge tree out of that stream." He cast her his devilish smile. "I suppose we could blast it out."

"Your pa put the kibosh on that, remember? Said it would ruin that stream all the more. So you're coming to help even if you have to help pick up that tree a splinter at a time, hear?"

"All right. I'll work right up to when school starts."

"And something else." She ticked her head toward Aces, sleeping in a patch of sunlight streaming through the window. "You make sure her pups gots good homes. You understand?"

"But Pa says to . . ."

Babe took a step closer to him.

"Okay, okay. I'll put a note on the bulletin board at the

post office. So, it's a deal? You don't tell?"

"Fine." She pointed to the door. "Now leave and don't you ever come in here without I say, understand?"

"Sure. Sure."

He left and Babe pulled the heavy door closed. Aces didn't even look up when Denny left. Babe knelt down and rubbed the dog's long, warm ears. "Don't you worry none, Aces. Ol' Babe'll see to your babies."

"Gosh, it's a bit chilly this morning," Lotty said. She, Babe, and Cleve wanted to get to the creek early. "We can barely see the creek. Why all this morning fog all of a sudden?"

Cleve draped his jacket over her shoulders. She wrapped the sleeves around her twice and tied them. "Sometimes happens in August. Reckon the whole Medford valley is fogged in. You warm enough, Babe?"

She noted there was nothing extra for her to put on. "I'm fine."

"Saw two woodpeckers working on the same tree the other day," Cleve said.

Babe and Lotty exchanged puzzled glances.

"Going to be a tough winter," Cleve went on. "Fog, woodpeckers doubling up. And have you heard the geese heading south already?"

"Ain't that normal?" Babe asked.

"Yeah, normal for forecasting a hard winter. If we're going to get this creek back, it better happen fast." He walked ahead.

"I don't like the sound of that," Lotty said, tapping Egypt with her handler's rod. "Come on. The others should be arriving pretty soon." She followed Cleve down to the creek.

Babe looked up through the fog and scanned the canopy of trees, looking for woodpeckers and listening for geese.

One by one, the others arrived. Hank rode up on a horse wearing a hauling rig; Denny had harnessed Ajax to a dump wagon. Boys from town and surrounding farms arrived with shovels and picks. Egypt stood, restless and chained, off to the side.

They all stood looking down at the giant, old cedar. The one last huge problem holding the stream back.

"Maybe Egypt could push it enough to break it loose," Lotty said.

"No, how about we fulcrum it up, maybe enough to break the suction and get some chains around it," Cleve said. He knelt down and drew his plan in the sandy bank. "See? Once we get a chain around it, then Egypt should be able to pull it free."

"Worth a try," Lotty said.

They set the strongest boys in a line, each one holding an iron pole or a sturdy piece of lumber. Babe chose a large-pole pine. They spaced themselves every three feet apart downside of the tree.

"Now, kids, we have to work together on this!" Cleve called out, taking a pole and securing it under the log. "Get your poles as far under the log as you can."

"This water's freezing!" Denny said, standing in the deepest part.

"Ready everyone?" Lotty called out from the shore. "One, two, *threeeeeee!*"

The team grunted, pushed, groaned. Then, snap! Crash! Two boys lost their grip, fell over the log and into the creek. Two of the wood poles burst in half. The tree didn't move an inch. Babe wondered if the creek didn't want to let the tree go or if the tree was just plain stubborn.

Two more tries. More spills, more broken poles, pulled backs and again, the tree didn't budge. Cleve called everyone back to the shore.

"Never seed a more orn'ry tree," Babe said. "Fighting us tooth and nail."

"Wait," Lotty said, shading her eyes and looking up-creek, then down-creek. "We're pushing against the current. We need to pry it downstream, not up. Why didn't we see that in the first place?"

"But then we risk that tree snagging downstream and then causing a logjam," Cleve said. "Might even dam the whole creek and then we have huge problems, not to mention killing the salmon runs."

"Well, if the tree is too big, why don't we just make it smaller?" Babe asked. "Cut 'er up. You know, get them two-man saws. Them long ones you got hanging in the barn."

"Sure! Once the tree is cut up into pieces, we can easily roll the sections out of the creek!" Lotty said.

It was Babe's idea to use the saws. But it was Denny's idea to make it a contest between teams. It was Hank's idea to place bets. And it was Lotty's idea to be the bookmaker.

"Okay, but how do we choose the teams?" Cleve asked. "I mean, we have to make it fair."

"Just like in softball at school," Denny said.

Cleve tossed an ax handle up in the air and six hands knew to grab for it. The order they grabbed, top to bottom, was the order they picked partners. Meanwhile, Lotty drove Ajax up to load the saws from the barn.

Babe hadn't been picked first for anything since they played tug-of-war at school. She stood next to Hank, who grinned ear to ear. The difference in their heights was comical.

Across the creek Luckett had stopped his panning and sat on his shoreline chair, watching the commotion. Babe reckoned they looked like a carnie—animals, equipment, people shouting, laughing. What an odd collection of curiosities and delights.

Saws were passed out and the teams had taken their places in the water.

"Everyone all set?" Lotty called out.

Six saws set on top of the log.

"Now, I know trees, Babe," Hank said. "Make sure we keep away from knots. And remember, you got to get a feel for how strong I can pull."

"You just take care you don't fly acrost the creek when I pull back," Babe said, grinning at him.

"That's what I mean, Babe. Pull back with the same strength as me. Otherwise, we'll get the blade stuck. This old saw is rusty to begin with."

"On the count of three! One! Two! Three!" Lotty shouted.

The teams began sawing, shouting, sawing, cursing. Sawdust and water flew all around them. You! Me! You! Me! Pull! Push! Pull!

"Take it easy, Babe!" She'd nearly pulled Hank over the log on her first few pulls. "Easy!" They quickly found their own rhythm. Five, six, seven inches into the tree, with six more inches before they would be sawing underwater. Babe stole a look over her shoulder at the team next to them. Their saw got stuck and *twang!* The cursing and blame went back and forth when their saw no longer did.

Within twenty minutes she and Hank knocked the spots off everyone else. Babe knew she looked a sight. Red, hot face dotted with sawdust and sand; hair undone and hanging in her face, soaking from head to toe, but she didn't remember ever having so much fun. She and Hank started for the creek's shore. Hank stepped into a hole and Babe was quick to grab him by his collar.

"I got you!" she said, pulling him up with a jerk.

"Thanks, pardner!" he said. He started to clap her on the back, then stopped. "I mean, thanks, miss!" He gave her a sweeping bow, picking up a hatful of water. "After you!" He placed his hat on his head and looked perfectly charming, red hair and all, muddy and drenched.

The declared winners reached land to applause, handshakes, and back pats. Babe glanced across the creek—even Luckett was standing, clapping.

"Babe! You were wonderful! I knew you'd win!" Lotty said, running up to her. "You should have seen Denny's face when Hank picked you!"

"First time ever, Lotty! First time I'm happy I'm he-man strong!"

Babe grinned, not caring a tinker's dam about her big red lips, her piano-key teeth. She had to figure this is what being a kid is like! Recess! Baseball! Socials!

But only two teams had cut through their section of the log, so Babe went back to work each time with a different boy working the other side. Soon seven sections of tree lay in the stream.

Now it was Egypt's turn. Lotty rode and commanded.

"No, Egypt!" she shouted. "We're not swimming today!"

"She doesn't want to work! She wants to play!" Denny

cried, laughing and pointing as Egypt filled her trunk with water. She lobbed her trunk back and forth playfully, splashing water toward the shore.

Babe was wading in the water next to Egypt, helping Lotty move the elephant toward the task at hand. "Should I?" Lotty asked, giving Babe a wicked grin.

"I think you should," Babe answered. "Let me get out of the way first."

On command, Egypt aimed her water-loaded trunk toward the shore. At first shocked, then delighted, the kids roared with laughter and it soon became one huge water fight.

But Lotty got Egypt settled and back to work. One by one, the sections of logs were pulled out of the creek. Bit by bit, the creek was becoming a stream again.

Then a rumbling sound—so far away, so vague, few noticed. Then a few rocks came tumbling down the hillside. Everyone turned, looked up. More of the hillside began to shear away. No one moved. A few more rocks stumbled down, followed by some rivulets of sand. Now everyone scattered back along the shore.

Lotty and Babe moved closer together. "Oh no. It can't start all over again, it just can't!" Lotty said, almost as a prayer.

"Hey! You kids! Get off that hillside!" Cleve shouted. Three little kids from town had been watching from above.

They scrambled away and the hillside was quiet and still once more.

It was a wonder to behold—slowly, inch by inch, the creek restaked its claim like a gentle incoming tide.

All and all, quite a day.

51

"Always working, huh, Babe?" Lotty said, bringing a glass of lemonade over from the house. "You spent the last two days cleaning up down at the creek and now this?"

"Them fence posts ain't made for elephant-scratching posts, so I'm digging deeper holes. Remember, Egypt can't never get loose again, Lotty."

"I know. Come on. Get out of the sun. Have some lemonade. I feel guilty with you out here doing all the work."

"Thought you was getting fitted for fancy school clothes for your fancy high school," Babe said, trying to keep the pinch of jealousy out of her voice.

"Well, we're just altering some of Miss V's old clothes. You know, she's really going to insist you register for school, too."

"We been through this, Lotty. Ain't going and that's a fact. Cleve said he'd help me with some primers. Ain't going until I can be with folk my own age." She downed the lemonade in a single gulp.

"If you think clearing that landslide was hard, wait until you go up against Miss V on this."

Babe handed the glass back to Lotty, then pointed toward the world beyond. "I'll walk away sure as anything before I'll go to school. I'm done with upsetting desks and dunce caps and all that."

"They don't have dunce caps anymore!"

"They'll make one for me! Ain't going to school!"

"That's another thing! *Ain't!* You're always wanting to speak better. Thought you wanted to lady up some," Lotty said. "You want to spend your life talking like a hick from the hills?"

"I *am* a hick from the hills!"

"Well, maybe that's where you belong!" Lotty shouted. "Maybe you should just go back to the hills! Go be a lumberjack now that Miss V can start up the mill again! Or, I know! Go be a hermit like that Luckett!"

"Why you so mad?" Babe demanded. Lotty was silent. She turned her back on Babe and looked into the empty lemonade glass. "Lotty?"

"Because you're still living in a barn, but I'm living high and mighty. You're digging fence posts and I'm getting new clothes. Because I've found a home and you've found . . . what?"

"I've found I don't belong here any more'n I belong sipping tea with the queen of England."

Lotty looked up at her friend. "I think maybe you might be right, Babe. But where? Where do you belong?"

Babe shrugged her giant shoulders. "Rosa said maybe she could find me a place if she gets that big house of hers. I writ her, but she ain't writ back."

"You wrote her?"

"Yes, asking if maybe I could come and help with her big house."

"What's this about a big house?" Lotty looked at her with narrow eyes.

"Said she was going to find her a big house for lots of folk."

"What? Like a boardinghouse? Don't make me laugh!"

Babe felt her face redden as the beast gurgled to life. "Stop that!"

"Sure, I can just see Madame de la Rosa passing the mashed potatoes and washing sheets once a week. Somehow, I don't think that's the kind of house . . ."

The sound of horses trotting up the road broke their argument.

Babe squinted toward the riders. Denny and . . .

"Lotty. We got trouble."

"Look who I found on the road!" Denny shouted, sliding off his horse before it had come to a stop. "This man was coming out to see us. Says he's an old friend! What's your name again?"

The man took off his hat, gave a dramatic sweep from atop his horse, and announced, "Phillipe Renoir. At your service."

Lotty stepped closer to Babe.

"No one here needs your service," Babe managed. Her whole body was pounding, and her hands formed into fists. He slid down off his horse and she smelled the gooey sweetness of his hair pomade. He handed the reins to Denny and walked toward them.

"Is that any way to greet an old friend?"

"There ain't nothing for you here, Renoir," Babe said.

"I'm going to tell Ma we have a guest for lunch!" Denny chirped. "A real circus ringmaster! Man!" he shouted, running backward across the barnyard to the house. "Yee-ha!"

"Ringmaster? Ha! Maybe of a flea circus!" Lotty said.

Renoir looked Babe up and down. "You know, Magnifica, I think you've grown. Maybe beefed up some. Tan as a roustabout!"

"You better just leave!" Lotty barked.

"And you," he continued, stooping down to speak to Lotty face-to-face. "I think you've grown smaller."

"Nothing for you here," Babe repeated, stepping into his light.

"I think there is."

"None of us are interested in you or your cheap dog and pony shows. We're done with that!" Lotty yelled.

"Well, actually, one of you *isn't* done with that."

"Get back on that horse and leave," Babe said.

"After that wonderful invitation to lunch? That would be rude."

He pulled out a piece of paper. Babe knew what it was even before he unfolded it. Miss V had framed the same newspaper article. "I'll happily leave. Once I get my property back," he said, holding up the article. "You can't deny this is Euclid."

"Babe," Lotty said, touching her arm.

"Just have him caged up and at the train station in Medford by this time tomorrow and all your troubles will be over."

"Euclid isn't yours! You cheated us! You left him off the inventory!" Lotty hollered. "You cheated us!"

"Perhaps you should read contracts a little more carefully, ladies."

"He's old and isn't fit for carnie life!" Lotty screamed, her beautiful face now pink with anger.

"The taxidermist can fix that. He'll have him looking young and ferocious in no time. Little stuffing here, little hair dye there, sparkling new eyeballs—nothing to it." He watched Babe's face as he talked. She wasn't scared, wasn't even worried.

"Lotty, go tell Sarah we don't got company after all."

"I think I better get . . ."

"Everything's fine, Lotty. Everything's just fine." For the first time ever, Babe had Phillipe Renoir just where she wanted him.

Lotty hesitantly backed away, leaving Babe staring down at Renoir. "Euclid's this way."

Euclid started shrieking and jumping up and down when Renoir approached. "Son-of-a-bitch beast!" Renoir shouted, pointing to the fresh, pink scar on his face. "Look what you did to me, you . . ."

Euclid charged at him, screaming, grabbing for him.

Babe handed him Euclid's leash and collar. She remembered when Lotty pulled the same stunt with Egypt. "Want him? Let's see you take him. Careful now, his cage door ain't locked." She pointed to his scarred face. "Reckon you know how he can slip a latch."

Renoir pulled out a small Derringer pistol from his vest pocket.

"That animal should be put down, I tell you. He's a man-killer."

"Well he ain't the man-killer sporting him a gun. Gimme that cap shooter." She easily snapped it out of his hand.

He fumbled for it, but Babe held it over her head and placed it on top of the main beam running through the barn.

"You and me got some fair commerce to trade on," Babe said. "Come in here where I got paper and pencil."

She slid the door to her room open. "Let's us get down to the last pitch. You took Euclid thinking I'd come after him. You don't want that ape any more'n you want me back in your cheap mud opera. I'm thinking it has to do with the California State Bank and your fancy back-east investors."

"You figured that all by yourself? You're quite the brain trust."

"There's paper on the desk. You write up Euclid is mine free and clear and you get your deposit ticket back. Been keeping it nice and safe all this time."

"You're bluffing. Why, you don't even know who my investors are."

"Sure I do." Babe stood her ground, hoping her voice didn't quaver in her lie. "Got it from good sources."

"Who?"

"Ina. Mina. Tina. Rosa and Serena. That's a powerful full house, don't you think? They all got the goods on you and handed 'em over to me."

He glared at her, twitching his lips in thought. He sat and quickly wrote out something. "There. I didn't use any big words, so you can understand it."

She gave it a squint, then handed it back. "You forgot something."

"Now what?"

"Eighty dollar."

"What the hell for?"

"Care and feeding of *your* ape lo these last weeks."

"You've slipped a cog, Babe."

"I got the ape and I got the ticket, Renoir. I even got your pretty little parlor pistol. Make that one hundred dollar."

She put out her hand and snapped her fingers. He sighed and counted out five twenty-dollar gold coins.

"Write it up. Fair commerce."

He added another line. "I assume this meets with your approval, Your *High*ness."

"Sign it."

"Okay, but pencil isn't legal for a document."

"Maybe you prefer blood?" Babe's heart was racing. Had she really done it? Outsmarted Renoir? Now, to just get him out of here!

"Okay, okay," he sighed, scratching his signature and handing Babe the pencil. "Now you sign. You can write your name, can't you?"

Babe scribbled her name. He held out his hand. "And

now, my deposit ticket, if you please?"

"Turn around."

He did and Babe pulled up the horsehair conjure bag from down her front. "You can turn around now." She handed him the ticket, still rolled tight.

She took the agreement he'd signed and placed it on top of a shelf, well out of his reach.

"Hey! Wait just a minute here!" he yelled. Euclid echoed his yell from his cage. He held up the paper. "All the ink's run on this!"

She gave it a casual glance and shrugged her mighty shoulders. "Well, how 'bout that? Must've got wet. Lots of wettning in these parts."

"You mean? You mean?" He shook his head. "You know, a lady would give me back my hundred bucks."

"I don't see no lady here."

He sighed heavily. "I have never met a freak who didn't lie, cheat, or steal."

"Ain't that a odd curiosity?" Babe said. "Even a delight."

He glared up at her.

"Never want to see you again, Renoir," she growled, still seething from all he'd done to her, wanted to do to her, tried to do to her. Wanting to kill someone and knowing you could—with your own two, giant hands—was a powerful and fearful thing, and the sooner he left, the better.

Euclid made one last swipe toward Renoir as he walked past his cage. Outside, Renoir untied his horse and turned to Babe. "Buy yourself something nice with that money. I know! A piano."

"What do I need a piano for?"

"Well, for the box, of course! Where else can a giant like you get a coffin big enough?"

She grabbed him by the coat and swallowed the urge to crush him like a cheap carnival trinket, but instead let go and shoved him into his horse. "It'll take a hundred hat boxes to bury you if ever I see you again, Renoir!"

He mounted up, giving her a last look of pity, spurred his horse, and disappeared down the road.

Before she could mumble good riddance, a shot rang out.

The barn!

Euclid was lying on the floor, not moving. Renoir's pistol was next to him.

"My god! What happened?" Miss V said, rushing into the barn with the others.

"Euclid's shot!" Babe cried. He was breathing, but his breath was fast, uneven, and short. He groaned when Babe picked him up.

"It's his thigh. Right there," Lotty said. "Quick. We need to stop the bleeding."

Miss V knelt down. "Denny, get the first aid box."

"I don't understand. What happened?" Cleve asked.

"He got a pistol I hid! Blast me! I should have locked his cage!" Babe stroked Euclid's head. His eyes fluttered. "Easy, ol' man."

Denny returned with the first aid box. "Where's that ringmaster man? Did he do this?"

"No, I did this!" Babe cried.

"Someone better tell me what's going on here," Miss V said.

"Can you fix him?" Babe asked Cleve, ignoring Miss V.

"Sit down and hold him still. If we're lucky, the bullet went straight through." Cleve moved the ape's leg, but Euclid swatted at the pain, growled, and flashed his teeth.

"I'm sorry, I'm sorry, I'm sorry," Babe whispered in his ear. She held him tight and rocked him.

"Babe, it's not your fault," Lotty said, reaching to comfort her.

"Hold him still," Miss V said, helping Sarah get his leg bandaged. "Denny, go call the vet in Medford. Get him up here. Don't tell him what it's for!"

He dashed out of the barn.

"Sarah," Cleve said, "see if there's any morphine in the box."

"No, Cleve, don't you remember? You gave it to Frank Mahan when he broke his hip," Sarah said.

Sarah picked up a brown bottle. "Babe, do you think

he can have laudanum? It'll help his pain and make him sleep."

Euclid started to whimper. "I don't know what to do. I wisht I knew more. What can I give him what won't make it worst?" Babe asked, looking at each adult. Then, to Sarah, "How much would you give a youngin?"

"Just a little." She pulled out the dropper and handed it to Babe. "Here. See if you can get this down him. Don't let him bite it off."

He fought it and twice spit it out, but the third time she clamped his jaw shut until he swallowed. She couldn't bear looking at his frightened eyes looking up at her.

"Come on, Babe. Put him in his cage and let him rest," Lotty said.

"I ain't leaving him. This is all my fault, and I ain't leaving him."

"Then I'll bring you something," Sarah said. "Come on, Miss V. You're looking exhausted."

"Operator said the vet's phone doesn't answer," Denny said, out of breath.

"Well, go back and keep trying!" Miss V snapped.

The barn grew silent as the adults exchanged glances. Euclid was fighting falling asleep but was soon in a deep sleep on Babe's lap.

"Come on. Everyone to the house. Lunch is getting cold," Sarah said.

* * *

Alone in the barn, Babe rocked Euclid in her lap. He seemed to be dreaming and jerked his head about. "Don't fight it," Babe whispered. "Sleep, sleep." She carefully carried him to her room, set him down on her bed, tucking her quilt around him to hold him safe and warm.

Several hours later, Babe left the barn for some fresh air. The heat of the day was beginning to peak. The screen door to the house slammed shut and Lotty walked toward her, carrying a tray.

"Here's something to eat. How is he?"

"Sleeping. That laudanum worked. Lotty, I dang near killt him. First by leaving that gun where he could get it and then I didn't lock his cage." She looked away, not wanting Lotty to see her cry. "How can I be so stupid? I was feeling so cocky pulling the wool over Renoir's eyes. Got him to leave, got him to give me money, got him out of our lifes, but . . ."

"Babe, you can't blame yourself. It was an accident."

"Everything in my damn life is a accident, starting with me."

"Come on, Babe. You know better. Here. Let's sit in the shade while you eat. Want some lemonade?"

"No, thanks."

"But . . . Babe . . ." Her words slipped away as she set the tray on a bench outside the barn door.

"You don't got to say nothing, Lotty," Babe said, giving her friend a slight smile.

Lotty began to back away. "Well, anyway, you better eat something. Your favorite pie is under that napkin."

Babe didn't eat. Didn't sleep. She did nothing but sit next to Euclid, watching him.

Several hours past dusk, Euclid stirred awake. "Ssssh, ol' man." Babe put her hand on his forehead to soothe him back to sleep, but her hand shot back fast, as though she didn't want to believe what she felt. She touched his forehead again, then ran her hand down his face.

Euclid was on fire.

Babe paced her room, talking to herself. "What're you going to do, Babe? Vet's in Medford. That's a piece away, even if he's around."

She looked out the barn door toward the house. The only light was coming from the moon. Euclid was now restless and moaning. Babe felt the weight of the five gold coins from Renoir in her pocket tapping her thigh as she paced. She jingled her pocket absently. "What good's gold for a vet if I can't get me a vet?"

Her hand dove into her pocket for her bandanna. Her fingers touched the gold coins. "Wait! I know!"

She quickly, but carefully wrapped Euclid in the quilt. Gently, she scooped him into her arms. He moaned and growled.

"Ssssh," she said. "Ain't getting you a vet. Getting you a doctor. Sssssh. You just let your ol' Babe tote you."

She knew he didn't understand her words, but he understood her voice. Her thoughts raged as she carried him out of the barn and into the night. She realized critters knew pain, maybe they even knew what death was. But did they know to fight for life? If he didn't fight for his, she'd fight for him!

She headed down the path to the creek. As well as she knew the path by now, she stepped lightly, careful to keep her balance, trying not to jiggle Euclid.

The creek wasn't as deep now, but it ran faster. It wasn't often Babe was happy for her size and her strength, as she easily and quickly forded the water. She scooped up a handful of water and patted some on Euclid's burning face. "Shhhshhh," she whispered, coming onto the shore. "Almost there."

But now what? Luckett had a house somewhere, but where? She followed the shore of the creek, passing through the gold-mining rig. Looking through the forest for a light, she caught the faint scent of wood burning.

She stepped over logs and snapped any branches that got

in her way. She passed Luckett's storage shed and waited for the moon to come out from a cloud to look for a path.

"Stop right there!"

Babe froze. "Mr. Luckett? It's me! Babe, the giant girl!"

"What the hell are you doing here?"

"Please, sir. I need help. My Euclid's gun shot. I need help."

Their eyes adjusted and the moon reflected the steely shine of his rifle.

"What? Who's shot?"

Babe pulled away the blanket. The rifle came down. Luckett looked up at Babe. "Your ape?"

"Please, sir. I seed you tend to Miss V. She called you doctor. You got to help me. He's got a bullet in his leg."

"Okay. Come on. Bring him up to the house. Follow me. Watch that log, there."

The path widened and the light from his house shone through the trees.

"Come on. Up here," he said, leading the way to the side of his house where a sign over the door read "Infirmary."

He opened the door, and Babe stepped inside. Cobwebs hung from the rafters, sheets covered the furnishings.

"Here, on the table," he said, lighting two more lamps and hanging them on poles. He pulled off the dusty sheet and the examination table under it gleamed porcelain-white in the lamplight.

"Can you get him to hold still?" Luckett asked, adjusting his glasses and unwrapping the blood-soaked bandages.

She held Euclid's head with one hand and forced his wounded leg down with the other. "Ssssh, Euclid. We got us help now."

"Small caliber. That's good."

"Just a dinky parlor gun," Babe said.

When he turned Euclid's leg over it was easy to tell some of the fight had gone out of the ape. "Don't you give in, *monkey*," she whispered down to him. Then to Luckett, "Can you take the bullet out? Will that fix him?"

"Hold his head. I don't want to get bit."

"Hesh, Euclid. He won't hurt you."

His eyes looked pleadingly up at her. His mouth opened, but only a trickle of blood came out.

"He might have internal injuries," Luckett said, seeing the horror on Babe's face.

"What's that mean?"

"His insides. Did he take a fall?"

"Yes. But he's got good balance and . . ."

"Maybe not with a bullet in him. I have to sedate him. He's moving too much. God, I hope chloroform doesn't kill him."

Babe thought her heart would break into a million pieces. She'd cut off her own leg to take away his fear and his pain. Luckett brought out a bottle and a wad of cotton.

"He'll probably fight this," he said, pouring some sweet-smelling chloroform onto the cotton. Babe held Euclid's head but in just a few breaths, he was asleep.

"If you're squeamish, you best stand aside," Luckett said, spreading the bullet hole open with his fingers. More blood gushed out.

"I ain't the swooning type," she said, stroking Euclid's head while Luckett took forceps and probed the wound.

"Got it!" He pulled the forceps out, the tiny bullet in its grip. He doused the wound with antiseptic, then stitched the hole up.

"Okay, hold his legs still in case he moves. I want to see if I can feel anything else broken inside."

He stopped and looked over to Babe. "What?" she asked.

"I'm feeling fluid. I wonder if it's blood pooling."

"Like he's maybe, what? Broke up inside?" She barely got the words out.

"Yes. It could be just that."

"Can you open him up and fix it?"

"Not on top of everything else. That would kill him. The best I can do is keep him sedated and see, well, see what happens." He took his stethoscope off the surgical tray and listened. "Does his heart usually run fast?"

"I don't know," she whispered, shaking her head, not caring that Luckett saw her crying. "I don't know."

Luckett's lips moved as he counted some beats. "I wish

I knew. I'll keep a chart and see how it changes. Maybe I can figure out what's normal for him."

Babe looked down, huge tears dropping onto the sheets holding Euclid on the table. Luckett touched her arm and smiled kindly. "Why don't we let him rest and I'll make us some coffee? The stove's still lit."

"I can make the coffee. Just show me where."

"That door there opens to the kitchen."

Babe stoked up the cookstove, filled the pot, and ground some coffee beans. Luckett came in, propping the door open so they could watch Euclid.

He sat at the table, ran his hand through his thick gray hair, and looked into his coffee cup. Babe sat on a barrel in the corner, holding her own coffee in trembling hands.

"Come sit here at the table."

Babe indicated the spindly chairs. "Here's fine."

"Come on. Roll the barrel over here. You're a guest and you'll sit at my table."

She did but still towered over the table and Luckett. He gave her a long, curious look. "When did you start? Growing, that is?"

"Giants ain't borned, they're made," she said.

"I know. You're the third person with gigantism I've met in my medical practice," he said. Babe returned his long, serious look. This Luckett was a far cry from the prospector at the creek.

"Folk told me I was right as rain till I was about three

month and then . . . *POOOOSH!*" She spread her fingers wide like Madame de la Rosa did over her crystal ball. "Well, up I come. And don't worry. I won't ask you to cure me. I know there ain't no cure for what I got. No magic potion I can drink and shrink down, like that Alice girl in her Wonderland."

"No, there isn't."

"Mind if I ask you something?"

"Depends."

"Are you a doctor for real?"

"For real, yes."

"Don't look like you get much business," she said, ticking her head toward the infirmary.

"That's because I haven't practiced since Val's mill stopped running. I was the company doctor. Lots of injuries, lumberjacking and mill work." He looked down into his coffee mug in his cupped hands. "Hard work, but nothing like battlefield work."

"You was a war doctor?"

"Yes. When the War between the States ended, I walked away, headed west. A man can amputate only so many legs and arms; pull out only so many bullets; listen to screams; watch boys die."

He sighed. Babe didn't know what to say.

"Anyway, not much call for a doc up here anymore, since they opened a clinic in the area. Fancy, back-east doctors. Fine with me. I like panning for gold. There's hope in that. Hardly any hope when a kid shows up with a leg blown off."

"And Miss V? You doctor her?"

"Also a long time ago," he stated flatly. "We were once . . . well, very good friends. But now, we stay on our own sides of . . ." He paused, smiled sadly, and added, "Heartbreak Creek. Huh. Never thought about that name before."

"Lotty and me figured that name out real fast. But Miss V says it's called that on account of there ain't no gold in that creek and that breaks a man's heart."

He smiled across the table at her. "No gold, but there *is* hope."

Babe looked past his shoulder. Euclid started to stir. Luckett followed her glance and they went to him. "He needs to sleep," he said, putting his hand on Euclid's throat and counting heartbeats.

"Laudanum worked before," Babe said.

"Good. We'll give him some and hope that keeps him quiet."

He dosed Euclid while Babe opened Euclid's mouth. He grumbled some, then fell back into a deep sleep.

"We better move him so he doesn't roll over and fall off the table. Over there. Can you carry him and we'll tuck him in good? And you can sleep right . . . oh, I guess you can't."

"It's okay. Floor's good enough."

"I'll bring in pillows, soften it up a bit."

He brought in an armload of linens. They got Euclid moved and secured. "My bedroom is just across the parlor. You'll come get me if he wakes or there's any change?"

"I will. Thank you, sir."

Luckett lowered the lamps so just a faint light shone down on Euclid, sleeping soundly. Babe wasn't going to be able to sleep, so she sat down next to him, took his hand and encased it in hers.

She smiled at the peacefulness in his face and thought back on all the times he'd stuck his tongue out at her, or folded his lips up or down to make a face. She wished she'd known him in his prime or that he could talk and tell her his life story. Was he caught wild and if so, where? What secrets did he hold inside his old, gray head? Did he have any babies? Who did that to his ears?

"Sure wisht you could talk," she whispered down to him. "Wonder what you'd tell your ol' Babe."

She leaned back on the wall, pulled a blanket up over her, and fell asleep.

Just before dawn, Babe's eyes flashed open, awakened by a sudden, horrible silence. She looked over at Euclid, picked up his hand, and gave it a gentle squeeze, wishing he could squeeze back just one last time. She cried in big, quiet gulps of grief. This is what aloneness feels like, she cried to the beast inside. This is what being the only person in the world feels like—no, more than alone—not even alive.

Her crying brought Luckett into the room. He knelt down and put his hand on her shoulder. "I'm sorry, Babe. We tried. We really did try."

"Bet you think I'm a fool, crying like a baby over just a critter. After all them men and boys you seed die, bet you think I'm pretty dang silly."

"No, Babe. Just the opposite. It takes a wise heart to care about creatures. Took a wise heart to let that bear go free."

She looked at him. "You know about my bear?"

"Where do you think he's been coming for handouts?"

"You've seed him? I thought for sure he was gone for good or spread out rug-like in someone's parlor."

"No, he comes by every day. I know I shouldn't have fed him when he first came around. He likes my huckleberry pie. Some folks would say I'm a fool for cooking pies for a bear."

Babe grinned, imagining Jupiter pulling a pie off a windowsill, just like they'd joked. "I'm glad ol' Jupiter's eating again."

"I've been calling him Brownie."

"Sure would like to see him. Been worried sick."

"He'll be here, don't worry. He's been trimming the blueberry bushes every morning."

She wiped her face with her sleeve, looked again at Euclid, and sighed deeply.

"Why don't you go heat up some coffee and I'll close up things here?" Luckett said, standing.

Babe pulled herself up and trundled into the kitchen. The door latched shut behind her. She turned but knew she couldn't, shouldn't open the door again. Quaking with grief and guilt, she wrapped her arms around herself.

Tighter. Tighter. Anything to comfort herself as she cried her heart out.

"Come on," Luckett said, handing Babe a plate overflowing with bacon, eggs, and thick slices of toasted bread. He'd given her time and space to grieve, then cooked them both a huge breakfast. "Let's sit on the front porch. It's nice and cool this time of morning. Can hear the creek babbling." He gave her an odd grin and added, "Of course, the creek babbles a lot louder after what you kids and that elephant did to it."

"Miss V should say she's sorry saying you made the landslide," Babe said.

Luckett put his head back and laughed. "Oh, she will! She's a stubborn old girl, but she'll set things straight. Hope I live long enough."

They sat on the sturdy log steps and ate.

"Reckon I owe you," Babe said, setting her plate down. She pulled out the five twenty-dollar gold coins from her pocket and placed them on the porch floor. "Think this will cover things?"

He looked at the money. "No. No charge. I won't take your money."

"Why not?"

"I don't need it."

"But, no doctoring, no gold strike . . ."

"Babe, no." There was a rustle in the bushes. "Here he comes. Right on time."

"Jupiter!" Babe cried out, rising.

Jupiter raised his head, sniffed. Then he lumbered over and up two porch steps. He grunted Babe a hello, then started to lick her plate.

"He's always been something of a sneak thief," she said, giving him a bear hug.

Luckett offered Jupiter the leftovers on his plate. Jupiter took it over to the bushes to finish it in private.

"He sure looks good. He was dang puny when I let him go."

"Nature will do that," Luckett said.

"Sort of funny," Babe said, looking out over the creek. "I lost Euclid but found Jupiter."

"Nature will do that, too."

She broke her stare. "You got a graveyard in these parts?"

"Well, all three churches have their own cemeteries over in John's Town. And there's Pioneer Cemetery. But . . ."

"You sure you don't want to be paid?" she asked, pointing down to the coins lined up on the porch.

"I'm sure."

"Then I'm thanking you for all you done," she said, scooping up the coins.

★ ★ ★

Babe pushed the door to the infirmary open. Just the sight of Euclid, now wrapped in her quilt, made her stop, but she set her jaw against the tears, let the beast inside her rest.

She had a job to do, and crying wasn't going to make it any easier.

"Oh, Babe, I'm so sorry!" Lotty cried when Babe told everyone what happened across the creek at Luckett's place.

"Can I make me a telephone call?" she asked Miss V.

"Why, of course," Miss V said, leading the way into the hall where the phone hung, dwarf-low, on the wall.

Babe looked down at it, then at Miss V. "What do I do?"

"We'll have to call up the exchange operator, and she'll get the number for you and make the connection. Want me to do it for you?"

"Yes, ma'am, please."

She turned the hand crank. "Who do you want to call?"

"Mr. Luckett told me you got a funeral man over to Medford. I want to call him."

"Funeral? Babe, why . . ."

"I'm getting Euclid a proper burying."

"But, Babe . . . ," Miss V began. "He's just—"

"He's *just* about the best friend I ever had." She felt the burn of tears, then her eyes landed on Lotty, standing in the hall. "'Cept you, 'course, Lotty. And hell, I'd give you a right fine burying, too."

Babe bought Euclid a child's coffin, mahogany and lined in satin, a funeral coach drawn by two black horses, with dashing black feathers on their heads. The plot she'd picked out had a fine view of the valley from the Pioneer Cemetery just outside John's Town. A real marble headstone marked his spot.

EUCLID

THE WORLD'S SMARTEST APE

DIED AUGUST 25, 1896

AGE 40 OR THEREABOUTS

The morning of the funeral, Babe visited Euclid. The undertaker made him look like he was peacefully sleeping, still wrapped in Babe's quilt.

Babe folded one of his hands around a sack of peanuts. "'Case you get hungry. Never knowed you to turn down peanuts. And here," she whispered. "Here's the hairbrush you was always pinching from your ol' Babe. It's yours now. I'm keeping the mirror, so's when we meet up again, we'll have the whole set. Goodbye, ol' man," she whispered, forcing back tears. "Ain't never going to forget you."

She closed the coffin lid.

"Babe, you in there?" Lotty called in as she peeked through the door to Babe's room.

Babe was on her bed, leafing through a scrapbook.

"Sure is quiet around here these days," Lotty said.

Babe looked through to the barn where Jupiter's and Euclid's cages now sat empty, still on the rickety wagon. "I know." She went back to the scrapbook.

"What's that you have there?"

"One of Miss V's scrapbooks from her carnie days. She said since I wasn't schooling, the least I could do was read some."

"Oh, yes, she showed me those after we first got here. Even has some family photos in it."

"I seed them."

"Seed?"

"Seen. Saw. Don't matter."

There was an awkward moment of silence, then Babe asked, still not looking up from the scrapbook, "How was school?"

"Oh, I love it! I got nominated for Harvest Queen! I just love high school!"

"Good on you, Lotty."

"Thanks. I have something for you."

Babe looked up. Lotty handed her a letter. "What's this?"

"It's an envelope, and that usually means there's a letter inside."

"Who's it from?"

"Who do you think? Rosa!"

"Rosa?" Babe's face brightened.

"Well, aren't you going to open it?" Lotty said brightly, popping up on the bed next to Babe.

"It's private. Maybe you could let me just read it alone?"

"Oh. Gosh. Sure, I just thought . . ."

She popped down off the bed and headed for the door. Babe's huge fingers struggled to open the envelope without tearing it. One look at the handwriting and she called out. "Lotty?"

She stuck her head back in the door.

"I can't read her writing. It's all dainty."

"Sure. Give it to me," Lotty said, smiling and taking the letter. She sat down and began to read.

"'Dear Babe; Thank you for your letter! I was sorry to see you so sad.'" Lotty stopped reading and looked at Babe. "You were sad?"

"Nothing was going good for me, Lotty. You know that. Does she say any more?"

"Yes. There's more." She continued reading. "'You don't need a two-bit mitt reader to tell you some days are happy and some are sad. I hope you are happier now. I left Renoir's outfit as soon as we hit the end of the line. I came down to San Francisco. I plan on taking the money I have saved and starting a new business on my own.'"

That brought Lotty's face over to Babe's. "Her big house? I wonder."

"Keep reading."

"'I enclose a railroad ticket—*not* in a cattle car!—so you can come see me. I will let you know about my plan when you get here if you still want to come.'"

Lotty shook out the envelope and sure enough, a ticket fell out. Babe picked it up, looked at it, then over to Lotty.

"Babe, maybe that's not such a good idea." Lotty shook her head.

"She write any more?"

Lotty continued. "'I think we can make a lot of money, and it will be fun! Please write and let me know what train you will be on. Your friend, Cora/Rosa.'"

Babe walked to the window. "I need me some fun," she said into the glass. The October rains had begun in earnest, and her body ached more than ever in the chilly damp.

"Then you're going?"

She turned around, a smile wide on her face. "I don't got Euclid, don't got Jupiter, and I don't got nothing else to do but read some scrapbooks of other folks' lifes."

For the first time in months, Babe was planning a change—for her, Fern Marie Killingsworth, not for Magnifica. A change—not for her critters, not for Lotty, not for Heartbreak Creek, but for her.

Two weeks later, Babe was packed and ready. She was still full from the going-away dinner Sarah and Miss V served everyone the night before, complete with her favorite foods, pies, and even a champagne toast to her good luck and the mysteries her future held with Cora/Rosa.

Babe took one last look around her room, making sure she had everything. She strolled past the two empty cages, running her hand along the bars and smiling at the memory of Jupiter and Euclid. She pulled out some of Jupiter's hairs stuck in the wire door, twirled them between her fingers, and placed them inside her conjure bag, still safe inside her blouse. She opened Euclid's cage and inhaled his memory.

Out in the barnyard, Cleve pulled up the wagon, her grip and trunk already loaded.

Babe went over to the pasture and lured Egypt with peanuts. Ajax and Honeycomb trotted over for their share. These goodbyes weren't supposed to be so hard. She felt an odd ache deep down inside where her beast usually resided.

"And you, Honeycomb," she said, kneeling down to see if the pony would let Babe pat her nose just this once. She flared her nostrils and nipped at Babe's outstretched hand. "Mean enough to bite yourself. You keep this little Calamity Jane in line, Ajax." She gave his great long nose a rub.

Egypt's trunk searched her for more peanuts and found her skirt pocket. She petted her trunk, leaned over, and gave it a kiss. "Don't you go places you shouldn't go. That sheriff has a job to do, and don't you be it!"

From there, she hiked her skirts and carefully walked the plank path through the muddy barnyard. These new skirts were not for dragging in the mud.

"Look at you!" Miss V cried.

Babe fidgeted with her waistband. "Think I'll take off this belt when I get on the train."

"Your pompadour is lovely!" Sarah said. "And the latest rage!"

"Got enough hairpins in here to build me a bridge," Babe said, sticking an escaping pin back into her hair.

"Have your money safe and sound?" Lotty asked.

Babe tapped the special linen bag Sarah had made for

her that hung from her waist, well-hidden by her skirt. She pulled the juju conjure bag from around her neck. "Got my good juju, too."

Finally, it was time.

Babe leaned down and gave Miss V an awkward hug. A giant can't hug a dwarf with grace and ease. "Got to thank you for all you done," Babe said.

"*I've* done? *You've* done! I have my mill back and running; I have my niece; I even have my elephant! Babe, thank *you*!"

"And thank you, Sarah. You been good to me, too."

"Got those pie recipes I wrote out?" she said.

Babe tapped the new valise she'd been given. "Can't wait to learn to cook."

Lotty walked her to the wagon where Cleve was waiting. "Babe, it's not too late to change your mind. You'll always be welcomed back here, you know."

"I'm doing right for me, Lotty. I know I am."

"Well, you can't say you don't have family," Lotty said, holding her hand.

"Now, if you start crying so will I!" Babe warned.

"I'm not crying." Lotty blew her nose. "Oh, I have something for you!" As she turned to pull something out of her apron pocket, Babe turned to pull something out of her valise.

They laughed as they saw what the other was holding. "No, you keep the set!" Babe said. "I'll just smash 'em along the way. They're too dainty for the likes of me."

Lotty held the cup and the saucer Lucretia the Lobster Woman had given them what seemed like a lifetime—two lifetimes!—ago.

"Do you mind if I pick you up?" Babe asked.

"Please." She set down the delicate cup and saucer and held her arms up to Babe, who gently picked her up. They gave each other long, sweet, arms-around-necks hugs.

"You're my hero. My champion," Lotty said. "I don't know what I'm going to do without you."

"Ain't no one's—not anyone's—hero, Lotty."

"Yes, you are."

Babe felt tears coming and set her friend down.

"Now, you have the telephone number. You have the address. You promised to write. If you don't, it's one of these!" She held up her tiny fist.

"You mean one of these?" Babe's huge fist went up.

"Yes!"

"Got to get going now, Babe. Climb aboard," Cleve called out, making room on the wagon seat. "And here. More books. So you can keep up your schooling." He tapped the small leather case next to him.

"Think I'll ride back here," Babe said. The wagon took a dip down as she sat on the tailgate, feet dangling over the end. She wanted to see Egypt, Ajax, Honeycomb, Lotty, Miss V, and Sarah disappear slowly. Her last glimpse might have to keep for a lifetime.

"Wait! Pa! Wait up!"

Cleve held the horse up while Denny came running. Aces ran and barked alongside.

"Here, Babe," he said, handing her a pup.

"Number three? Pick of the litter?" she said. "Thought she'd be the first to find a home."

"I saved her for you. Everyone wanted her, but I saved her." Denny beamed while the pup jumped up and tried to land kisses on Babe's face.

"For real?"

"Of course for real! She's all yours." He shook her hand and added, out of his father's earshot, "And thanks, you know, for . . . well, just thanks." His face went serious as he looked down. "Oh, and I finally owned up to the whole blasting-cap thing. Me and Hank have to work for Mr. Luckett to makes things even."

"I'm real glad I met you." Babe had to wrestle the pup into a sitting position.

Denny took off his hat, bowed, and said, "Me too, Babe. You're one hell of a big . . . no, you're just one hell of a girl."

She smiled as the wagon rounded the bend and the forest enveloped them. Babe kissed the pup, then held her up high. "Hesh. Your Babe's got you!"

58

January 3, 1898

Dearest Babe,

I know it's been a while since I wrote and for that, I send you my apologies. So much has happened this last year that it seems just as soon as I sit down to take pen in hand, something else comes up and I need to start all over again.

Your last letter was wonderful! I am glad to see your handwriting has much improved, as well as your spelling and grammar. That night school has served you well.

The photograph I enclose was taken by Hank. That boy and his camera! As you can see, we are at a party. A going-away party—for me! I will write more later, but wanted to let you know the latest.

I am heading for a nursing school in Chicago! Yes! Mr.

Luckett, although he's really Doctor Luckett, said he knew of this nursing school. Seems that I can enroll and because of my size, they want me even more! There is an orphanage that takes in sick babies and children with deformities. The poor kids who probably won't ever get adopted. Like you and me. All I had to do was sign an agreement to work for them for just room and board for three years after I graduate! Can you believe it? I get to be a nurse after all!

You asked about Miss V and Dr. Luckett. Oh, what a mystery! They sometimes sit on their own sides of the creek and just look at each other. But get this—the other day I saw Miss V sitting on his side of the creek and he was showing her how to pan for gold! (I don't ask, and she doesn't tell!) My guess is they are still in love! Can you imagine?!?

Oh! Denny! He's president of the senior class. Hank is always in detention, though. Please let me know how your trip to the Midwest goes. I can't wait to hear what your big surprise is, so please do write and let me know when you get there. Remember, you promised not to go back to the carnie life. No more Magnifica or anyone else you aren't!

One of these!

Lotty

P.S. How is your beast? Mine seems to have faded away!

March 20, 1898

Dear Lotty,

Do not get mad when you read this! I am in Omaha, Nebraska, but I'm not moving a landslide or going to night school. I am performing on a stage. They call it the Trans-Pacific Exposition, which is a fancy great big fair. Not sideshow, carnie, circus, dime museum, or nickel peepshow. <u>Exposition</u>. So, I'm keeping my word. I am not lifting weights, looking like a monster, scaring children, or tossing drunks out of the fighting ring.

I am writing this to you now in my own dressing room in a theater that fills with customers every night and twice on Saturdays. Guess who is right here next to me. Denny's puppy number three! She comes with me everywhere. When did you know your Babe not to tote her a critter? Did you tell Miss V I named her Valentine?

The show is called C. Epstein's World of Unique Considerations and I am one of them. And that's my biggest surprise! Yes, C. Epstein is Madame de la Rosa!! As you know, I have been with her since I left you and Miss V. She's been a good friend and had enough money and connections to build this show. <u>This</u> is the big house she wanted! House, as in theater! Ha! Ha!

I'm billed as the world-famous giant Miss Fern Killingsworth. I come out and look pretty in a spot of light. My spiel is simple. I tell them how big I am—oh, I have just hit seven feet! I tell them about how I grew up and my time in a cheap carnie. Sometimes I show them my tattooed biceps and sometimes I lift a man. The audience gets to ask questions and I have heard some humdingers! But the best part is they clap FOR me, not AT me. What a world!

I like being a unique consideration instead of a freak, but well, you and me, Lotty, we're lots of things, ain't we? Ha ha! I wrote "ain't" to make your eyes roll! We're lots of things, isn't we? I'm not getting smaller and you're not getting bigger. And my beast? She's still there. Still trying to grumble and growl to life. She sure keeps me on my toes!

What will we do when this booking is over in a few months? Rosa says all things are possible, and I think I believe her. Did you know they discovered gold up in Alaska someplace? There's a man here making big money teaching folk how to pan for gold. I wonder if Dr. Luckett knows him! Ha! Ha!

Well, it's showtime! More later.

One of these!

Your Babe

P.S. Some college man came and asked me if I wanted to play a game called football and if I did I could get more schooling. For free! Ha Ha. I wonder what football is.

Author's Note

When an author creates a cast of unusual characters, usually the first question they get is, "How in the world did you come up with this?" I know I'll be getting this question a lot now that Babe and Carlotta and their friends have been introduced to the world.

Babe and Carlotta are old friends of mine. They first appeared in an earlier novel about a half-Chinese, half-Caucasian Albino girl who becomes a sideshow sensation in 1918. In that book, *The Likes of Me*, Babe and Carlotta have supporting, but important, adult roles. Ever since it was published, readers have asked about Babe the giant. They wanted to know what her life could possibly have been like as a child and as a teen. Turns out I was curious, too. So I began my research and the task of getting to know these characters and the carnie world they inhabited.

I have always had a deep love and concern for animals. I was the kid bringing home strays, working for free at the stables, reading every animal book I could get my hands on, and then finally, adding a critter to just about every book I've written. So it was very natural to introduce Euclid the chimpanzee, Jupiter the bear, and Egypt the elephant. One can't love animals and not be concerned about their plight and exploitation. Researching the early days of traveling circus and carnival life was difficult at times. But here is where being an author rocks. Authors can create characters who see wrongdoing and then make changes in not only their own lives, but in the lives of the animals they care for in their stories.

Every writer loves words, and I especially love slang! I love the many colors and shades in our language—after all, we don't speak in just black and white! Because of this passion and the fact that historical fiction uses words and expressions that are seldom encountered in modern times, I developed my own database of slang and expressions. Carnival, circus, and show business slang terms from a century ago are extra colorful and, perhaps to today's ears, a bit insulting, derogatory, or even hurtful.

At least some of the power has shifted recently, and thankfully, girls like Babe and Carlotta and other individuals with mental and physical differences and disabilities have more rights today than ever before. At the same time, slang terms show us what real life sounded like in a particular time period and are great for sparking conversations about how people who were born different were treated in eras past. Studying how slang morphs and grows and even dies over the years is fascinating. What may have been acceptable—and even common—then is seldom heard now.

It's my hope that this information will add to the reader's enjoyment and understanding of this book.

Randall Platt